The HIGH COUNTRY

A Novel

Richard Perce, DVM

Fitch Mountain Press
Healdsburg, California

To Chari

Acknowledgements

This book would not exist without the support and encouragement of my wife, the love of my life, Chari. Her patience and understanding have made the project a pleasure.

Many thanks to Jan Flores and Eileen O'Farrell for their help in editing the manuscript and Wanda Smith for the cover design. To the members of our writing group, Marie Butler, Bill Hanson, Katie McMurray and the late Preble Franklin; your ideas have been invaluable. Thank you Sarah Murphy your graphic art expertise has been a blessing. To the clients and patients of forty years; the experiences we've shared provided the material and inspiration that have made it possible to tell Clay's story.

Table of Contents

Chapter 1

The Last Race

*T*he dawn broke clear and bright without a hint of the disaster that would end my career. As I climbed into my truck and headed for the racetrack, my thoughts were of coffee and hash browns at the Horseman's Café.

The screen door twanged, vibrating as the bottom corner popped loose. Its white paint, stained by thousands of grubby hands, was chipped and peeling with the previous coat, a bright blue enamel, showing through on every surface.

"Damn, Doc! How many times do I have ta tell ya? Pick up on the handle an' it won't stick," Billy yelled from the grill, pointing at me with his spatula.

"A couple of tools and a half hour would fix that door, and nobody would dislocate a shoulder trying to give you business," I said, stepping over near the counter to order.

"Over easy, bacon and hash browns?" Billy asked, pouring a mug of coffee and setting it on the counter. "Wheat or white?"

"Wheat, if it's fresh, and make those eggs sunny side up," I said, inhaling the smell of hot bacon grease and coffee.

"That's your coffee, Doc. Sit and I'll bring your eggs. I've got a few minutes till things get busy."

"Thanks," I said, looking at the lighted Coors clock and trying to read 6:10 through the bubbling of the Rocky Mountain Spring Water. The morning workouts would be ending soon, turning the nearly empty Horseman's Café into standing room only; a blue haze of cigarette smoke and its accompanying stink would soon replace the aroma of bacon and coffee. I pulled out the nearest red vinyl chair, its legs scrapping loudly on the cracked linoleum floor. Sitting down with my coffee I began to peruse the day's racing program.

"I see you haven't gotten the damned door fixed yet, Billy," Don Parker said as he tried to open the screen. On his second attempt Don put his back into it and the door flew open, shuddering louder than ever. "Do I have to rip the hinges off this thing to get you to fix it?" Don shook his head.

2

"If you'd pay your bill maybe I could afford to get the door worked on… but, oh, no, it's 'Put this on my tab, Billy.' 'Charge that to me, Billy.' You'd think I was the Raton State Bank," Billy said, pulling the stubby pencil from behind his ear. "Well, what's it gonna' be, Doc? I don't have all mornin' to listen to your complainin'. I got other veterinarians to feed, and they pay their bills." He looked my way and winked.

"I'll risk the Denver omelet again if the ham's not rancid," Don said, coming over to sit at my table.

"I ain't carryin' the coffee over like some little waitress," Billy said, slamming a mug on the counter for Don.

"We'd never mistake you for a waitress, would we, Clay?" Don said as he stepped back to the counter for his coffee.

"Don't get me involved," I said. "I haven't gotten my breakfast yet and I don't want to be eating burned toast."

Don returned laughing and reached across the table to shake my hand before sitting down. "How many you got runnin' today?" He motioned to my program with his chin.

"I'm not sure; I was just countin' up. I think it's gonna' be a light day for me though," I said, turning a page in the narrow program. The door was twanging and slamming with increasing frequency as the trainers filtered in for coffee and gossip.

"Eat up, boys, an' I'll bring ya' more coffee," Billy interrupted our conversation slapping our plates on the table.

"Gee thanks, Billy, you are quite a waitress after all," I said, holding up my heavy mug.

"Don't get used to this kind of service." Billy took the cup and turned to leave.

"Wait a second, these are mighty anemic looking bell peppers," Don said, poking his omelet with a fork.

"I meant to tell ya' about that." Billy looked a little sheepish. "I'm out of peppers so I substituted green chile. Figgered you'd like it better anyway."

"Ought to get a discount for the chile," Don said, still stirring his eggs around.

"In your dreams, Parker." Billy reached down as if to remove the plate but jerked back when Don's fork slammed into the table just missing his hand. "You can get your own damned coffee. I only waitress for folks with manners," Billy added, waving my cup as he left.

"I just come for the entertainment," Don said, leaning close. "The food's crap."

"I heard that, you over-educated stall cleaner," Billy said, returning with my coffee and carrying the pot to fill Parker's cup. "Any more refills?" Billy raised the coffee pot above his head. Better get 'em now, 'cause I won't be back!" His invitation was followed by catcalls and raised cups into which Billy sloshed the strong brew.

"We're in for it now, boys," Skillet Gillespie announced as he came through the door. "We've got veterinary collusion goin' on so prices'll be up come Monday!" He stopped, smiling like he'd just won the Kentucky Derby, slapped me on the back and, leaning in close, whispered, "Stop by 'fore you leave tonight, Doc. I've got Peter in tomorrow." I nodded and continued eating my eggs as Skillet moved off to harass a table of jockeys and their agents.

"Ya think Skillet's gonna turn Peter loose tomorrow?" Don mumbled between bites.

"Good luck figuring that out. Did he whisper in my ear so trainers would notice or so they couldn't hear? The only thing I know for sure is that sometime this meet he'll do whatever it is he does to the horse and Peter Don't Bite will win going away."

"He lets Peter go when the odds get high enough to suit him. I've been trying to figure out when that is for three seasons and I've only been to the pay window once. Nobody plays it any closer to the vest than Skillet." Don wiped up the last bit of omelet with his wheat toast. "It's time to get out of here; the smoke line is

4

down to my eyes." He pushed his chair back and uncoiled his six-foot-four frame, fanning the blue haze away from his face.

"I'll be right behind you," I said, downing the last swallow of coffee.

"See you around campus," Don nodded in my direction then turned toward the door.

The air seemed especially fresh and crisp after the warm smoky café as I crossed the gravel parking lot to my pickup. I pulled off my jacket as I walked and rolled down the driver's side window while starting the truck.

"Hey, Jimmy, you stayin' warm enough?" I waved offhandedly to the security guard. Jimmy bowed from the waist, clad in a huge down coat that hung almost to his knees, and motioned for me to pull through the gate into the barn area.

"I'm doin' okay, Doc, how about yourself? Billy poisonin' you with that rot gut he calls coffee?" Jimmy laughed and zipped his coat a little tighter.

I gave him a thumbs up and eased along the first shed row looking for Harvey Baker. I shoved the truck into park when I spotted Harvey's blue baseball cap through the open door of a stall in the middle of the barn. The cap bobbed just above ground level as the trainer bent to run his hands over a two-year-old's ankles.

"I saw High Command got in; his left knee's not gonna' hold up, Harv." I said, approaching the stall.

"It's tight, Doc. I think he'll be fine. Doctor Simms insists on running him." Harvey stepped away from the colt he was working under. "See what you think of these ankles." I wrapped both hands around the left front leg starting below the elbow and slowly worked my way down the limb to the hoof, repeating the procedure on the opposite limb.

"A little filling in his left knee, and both ankles have some filling. The left one is warm. Is he sore to flex?" I stepped back and tilted my head looking at first one ankle then the other.

5

"He flexes okay; maybe I'll give him a week or so off," Harvey said, handing a tray of leg wraps to his assistant. "Do him up, Jerry, and take him off the schedule."

"What I'm really worried about is High Command, Harv. He needs at least another week. I'll talk to Simms if you want. The colt needs to be scratched."

"You're right, Doc. I'll talk to the owner and get him to let me scratch the colt," Harvey said going to the next stall.

"Good. If you need any backup I'll be here."

The rest of the morning went without incident, and at a quarter to one I was under an elm tree just outside the saddling paddock almost asleep in the cool shade.

Fourteen two-year-old Quarter Horses with their lead ponies and outriders paraded onto the track as the last notes of the "Call to the Post" echoed away.

"Hey, Clay, how's it going?" Don Parker asked, stepping up beside me.

"I guess everything's fine, but to tell the truth I've been catching up on my sleep." I shook my head to clear the cobwebs and pointed toward the collection of horses as they trotted past the grandstand finishing their warm-up.

"I was surprised to see your Scottsdale horse in. I thought he'd been scratched," Don said, climbing up on the fence beside me.

"High Command?" I turned to look at the older veterinarian. "He has been scratched."

"I saw Harv less than an hour ago getting him ready," Don said, scratching his head.

"High Command sprained his knee last week and they took him out of the race," I said. "Are you sure we're talking about the same horse? He's a big chestnut."

"With a star and one white sock, right?" Don pointed to the big horse as he circled behind the starting gate. "Well, he's sure

6

out there." He sat up straighter to get a better look at the colt. "He's the number four horse, with Billy Hunter up."

"That's him, all right! Where the hell's Harvey Baker?" I said, looking around the immediate area. "I need to have a chat with him."

The first two horses were in the gate, but Luckee Lady was kicking at anyone who came near as they tried to load her in the third position. High Command nervously trotted in place tossing his head. Men from the gate crew moved in behind him, easing him into the fourth spot. The hind gate banged shut, and instantly High Command launched himself straight in the air. Rearing nearly vertically he struck the back gate with the saddle as his hind feet went out from under him. Billy was quick enough to jump clear, pulling himself onto the wall of the chute and ducking High Command's flailing front feet as the colt's hindquarters slid forward and he landed on his back. One of the attendants jerked open the loading gate and the colt scrambled to his feet, banging his head. A few seconds passed as the starter and the track veterinarian looked the colt over. Then, still shaking from his ordeal, High Command was reloaded into the four position.

"They should have pulled him after a wreck like that," Don said as the rest of the field was loaded into the gate.

"Harvey was in agreement when I told him the horse needed to be scratched. The damned owner is gonna' get a good horse crippled."

"Hell, Clay, his knee is bound to hurt enough to slow him way down. Maybe he won't make things worse," Don said.

"I hope you're right."

"We'll know in about eighteen seconds," Don said as the gate crashed open and "They're off!" blared over the loud speaker. The grunts of exertion as the horses blasted from the starting gate were clearly audible over the sound of pounding hooves. I jumped off my perch and moved to the trackside rail. An Oklahoma colt in the middle of the track got out well with a length lead by the third stride. High Command was second by a neck over the filly in the three position. Fifty yards into the race the horses were still accelerating, and High Command was second by less than half a length.

Suddenly he veered toward the inside rail smashing into Luckee Lady. Her jockey wasn't prepared for the collision and catapulted off her right shoulder, landing between the two horses. The screams of a capacity crowd were deafening. Billy Hunter was standing in his stirrups and leaning back to pull High Command's head up and prevent him from falling as his left front leg flopped uselessly. Manuel Ortega riding the two horse was being badly outrun so he had time to pull his colt to the outside and avoid the disaster, but Charlie Brendel tried to get by along the rail and High Command struck the number one horse just behind the saddle, rolling her over the rail in a flurry of thrashing legs. Bird's Song landed on her back in the infield with Charlie still in the saddle. She scrambled to her feet wobbling dazedly across the infield grass, her reins dragging. Charlie didn't move. Billy Hunter jumped to the ground as High Command pulled up to stand trembling with pain. The wreck was over in seconds, and the siren's blare drowned out the announcer as he named the winner.

The ambulance raced to the injured jockeys as the first help arrived on foot. Don hopped the inside rail, and I was close behind him. "Don't move, Charlie," Don said, kneeling beside Brendel. "Bird fell right on top of you. You're gonna be alright, but don't try to move 'til the medics have a look at you."

"Doc, I wanna' sit up." Charlie tried to raise himself up on his elbows. "Ahhh… shit!" He fell back moaning.

The paramedics were maneuvering a stretcher over the rail, and I hurried over to lend a hand. "Charlie's back might be broken," I whispered to one of the attendants. "The mare landed with her withers right over his lumbar vertebrae."

"Don't worry, Doc, we'll be careful with him," the older of the pair said as they moved to Charlie's side.

8

I stood looking around at the scene. Some of the starting gate personnel were trying to catch Bird's Song as she wandered around the infield, and the track veterinarian had already sedated High Command. He was about to be loaded in the trailer used as a horse ambulance. It had been backed next to the colt, and a sling was being placed around his body to lift him aboard. Luckee Lady was at the far end of the track, and her rider was leaning against the rail a few yards from me, gingerly brushing dirt from his shirt.

"Doc! Doc! Over here!" Harvey yelled, waving me over to the horse trailer. "Can you meet me at the stalls to check out High Command?"

"I'll bring my x-ray," I said, shaking my head in disgust as Harvey left riding in the horse ambulance.

Charlie Brendel was being lifted into the ambulance with Don Parker at his side. "Hey, Don," I yelled. "You riding to the hospital?" Parker shook his head. "I'm headed to Harvey Baker's stalls if you'd like a ride," I added.

"Damn straight," Don said as we crossed the track heading for my truck. "I wanna' see what that son of a bitch has to say for himself."

"Doc, I know...you were right. We should have scratched him," Harvey said as Don and I climbed out of the truck. "It was Doc Simms. He wanted to run the colt."

"I thought you were better than that, Harvey," I said, brushing past the trainer. "Leave him in the sling for a minute, Jimmy. Let me have a look at him while he's reasonably comfortable," I said, waving to the trailer crew as I approached the horse ambulance.

"I'm sorry, Doc, but the owner insisted and...well... I've got three more of his in training. The colt'll need some rest and maybe a cast or something for the sprain, but I'm sure you can fix him up good as new." Harvey was trailing in my footsteps looking like an elderly Bloodhound.

"Let's see what this knee feels like," I said, climbing into the trailer and bending over to examine High Command. The colt's carpus was almost twice its normal size. He stood trembling with the toe barely touching the trailer floor. "Easy boy," I said as I gently placed both hands around the joint and started to palpate the injury. Mild pressure produced crepitus, the unmistakable feel of bone grating on bone and a sure sign of fracture. As I moved over the joint I could feel pieces of bone moving around as if I was squeezing a bag of rocks. I turned to Don, shaking my head as a stick-thin man elbowed his way through to the trailer.

"What do you think, Harv? Let's get him out and have a look at him," the man said, whining through his pencil thin nose.

I stood and stared at the rat-like creature. "You must be Doctor Simms," I said, stepping away from the injured colt.

"You're Williams…Harvey speaks highly of you. How's my colt?"

"Multiple carpal fractures, I'm afraid," I said, offering Simms a hand into the trailer.

"Are you sure?" Simms asked, his mouth dropping open. I reached further to help him step up, but he recoiled.

"As an orthopedic surgeon you've had a lot more experience palpating injuries than I have. Perhaps you can ascertain how many fractures we're looking at," I said, stepping down the ramp and offering Dr. Simms room to examine the colt. The owner stood wide–eyed, staring up at High Command, then he shook like a Labrador Retriever coming out of a lake.

"I trust your judgment," he said, coughing and backing away. He took Harvey Baker by the arm and turned away.

"He'll never be worth anything as a breeding horse, Harvey," Simms said, shrugging his shoulders. "We'll have to put him down."

"Ain't there somethin' we can do?" Harvey peered back and forth between me, Dr. Simms and Don Parker.

"I think we've already done it," Don said, his teeth grating as he clinched his jaw.

"You practice a lot of sports medicine, don't you, doctor?" I asked, stepping in front of the surgeon.

"Why, yes, I do," Simms said with an even bigger smile.

"Probably work on a lot of high school athletes."

"Of course," he said, starting to look a little confused.

"I was wondering," I growled. "How does your program work on injured football players? Can you pat them on the back and put them right back in the game?" Simms backed away, his face turning crimson.

"Just what do you think I am?" he huffed. "What kind of a doctor do you take me for?"

"Doctor? I'd never take you for a doctor, you sleazy bastard. Assholes like you are what give racing a bad name!" I made a lunge at Simms, but Don stepped between us.

"I r-r-refuse to be insulted... by a veterinarian," Simms stammered, backing away. He grabbed Harvey by the arm, turned on his heel and stomped down the shed row.

"I'll be right back, Doc," Harvey shouted over his shoulder. "Don't leave."

"Wow, you all right, Clay?" Don asked, patting me on the shoulder.

"That weasely little bastard shouldn't be allowed to own a horse!" I hissed, leaning on the trailer.

"Steady there, boy, we've dealt with his kind before and we'll have to deal with his kind again," Don said.

"I won't," I said. "I won't deal with that kind of human. I'm done with the track. You can have all the Dr. Simmses."

"Yeah, right, Clay. You love the track. I can see it in your eyes every time they open the starting gate. You're not leaving," Don was slapping me on the back. "Boy, you sure did unload on our surgeon!" The trailer crew had joined us.

"I thought that guy was gonna' shit himself when you made a grab for him," Jimmy chuckled.

"I guess I kinda' lost it there. I can't believe the skinny little S.O.B. is allowed to own a horse. I'd like to know how we can get him ruled off the track!"

"Truth is, we can't, Clay. He'll deny everything and he's got the bucks behind him," Don nodded toward the trailer. "You want me to take care of High Command?"

"Thanks, but no, I'll finish the job. I want to x-ray that knee when he's down anyway, just in case Simms wants to claim it was misdiagnosed."

"Can we haul him out behind the maintenance shed, Doc? We've got power real close there."

"Sure, Jimmy, I'll be right behind you," I said and turned back to Don. "I do like seeing them run. They were born to run, but I don't like this kind of crap and I've been toying with the idea of moving to the high country. I just might do it now."

That evening I started my research. I wrote to the Chambers of Commerce in any towns that interested me, collecting and reading through the material they sent. By the end of the race meet I'd narrowed the field. I was ready for a road trip.

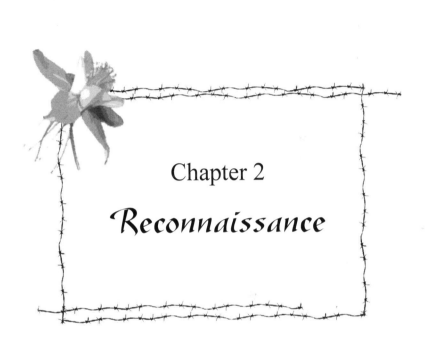

Chapter 2

Reconnaissance

*H*ighway 40 made a ninety-degree left turn heading almost due west and became the main street of the small ranching community. I was sure I could find a pay phone here, and the number I'd copied from a property sign just outside of town was beckoning to me from the slip of paper on my truck seat. I smiled as I read the Colorado State road sign, "Steamboat Springs, elevation 6995 feet - population 6822." More elevation than population. Somehow that thought appealed to me. I continued on, crossing a small creek and passing two grocery stores on opposite sides of the street. Mid-afternoon on Sunday and they were both closed. *Small town*, I thought with satisfaction.

Most of the main street was empty. In fact, the only activity seemed centered on a red brick building on the left where several cars were parked. As I eased past, the sign surprised me: Steadman Realty. Amazing that they would be the only business open; it was their number lying on my truck seat! *Sunday afternoon,* I thought. *What's the chance of that?* I parked across the street, in front of the courthouse, and headed for the realty office. Two large plate-glass windows edged with pictures of properties that Steadman represented allowed me to observe the beehive of activity inside. A large central room was filled with desks each occupied by one or two people with clipboards and everyone feverishly pounding away on adding machines. Some of the machines were old with spring-loaded handles, reminiscent of a slot machine. I stood just inside the door trying to determine what all the activity meant when a sandy-haired man spotted me.

"You buy one?" He stuck out his chin, nodding in my direction.

"Me? No!" I answered, foolishly looking over my shoulder to see if he was really addressing me. I must have looked as confused as I felt, because he stopped working and came around the desk with his hand outstretched.

"Joe Adams," he said.

"Clay Williams," I countered, shaking the proffered hand.

"You here because of the auction?"

14

"No, about a property listing." I held up my slip of paper.

"Sorry, we're all tied up with the auction," he looked around. "Otherwise I'd be glad to help. You know about the auction?" I shook my head. "Condo complex at the mountain went under," Joe said as he reached for an auction brochure on his desk.

"Oh," I said, still confused.

"The mountain, Mt. Werner, the ski area?" He pointed southeast toward the back corner of the office.

"Oh, sure, I passed the turnoff on the way into town." I said, finally beginning to understand.

"That's the one," Joe smiled. "A condo project, about three-quarters finished, went belly up, and this morning we auctioned everything: Condos, dozers, tractors and pickups, even hand tools." He gestured around the office. "We're adding it up now."

"I see," I said looking around the room. "I just drove over Rabbit Ears Pass and noticed a Steadman sign on some property south of town."

Joe glanced around. "Tom's in his office." He jerked his thumb toward a room on the left. "He can probably help you out. If he can't, stop back and I'll give you my card. We could talk tomorrow."

"Thanks," I said. "I'll do that." Joe went back to his adding as I walked across to Tom's office. The door, a big glass slider, was standing half open. A large man, maybe six-foot-two, wearing a red plaid, Western cut shirt, was behind a hard-used, glass-topped desk. Two days' growth of jet-black beard covered his large square jaw, his legs were crossed and he was reared back in his chair, cowboy boots resting on the desktop. Smoke curled up from a large dark cigar clinched firmly in the corner of his mouth. I knocked and stepped through the ample opening. The rank cigar odor assaulted me. *It must be a great cigar,* I thought, remembering a high school friend whose father taught me that, in cigars, the worse the smell, the better the taste. A brass nameplate, a huge red ashtray and his size twelve boots were the only items sitting on the cracked glass. The nameplate read, Tom Steadman, Realtor.

"Mr. Steadman?" I inquired. He nodded an invitation, and I quickly took a seat, hoping I could get below the hazy cloud of foul cigar smoke.

"I'm Clay Williams," I introduced myself. Tom squinted at me through the smoke saying nothing. "I just drove into town and noticed your sign on a piece of property out past the Holiday Inn."

Tom nodded, "Know the one you mean," he said with a hard stare that reminded me of the caged lion I'd seen at the Denver zoo.

"Well, I was wondering about the price," I said, scratching behind one ear and trying to stimulate our conversation.

"Why?" Tom continued to puff on his cigar unblinking.

"I'm thinking seriously about moving here," I continued, sitting a little straighter. "I'm a veterinarian and thought that acre with its house and steel building would work well." Steadman looked me up and down.

"It wouldn't," he rolled the cigar to the other side of his mouth and grunted around it. I was surprised and it must have shown because he added. "Set up to be a restaurant, might even be a service station, and store. Not a vet hospital."

"Well, if it's zoned to be a restaurant, I'm sure a veterinary clinic would be allowed." I smiled meekly.

"You can't afford it!" Tom said, as if he were my accountant.

Still trying to get along, I laughed. "You're probably right. I was just curious about the price."

Tom pulled his boots off the desk and sat up, arms spread, hands flat on the glass top.

"We've got one veterinary hospital around here and we don't need another!" he growled, leaning forward over the desk.

"Excuse me," I blinked, "what was that?"

"I said, we don't need a vet hospital on that edge of town." Steadman sat and rubbed his hands together as if he was washing them. "In fact, we don't need another vet around here at all."

"Well, thanks for your time!" I said in the nastiest tone I could muster. Rising quickly, I didn't look back.

"Don't mention it," Steadman muttered.

"*Welcome to Steamboat Springs,*" I thought as I left. Joe looked up as I passed his desk.

"I'll take one of those cards now." I mumbled between clinched teeth.

"Sure, no problem." Adams gestured to the cardholder on his desk. "What did Tom have to say?"

"Said you don't need another veterinarian around here." I slipped his card into my shirt pocket without slowing my pace. Joe nodded knowingly.

"Call me," he said.

I recrossed US 40 to my pickup, vowing not to let Steadman get me down. I thought of how I'd felt less than an hour ago coming over Rabbit Ears Pass with its meadows of dried grass and the deeper gold of aspen leaves shimmering in the mid-September breeze. Snapping out of my daydream I slowly drove the remaining few blocks of Main Street watching for a place to turn around on the edge of town. I spotted the Westside Veterinary Hospital, a tan block building. Two cars were in front so I parked and went in to the small animal reception area. I could see into the first of two exam rooms where an Australian Shepherd pup was lying on the stainless steel table. The doctor, a man of about 50 with light red hair, ruddy complexion and large freckles, stepped back shaking his head.

"He's going to need some work, Don. I'll just hang on to him and give you a call tomorrow," the doctor said, bending over to pick up the pup. It was then that he spotted me. "I'm going to be here awhile," he said, nodding in my direction. "Is there something I can help you with?"

17

"Just thought I'd stop in and say hello. I'm a veterinarian and I noticed the cars out front," I replied, moving closer to the door.

"Great!" he said, straightening up and patting the dog on his head. "If you've got a few minutes, I can use some help with the anesthesia. Would you mind keeping the dog occupied while I get a little information from Don so he can be on his way? Otherwise he'll be late for work."

"No problem," I said, stepping up to the exam table and scratching the frightened Aussie behind an ear. "How bad is he?"

"Fractured femur and road rash." He pointed to the pup's hind leg bent at an odd angle above the stifle. "This is Don Pendergast," he added, gesturing toward a tall, thin man in his early twenties. Don was backed into the room's far corner. He had streaks of blood and dirt on his shirt and appeared to be very uncomfortable.

"Come on, Don," the redheaded veterinarian said. "Let me get your phone number at home and at the steakhouse." Don, looking relieved, followed the doctor into the reception area, and I could hear the murmurings of their conversation. A moment later the doctor returned with his hand outstretched. "Ed Sims," he said, "but everyone calls me Red."

"You're Red Sims?" I exclaimed in surprise. "Your brother taught our small animal surgery class!"

"I figured as much," laughed Red, "Everybody knows Benny. He's been at CSU forever!"

I didn't have much chance to try and remember any of the things I'd heard about Red because he started to clean the Australian's wounds and my help was required holding the young dog.

"I thought I'd clean up these wounds a little before we knock him out," Red said, pausing as if he'd had an unusually good idea. "In all the excitement, I didn't get your name!"

"Clay Williams," I answered.

"Well, Dr. Williams, what brings you to Steamboat?" Red asked, gently cleaning dirt and gravel from his patient's shoulder and chest.

"Racetrack burnout. I'm looking for a place to relocate," I said, holding the pup around the muzzle with one hand while I held his front legs with the other.

"You plan on doing large animal work?" Dr. Sims asked.

"Horses entirely, if that's possible, but it looks like I may have to do some small animal, and maybe even cattle work."

"Come here, to Steamboat." Red said, rinsing out the wounds and spraying them with antiseptic. "My partner is the only large animal practitioner in the area. Nice as he is, he shows up days late and never calls anyone. You'll be doing all the large animal work in the county within three months."

I was at a loss for words. I just stood with my jaw dropped.

"Well, hey, it's true. Bill just wants to stay home and ranch. All the livestock owners will line up to switch," Sims continued as he worked on the dog.

I don't know about this town, I thought. *A realtor who doesn't want to sell property and a veterinarian promoting competition.*

"I've about got him cleaned up," Red said. "I'll pull up some Rompun and ketamine. I just need a few minutes to splint the fracture and bandage the rest of him." I held off the cephalic vein for Red's I.V.

"The pup has a T fracture, but I'm not putting any hardware in there till I find the owner!" Red said as he sedated the sheepdog.

"Don's not the owner?"

"No, Don hit him, and he's not too excited about having to pay for the repair. He's a good kid, though and he feels sorry for the pup," Sims said, injecting the ketamine. I held the dog until the drug took effect, then eased the unconscious animal onto the table with the fractured leg on top. Red deftly adjusted an old Thomas splint and taped it in place, stabilizing the fracture to prevent further damage. "I'll bet we have an owner calling by morning. After all, he's a nice dog and this is a small town," he continued as he quickly bandaged the other wounds.

We chatted for a few more minutes, then I checked my watch. "I'd better hit the road. I told my brother I'd buy him dinner at seven, and he lives in Fort Collins."

"Better call him and make it eight o'clock," Red cautioned. Then he added, "I'm serious, Clay, you should move up here. You'd do well."

"I might just do that!" I replied, turning to go. "Thanks for your time, Dr. Sims."

"Dr. Sims is my brother; I'm just Red!" He laughed tousling his red hair. "I'm the one to thank you for the help," he added.

"Thanks again, Red," I said, heading out the door.

"I'll let Bill know you're coming," Red said. I raised an eyebrow in surprise. "No, no," Red said. "Bill will want to introduce you to all the ranchers."

I retraced my route through town, but before climbing back over Rabbit Ears Pass I pulled into the property that had brought me to Steadman Realty. A thin man, dressed all in khaki, was working around the outside of the house. He was draining a hose as he rolled it, and there was new insulation around the hose bib where it had been hooked.

"Doin' a little winterizing?" I climbed from my cab and went to shake hands.

"Yup, usually I wait till right after the pipes freeze and break!" he replied. "I'm trying to avoid that for a change."

"I saw the sign and wondered about the price!" I told him, pointing to the large red, white and blue piece of plywood supported on either end by treated posts.

"We're asking $70,000," he said, carrying his hose toward the garage.

"Steadman was right," I mumbled.

"Oh, sure. Tom knows what we're asking," he said, opening the overhead door.

"He never told me the price. He just said I couldn't afford it. Unfortunately, he was right." I turned toward my pickup more than a little discouraged.

"You could make us an offer. We might be able to negotiate a little."

"I really don't want to insult you. It's probably worth the money, but it's way out of my league!"

As my pickup climbed the pass I reflected on my day; what would it be like to call the little ranching town home? I scratched my head wondering if Steamboat Springs really needed another veterinarian.

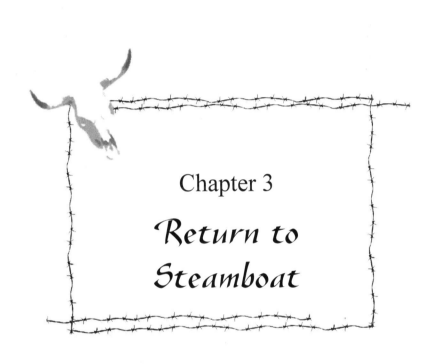

Chapter 3

Return to
Steamboat

*M*y next visit to the Yampa valley was over the long Thanksgiving weekend. I had turkey dinner with my mom in Albuquerque on Thursday and then started north about four that afternoon. Joe Adams had made a reservation for me at the Iron Horse on the east edge of downtown Steamboat Springs. He had told me that my late arrival was expected, but the little motel was completely dark when I pulled in well after one in the morning. I stopped so that my headlights would illuminate the entrance as I tried to awaken the night attendant. There wasn't a bell anywhere in sight, but taped to the door was an envelope with "CLAY" printed in large block letters. Inside was a key to room nine, no note, no bill. I parked in front of number nine, the last room on the left, and even before I'd opened the door I could hear the Yampa River making music. The first thing I did was open my window and the last was to set my alarm as I lay back to the river's song.

The next morning I stumbled from the shower trailing a towel as I lurched across the bed to grab the phone. "Hello, this is Clay. Oh, hi, Joe. Sure, breakfast sounds good. Okay, I know where it is; I passed it last night about a mile south. Yeah, thirty minutes, I'll be there."

Quickly dressing, I made a stop at the motel office. "Hi, I'm Clay; I'm in room nine." I drew a blank stare from the elderly lady behind the counter. "The room by the river," I said, hoping to jar her memory.

"I know which room it is," she growled, raising an eyebrow.

"I thought I'd give you a credit card number to hold. I'll be here another night." I pulled my wallet from my Levi's and started to fish out the card.

"Don't see you registered," the old woman scowled as she adjusted some kind of strap beneath the shoulder pad of her flowered dress.

"I came in late; the key was taped to the door," I said nodding.

24

"Don't know nothin' about it," she said and turned to shuffle some papers behind her.

"Well I, er, I just wanted to give you my card number," I said.

"Boss'll be in later," she mumbled as she walked into the back room.

"Why don't I stop back later?" I fumbled with my wallet trying to get the card to slip back into its too small pocket. "I think I'll stop back this afternoon," I said, raising my palms to the now silent office.

When I arrived at the Holiday Inn coffee shop Joe waved me over to a table by the window. Hay meadows covered in snow led to the base of the ski mountain and the early birds were visible carving turns on runs groomed during the night.

"We'll be able to make snow on the lower mountain in a year or two," Joe said, motioning with his chin toward the skiers. "That'll give the economy a big shot in the arm."

I pulled out a chair. "Looks like there's plenty of snow up there to me," I said.

"Some years we don't have snow on the lower mountain 'til January," Joe said. "The business owners start sweating when Indian summer lasts into December and reservations are canceled."

"That would make any retailer sweat," I said, picking up the menu and selecting French toast with bacon and over easy eggs.

Joe moved his coffee cup to the edge of the table as the waitress arrived with the pot. She nodded in my direction.

"Sure," I said, turning the heavy mug right side up.

"Cream and sugar?" she asked, already setting the cream pitcher on our table. "You guys ready to order?"

We ate with pleasant conversation, and I readily agreed to let Joe drive me around to look at the available office space.

"What I'd really like is something with enough room for a small animal clinic and enough of a parking lot for horse trailers.

25

Ideally it needs to be on the opposite side of town from my competition," I said as we walked to Joe's Chevy Blazer.

"The most important reason though," Joe said as he climbed in motioning me around to the passenger side, "is that most of the growth is going to be from town to the foot of Rabbit Ears Pass. I think I know just the spot for your clinic. It's a new little strip of offices between town and the mountain."

We drove around looking at property for a couple of hours, and it was obvious from the start that Joe's first idea was by far the best. The strip of six spaces was a quarter of a mile from downtown. It had recently been built in the corner of a twenty-acre alfalfa field. There was an ample graveled parking lot in front with room behind the offices for a truck and trailer to loop around the building. Two units on the left were vacant, and I decided that the end one would suit me fine. The eight-hundred-square-foot office was empty space except for a small bathroom in the corner next to the steel rear door. A covered front porch ran the length of the building with redwood decking. It was two steps down to the large gravel parking area.

"Sign me up," I said after a brief examination of the interior. "Who do we need to call?"

"The owner's out of town. He's jumping out of airplanes in Arizona, but don't worry, Craig will be happy to have you as a tenant. Next, we'll find you a place to live," Joe said moving toward his car.

"I'm up for anything." I climbed into the passenger side. "I planned on spending another night, if I have a room."

"I made the reservation through tonight. There shouldn't be a problem," Joe said.

"Oh. It's just that this morning the woman at the desk had no knowledge of me being there at all."

"Okay. Let's run over to the Iron Horse right now. I'll get Wilma straightened out and you can meet her boss. Terry's the guy I need to talk to about those condos anyhow," Joe said, pointing across the highway at a row of three-story units just visible on the hillside closer to town. "He told me the other day that his neighbor was moving back to Denver, and they've always been a good value because the driveway is steep and it takes a four-wheel drive to make it home in the winter."

"I've got the four-wheel drive, but things seem to be moving along pretty fast and I haven't even decided for sure about moving up here," I said, shaking my head.

"Let's get your room straightened out, then join me for lunch at Rotary. That'll help you decide," Joe said. "The weekly meeting was moved to today because of Thanksgiving. I'll introduce you to a number of local businessmen and they'll give you a better perspective of the community."

"Wow, Wilma, I just love your dress. It makes the whole room smell like flowers," Joe said as we walked into the lobby at the Iron Horse.

"Mr. Adams, how you make a girl blush," Wilma giggled.

"I think you've met my friend Clay," Joe said. "We need to get him registered."

"He's been in," Wilma hissed glaring at me. "Looks like a damn Texan up to hunt elk."

"Dr. Williams is the new veterinarian in town," Joe said, nodding in my direction. "He'll have to meet Lilly just as soon as we get him moved in next to that beauty shop you love so well."

"Oh, that would be convenient," Wilma batted her eyes at me. "My Lilly does hate those long car rides."

"I'll make sure to bring you a card as soon as I'm open," I said, approaching the desk. "What do you need for me to register?" I pulled out my credit card for the second time.

"I'll just handle everything, doctor," she said smiling. I reached out to place my card on the desk and Wilma patted me on the back of the hand. "That's all been taken care of, you just don't

27

worry about a thing," she cooed in a newly acquired Southern drawl.

I looked over at Joe. "What's going on; what's been taken care of?" I asked.

"Just Steamboat hospitality," Joe said. "I told you this was the best place in the world to live." I looked from one to the other and all I got were smiles.

"Now wait just a minute," I said.

"Terry, you're just the guy I want to see," Joe said, turning with an outstretched hand as a tall, rugged-looking fellow about thirty came in the front door. "I'd like you to meet Dr. Clay Williams, Steamboat's newest veterinarian."

"Joe told me you'd be moving up here when he reserved number nine for you," Terry said as we shook hands. "I told Joe it only takes one night in that room for the Yampa to weave its spell, but he insisted on two nights to cement the deal."

"Realtors and lawyers, can't trust either of them," I said shaking my head.

Terry confirmed that his neighbor was moving, and since the two condos were identical we visited his. The building wasn't overly impressive, but the view was incredible. Built on a hillside at the east end of Main Street, the living room with its large picture window faced downtown. Standing at the window I looked straight down the main street, and the entire community lay at my feet. The rodeo grounds and Howelson Hill were on the left beyond the river with the residential side of town on the right. Reclining several miles to the west was the Sleeping Giant, formed by the ridgeline of Elk Mountain.

"I never get tired of seeing the sun set behind the Giant," Terry said.

"I'm sure that's true, the view is terrific," I said. "But what about the driveway; Joe tells me that I'll need my four-wheel drive to make it up the hill in the winter."

"Occasionally that's true," Terry said. "But that's not the biggest problem. The scary part is leaving. When the driveway is icy it's like driving a toboggan; there's no control. You slide the length of the hill trying to time it so that when you skid onto the highway you don't crash into any vehicles. It helps if your car is sliding sideways for the last fifty feet so that you can accelerate, spinning tires and fish tailing, to merge with the west-bound traffic. Then, if you need to go east, just turn around in the Safeway parking lot."

"That sounds like loads of fun," I said.

"It definitely will get your attention," Terry said, pointing over toward the drive. "The locals all know that we're out of control coming off the hill and they watch for us. It's the unsuspecting tourists that provide the thrill and get your blood pumping in the morning."

Joe jangled his car keys. "We're gonna' be late for Rotary," he said. "You guys can continue the discussion at lunch."

During the Rotary luncheon I'd heard about several houses for rent in town, been invited to stop by the hospital for a tour, open an account at the local bank and enjoy an evening sleigh ride that included a guitar player singing cowboy songs and a steak dinner prepared over a campfire. In addition at least twenty Rotarians had introduced themselves and wished me luck. My head was spinning when the last of my new friends left Joe and me at the restaurant.

"Follow me out to my place at Stagecoach and I'll show you some condos that are for rent," Joe said. "We think Stagecoach is Routt County's best kept secret."

"I'll have to pass," I said. "I'm beat. I think I'll wander around town for a while and turn in early. I've got a lot to mull over."

"I'll give you a call in the morning and see what you're planning," Joe said shaking hands as we parted in front of the restaurant.

I spent the afternoon sniffing around town and finished with an early dinner of Chinese food in the Harbor Hotel. I smiled as I stepped out of my truck back at the Iron Horse. It was 6:15. *The Yampa River is weaving its spell*, I thought as I heard it caressing the rocks. A note was wedged into the door jamb just above the knob. Turning on a light I read the shaky script. "Come by the office, we have hot chocolate for you." It was signed "Wilma and Lilly."

"Oh, doctor," Wilma called from the back as I entered the lobby. "Just have a chair. I started heating the chocolate when you drove in and it's just about ready. I'll slice the bread and be right there."

"Don't hurry, I've got plenty of time," I said, pulling a chair back from one of the small tables in the area used for their weekend continental breakfast program.

"The girls at the beauty shop were all excited about your clinic," Wilma said, setting two steaming cups of chocolate and a plate of sliced pumpkin bread on the table. She pulled out her chair but had to go behind the lobby counter and answer the phone before she could join me.

I picked up my cup and I was about to take a sip when my right foot was violently jerked under the table. "Whaa…!" I yelled. Lashing out with my left foot I made contact with a large solid object as scalding hot chocolate splashed down my chest. I leaped to my feet knocking over my chair with a crash that went unheard, buried by the ear-piercing squeal from under the table. I was too busy ripping my shirt off, buttons flying around the room, to notice that the table was leaving in a series of violent jerks punctuated by incessant squeals and the crash of porcelain as the plate of pumpkin bread followed by the remaining cup of chocolate smashed on the floor. The table spun on one leg, flipped in the air and landed on its top exposing the largest pot-bellied pig I'd ever seen. The pig, still squealing in terror, ran.

"Watch out, Wilma," I yelled, regaining my senses as the pig, racing through the lobby, rounded the counter sliding on slick hooves and launched herself toward Wilma. I charged behind hoping to save the old lady from the ravages of an insane hog.

"Lilly, Lilly, calm down! Dr. Williams didn't mean to hurt you. He's your friend, baby. Let mommy scratch your back," Wilma cooed.

"Lilly?" I croaked. "That's Lilly?" I stopped, leaning heavily on the counter, mouth agape as I stared down at Wilma bent over scratching the sow behind an ear.

"Mommy's right here, baby. You just scared the nice doctor. He didn't mean to hurt you. It's okay, mommy's here." The pig snuffled and darted her eyes in my direction. "I won't let the doctor kick you again, honey," Wilma said, continuing to scratch her pet.

"It wasn't like I intended to hurt her. She bit me and I just reacted," I said.

"We're the adults. My little girl doesn't understand; she was just looking for affection," Wilma said. "I won't let him hurt you again, darling."

"Ahem." The sound of a man clearing his throat caused me to look toward the entrance. A young couple, each with a small suitcase, was standing just inside the front door. I looked back and forth between the pair and Wilma, suddenly realizing that I was leaning over the counter with my shirt ripped open and that Wilma and Lilly were hidden from their view by the counter.

"Wi...Wilma," I said, still shifting my attention between both parties. "There's a couple..." The woman was tugging on her husband's jacket and whispering in his ear.

"No, wait. I can explain," I said as she turned dragging him out the door. Laughter erupted from the back room and Terry's head appeared around the door frame. "I think I cost you a room," I said.

31

"It was worth it," Terry said when he'd had his laugh. "I can't wait for the next Rotary meeting." He bowed and ceremoniously handed me a button, which started him laughing all over again. "I'll bet they think Lilly is a teenage rape victim."

"Oh, no. How long had they been in the lobby?" I looked around for an upright chair. I needed to sit down.

"Long enough that we can expect a visit from the police in the next few minutes," Terry said.

"In town less than twenty-four hours and I'm to be arrested," I said. "Maybe some other town would be a better place to settle."

"You've already met half the business community, and by next week you'll be famous," Terry said. Now we were all laughing, all of us except for Lilly who had emerged to snuffle up the pumpkin bread and lick at the chocolate. All the while she was making contented little grunts.

"Don't get cut on the broken dishes, dear," Wilma said, coming over to give her pig a pat on the back.

"If Joe Adams calls in the morning tell him I left town at first light," I said, righting my chair as we started to clean up the mess.

Chapter 4

Getting Started

"Come on in," I yelled, hearing someone on the porch stamping the snow off their boots. It was Friday; my third week in town and February was half over. I was expecting Wally Watkins, the contractor I'd met at Rotary just after Thanksgiving. Wally was about thirty-five, an athletic five-foot-ten with black hair, dark brown eyes and a kind face with a big charming smile. His Wranglers were always starched and pressed with a crease breaking in the exact center of his Tony Lama boots, which I'd come to realize were a remnant of his Texas heritage.

Wally had been helping me turn the leased office space into a clinic and was becoming a good friend in the process. During the last week he'd helped me build the interior walls and ceilings, install the plumbing and upgrade the electrical service.

Is that you, Watkins?" I asked as the front door opened with a high pitched creak, the kind reserved for mornings when the hinges are almost frozen solid.

"Wow, Doc, it's colder in here than it is outside," Wally said, stepping around the partition to watch as I organized my first shipment of supplies.

I looked up in time to see a large foggy cloud as Wally exhaled. "I turned the dial to fifty before I left last night. I didn't know that fifty is actually 'Off' on the thermostat," I said.

Wally pointed with his chin to the back corner of the clinic. "It's lucky we haven't tied in the new sinks to the water lines yet, but when that bathroom thaws there'll be broken pipes for sure," he said.

"The bathroom never warms up much so I left a little space heater in there and the water's running fine," I said. "I just hope I can get it warmed up in here before these drugs freeze," I held up a vial of lidocaine I was unpacking and swirled the liquid looking for ice crystals.

"That's the high cost of education," Wally said. "You're learning about our chilly nights."

"Learn or freeze to death," I said looking toward the front door. "Is it warming up at all out there?"

"It's a lot warmer than yesterday. It was only minus fourteen when I started down here."

"That's an improvement. My thermometer read twenty-two below when I left home," I said.

"I was planning to texture your exam room and the surgery today so we can get the whole place painted, but I think I'd better wait 'til it warms up in here," Wally said. "Anything else we can get done?"

"Maybe we'd better let it thaw; working inside with a parka doesn't make a lot of sense," I said. "Besides, I'm leaving in thirty minutes; I've got my first horse call this morning."

"All right," Wally said with a smile. "Where you headed?"

"Fella' name a Charlie is comin' to escort me to the Damon Ranch," I said. "It's just for some vaccinations, a Coggins test and health certificate. You know Carl Damon?"

"Carl, Ellie and Charlie Smith, too," Wally said moving toward the door. "Carl must be headed to Phoenix. He goes down there to rope during the annual February cold spell."

"Looks to me like he missed his chance by at least a week," I said, rubbing my hands together hoping to relieve the numbness.

"I hate to be a wuss, but I'm goin' to warm up with a coffee an' a doughnut at Ken's. You care to join me?"

"I'd like to. I end up dropping half the vials I try to pick up because I can't feel my fingers," I said. "The problem is that I need to wait for Charlie."

"Come on, then," Wally opened the door. "You'll hear Charlie's Harley. Might even hear it better at Ken's 'cause you can raise those ear flaps."

"Charlie rides a bike in this weather?" I said pulling off my hunting cap.

"Only guy in the county," Wally said.

I was stirring sugar into my to-go cup when I heard the rumbling of a large motorcycle as it coasted through the parking lot. Snapping on the plastic lid I stepped out the door and waited for Charlie to remove his helmet. "You want a cup of coffee?" I yelled still holding the door knob.

"No, thanks, I've had too much already," Charlie said, leaning the Harley on its kickstand.

"I'm Clay Williams," I said walking over to shake hands. Charlie pulled thick leather gloves off the biggest hands I'd ever seen. He was six-four, a bear of a man with a bulbous nose, bright red from the cold and a full beard almost snow white from ice crystals. His huge barrel chest appeared even bigger because it was contained in an enormous down coat.

"Charlie Smith," the bear said in a low growl. "Good to meet you, Doc. You wanna follow me out to Carl's?"

"Unless you need your bike out at the Damon ranch, why don't you ride out with me?" I said looking at his big Harley.

"That'll work," Charlie said. "Where do you want me to park the bike?"

"It's good right where it is," I said, walking around to the driver's side of my green Dodge. Charlie climbed in and we turned right onto Highway 40 driving south up the Yampa Valley. "You can push that seat back," I said, noticing that Charlie's knees were right against the dashboard. "I've never been to Carl's; you'll have to give me directions."

"Just take 131 and then make the first right to Sidney," Charlie said as we passed the turn to Mt. Werner ski area.

"You ski, Charlie?" I asked, looking across the blindingly white snow covered fields to the slopes.

"Na, Doc, never learned," Charlie said.

We continued on past a ranch or two, hay fields covered by three feet of snow on both sides of the highway, and turned right onto Highway 131 toward Oak Creek. The pristine snow was furrowed on the left by a pattern of tracks forming loops and circles then following the fence line for a ways only to loop around again. "You snowmobile?"

"Naw, Doc, never tried it," the big man said grinning through his beard.

"What do you do all winter, Charlie?"

He pointed to a snow-covered lane that turned off the highway between two fences. "There's our turn," he said, realizing I hadn't seen the road.

The turn to Sidney was almost invisible in the bright sun with the glare coming off unblemished snow. "Damn, I almost missed it," I said aiming for the turnoff. I touched the brakes and the Dodge seemed to speed up as all four wheels locked and the truck slid past the intersection heading for the barrow ditch. I tried to steer toward the middle of the highway getting off the brakes as I frantically checked my mirror for traffic. I over-corrected, throwing us into a left-hand skid. Steering back to the right caused the vehicle to fish-tail wildly. Each correction seemed to make our predicament worse. I jammed on the brakes out of desperation and the left rear wheel slid off the edge of the pavement. The corner of the bumper buried itself in deep snow that whipped the front of the now almost stopped truck to the left. We came to rest with the front wheels still on the pavement and the truck facing any oncoming traffic.

"That was fun," Charlie said the seat shaking from his laughter. "You ever driven in snow, Doc?"

"Is that what this white stuff is?" I tried to smile and open my door, but realized it was as impossible to smile as it was to open the driver's side door that the snow had blocked. "I'm gonna have to crawl out the window."

"I can climb out and you can slide over," Charlie said opening his door. I climbed out and reached behind the seat to drag the canvas bag containing my chains out on the highway.

"These should do the trick," I said, opening the bag to remove the chains. I held one set up and tried to find the center while Charlie did the same with the other.

"If you take a little piece of baling wire or even a quick tie from the produce section of the grocery store you can put it on the center link of the outside chain. Then just center that on the tire and you'll save time when it's this damn cold," Charlie said, stopping to blow on his hands.

"Hands cold already?" I asked looking up at Charlie as I slid under the truck to fasten the inside chain. "I'll get that side, no use both of us wallowing on the pavement." I slid myself to the other side of the pickup by grabbing the bumper.

"I suppose you're hands are plenty warm," Charlie said fastening the outside chain on the second tire. "Tension bands in the bag, Doc?" he asked, warming his hands under folded arms.

"They should be," I said, rolling out from under the truck. By the time I'd brushed the snow off my pants Charlie had the bands clipped on.

"Turn around and I'll get your back," he said as I rubbed numb fingers together trying to get some feeling back.

"Let's get out of this cold," I said, opening the passenger door. I couldn't remember a truck heater ever feeling as good as I slid across the seat.

"I'll stay here and push if I have to," Charlie said, closing the door. I slipped the four-wheel drive lever into the low range before pulling ahead. The front wheels spun for less than half a turn before catching. The truck lurched forward roughly and the rear bumper came clear of the snow.

"Hop in and I'll turn around. We can pull the chains off as soon as we get off this highway."

"That'll work," Charlie said. "But I really don't think anybody else is crazy enough to be out in this cold."

We removed the chains on the lane to Sidney and threw them in the floor on the passenger side. The truck's heater had sufficiently warmed our bones by the time we'd reached the Damon ranch that we could once more brave the environment. The horses were stalled in Carl's barn and their presence raised the temperature

38

noticeably. Still, we didn't waste time. The horses were vaccinated and blood was drawn for Coggins testing before my cab had time to cool down. The ride back was uneventful and we'd nearly reached Steamboat when I remembered our earlier conversation.

"I think," I said, grinning over at the bear, "we were having a conversation before we were almost killed because my navigator forgot his job. You'd told me that you don't ski and you don't snowmobile. So what is it you do all winter, Charlie?"

"I wait for summer," Charlie said.

"I don't think I could live here if I didn't have something I liked to do all winter," I said pulling into the clinic parking lot. "I'm not sure I could stand it."

"That's because you haven't been here for a summer yet, Doc," Charlie said with just the hint of a smile.

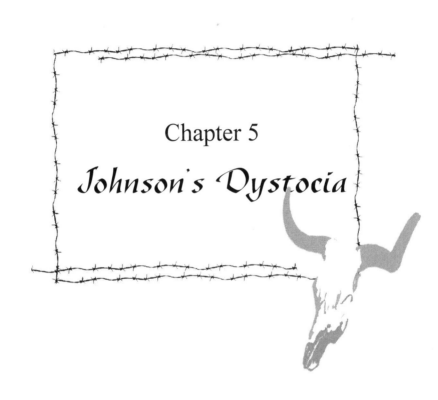

Chapter 5

Johnson's Dystocia

I answered on the first ring that Monday, anxious for some work. "Routt County Veterinary Clinic. May I help you? Yes, this is Dr. Williams," I said, accepting a call from Dr. Bill Belman. I'd only met Belman once. It was the week of my arrival, and I'd made a special trip across town to introduce myself. Bill had seemed genuinely friendly at the time; he'd had the staff show me the entire hospital. Dr. Belman was the long established large animal practitioner in town. He'd called this morning to invite me to go with him on a call the next day. He said he wanted to introduce me to some of the local ranchers.

Tuesday dawned crystal clear. I stepped off my porch to the crunch of frozen snow; it had warmed to 34 degrees a week back and the thaw created a frozen crust. Now the jet stream was back over Canada. Northern Colorado was clear and cold. *It was 47 degrees below at 9:30 last night,* I thought. *It may warm up to a minus 15 by noon.* I unplugged the engine heater and started my pickup, allowing it to warm up while I scraped thick frost from the windshield. Arriving at my new office, a few hundred square feet in a small strip of six rentals, I inhaled the odor of fresh paint mingled with the familiar smell of disinfectant and checked all four sinks to be certain that no pipes had frozen during the night. Walking along the front porch brought me to the doughnut shop two doors down. Ken was in the back, cranking out his specialty.

"Those French guys done yet?" I hollered, as I opened the door.

"The first batch are cooling. Help yourself!" I grabbed a napkin and lifted a warm, chocolate glazed, French cruller from the rack and poured myself a cup of coffee, black as night.

"I haven't made fresh coffee, so drink at your own risk!" Ken called. "What's up? You're over early."

"No breakfast, and I'm going up to Yampa with Bill Belman."

"Take a couple of cinnamon rolls with you. They're Bill's favorite." Ken said.

"I didn't know Belman was a regular,"

"Hasn't been for a few weeks. Either a New Year's resolution, or he's steering clear of the competition," Ken answered.

"You mean because I moved in?" I laughed. "Somehow I don't think I bother Bill."

"You never know," Ken said coming out from the back room, flour splotched on his face and arms as usual. I'd known Ken for about a month, since the first day I'd moved in to the little row of rental spaces. He might have been the cartoonist's model for Popeye. He had huge forearms with the Navy's anchor insignia tattooed on both. Ken always wore a white tee-shirt beneath his baker's apron, and peeking from under his right sleeve was a red high-heeled shoe and the blue outline of a slender calf. He wore a big smile and had a deeply dimpled chin. His hairline had receded almost to baldness with only a wisp slipping from under his baker's hat in front. Ken pulled two cinnamon rolls from the case and bagged them. "You take Belman these from me; maybe I can get him coming back even if he resolved to shed that little paunch of his."

"I'll tell him you said that an' see what he thinks about this dive."

"Whatever he thinks, he won't say much!" Ken said, his grin widening. "Better take reading material; Bill's famous for his silence."

"Hey, he called me, so I figure he can't be as quiet as everyone says." I picked up the bag of cinnamon rolls and went back into the cold. A few swallows of coffee, and Bill was pulling up to the clinic in his blue Chevy Bel Air. Wasting no time I climbed into the warm sedan.

"Good morning. Ken sent these rolls for you," I said, holding out the bag before reaching down to fasten my seat belt.

Belman nodded wordlessly as he backed from the parking space.

"If you'd like a cup of coffee, I can grab one for you," I said. "Ken just made a fresh pot."

Bill patted the stainless steel thermos lying on the seat beside him, put the Bel Air in gear and started south toward Oak Creek and Yampa. He was dressed from head to foot in khaki. A thermometer and two pens were sticking out of the left breast pocket of his long sleeved shirt. Thick bifocals with small round lenses perched on his nose, with wire frames that wrapped around his ears.

We drove in silence, the valley incredibly white on that February morning with patches of mist hanging low over the frozen river. Thick frost covered every surface, making the fences and willows as white as the snow. The cloudless sky was the deep blue of the high country.

"It sure is a beautiful day," I said, hoping to draw Belman out. There was no reply. "Cold though." Still no response. "Lots of snow in that last storm." Nothing from Bill. I was rapidly coming to believe the stories I'd heard about his silence. We drove along and I changed tactics. "Where is it we're headed?"

"Johnson place," Bill replied, glancing in my direction.

Now we're getting somewhere, I thought. "Is his place on the left where the road comes out from Yampa?" I asked, knowing the answer.

"That's it," Bill said.

"He's sure got a nice spot there on the river. Don't you think?" More silence.

"Does he do well with the Shorthorns he raises?"

"Trust funder," Bill said with a frown.

"Bob Johnson's a trust funder?" I asked. Bills answer was a single nod. "I thought he grew up on that ranch," I said, forgetting to make it a direct question.

"Bob's had the ranch about six years. Houston oil money." Bill looked over at me.

He's warming up to the conversation now! I thought. "I'm surprised; his place looks well-kept even though it's obviously not new. I thought he'd been ranching all his life."

44

"It's always been a good ranch; he works hard, but knows next to nothing," Bill said.

"I saw him at the El Rancho one day. Nice guy. He seemed to fit right in at the table," I said, thinking of the morning hangout where a large table was always reserved for the locals.

"He's well liked," Bill said. "Doesn't flash his money around, but it's there. Conoco, I think!"

"I'd never have guessed him for a Texan," I said, shaking my head.

"Educated back east from grade school, then went to an Ivy League college. I can't remember, maybe Yale. He keeps his Texas roots quiet, and nobody holds it against him. It was an accident of birth." Bill smiled, pointing across the highway to a small group of Johnson's red roan cows. They were in the willows on the far side of the river peacefully munching grass hay. The feed trail, a large loop of packed snow circling the pasture, bore the unmistakable tracks of a horse-drawn feed sled and held several groups of cows. They were all near their calving dates by the looks of them.

"What are we coming to see?" I asked, as we turned left into the Ranch Drive.

"Dystocia," Bill said. "I think she's been trying to calve for several days."

"Several days! This may be real ugly," I said. Looking around as we bumped over a snow-covered cattle guard I noticed that the snow stood more than 10 feet high on either side of the drive. We entered the ranch headquarters. All the snow was removed from the ample yard area, with the house and equipment sheds on the right and the barns and corrals on the left. "Johnson sure has a good blower," I said.

Directly in front of us, in what would be a pasture in the summer months, was a veritable mountain of snow. The stored snow covered an area as big as a football field and stood 20 feet high. Dozer tracks on the top testified to the packing job. I'd barely taken it all in when we pulled up to the main barn. On one side, a set of small sorting pens with an approach chute and a squeeze chute were all housed under a metal roof. Behind this was a much larger set of pens with a long curved approach chute, the latest innovation, and a brand-new hydraulic squeeze. This set, without the benefit of a roof, was covered with three feet of heavy snow. Bill's trust funder comment flashed through my mind, and I smiled inwardly realizing that whatever the rancher wanted he could afford.

Bob Johnson came out of the barn. He was just over six feet, but his lean body and small frame made him look even taller. A pleasant face and soft brown eyes made him appear to be at peace with himself. He gestured toward the covered chute. "In there," he said, pointing to two cows standing in the covered pens. "I hope you don't mind, I found a bad eye this morning and ran her in, too."

I noticed the larger of the two cows had tears and discharge matted below her right eye. Bill was already out of the car opening the trunk. A frigid wind hit me as I climbed out of the Chevy, causing me to gasp and shiver. I zipped my heavy goose down parka to the neck and pulled my knitted ski cap over my ears.

"This is Dr. Williams," Bill said, gesturing in my direction.

"Clay Williams," I said, as Bob, pulling off his glove, approached with outstretched hand.

"Bob Johnson," he said. "You look familiar. Have we met?"

"The El Rancho at lunch last week, maybe Tuesday."

"Oh, yes, now I remember, but you didn't say you were a vet."

"I didn't know it mattered. Most people will eat at the same table with me, even when they know what I do for living!" I laughed.

"I'll get one of them in for you, Doc," Bob said, ignoring my banter as he started opening gates to move the cows.

Dr. Belman winked and, leaning close, whispered, "Educated back east, Clay, just like I said."

The first cow through was the eye. Bill quickly examined her and then handed me his magnifying loop as he went to the car for supplies. I pulled the plastic headband on, adjusting it to keep the lens in place. As I moved my head closer, the cow's eye came into focus. No sign of cancer, just a lot of inflammation. Pinkeye. I finished my exam as Bill returned, syringe in hand.

"What do you see?" He asked.

"An uncomplicated pinkeye," I said, handing him back his loop.

"Me, too," he said, handing me a pair of nose tongs with a short piece of 3/8" rope attached.

I grabbed her nose with the blunt instrument. Keeping the tongs squeezed tight, I wrapped the rope around a pipe on the cow's left, and pulled her head in that direction, exposing her right eye and limiting any attempt at head movement.

"OK," Bill said as he pushed his right hip against her nose. Everting her upper eyelid with his right thumb and forefinger, he injected a mixture of antibiotics and cortisone under the conjunctiva. Then he surrounded the eye with black paint from a small roll-on container. "Let's paint her other eye," he said, stepping away from her head. I unwrapped the rope and brought her nose around to the right so that Bill could paint around her left eye to reduce sun exposure. "Next victim," Bill said, opening the head gate and allowing the cow to clang and bang her way to freedom. He went to his car for more supplies and equipment, and I helped Bob by running the chute as he pushed the next cow through. With her head safely caught, and the squeeze tightened enough to reduce movement, I retired to perch on the wooden fence out of the wind. I wondered what the chill factor was as the breeze stiffened. Zipping my parka all the way to the top I pulled the collar up over my chin and adjusted my cap, tugging it as far down as it would stretch.

"I think it's getting colder," I said.

"That's the one thing about this ranch," Bob replied, pointing to the west. "The wind comes off Shingle Peak over there and howls right through here!" Almost on command, the breeze increased kicking up granules of snow anywhere the crust had been broken. I shivered involuntarily.

"How long has she been trying to calve?" Dr. Belman called over the moan of the wind.

"At least four days," Bob replied without a trace of guilt in his voice.

Four days, and I don't think he's kidding. I tried to get a look at Bill, but the open trunk obscured him. Fleetingly I wondered what he was doing; maybe slashing his wrists so he wouldn't have to deal with this. After four days the calf would most certainly be dead and rotting.

"Is that water heater still in the barn?" Bill asked.

"Oh, sure," Bob said. "Would you like me to draw you a bucket?"

"That would help!" Bill set out his 3-gallon stainless steel bucket. Bob went for warm water and I hunched over to reduce the wind exposure. *I'm in a sheltered spot,* I thought. *I wouldn't want to be Belman in this wind.*

"Anything I can do?" I asked, hoping Bill would want me to wait in the car.

"You just sit up there, keep warm, and let me know if you've got any ideas!"

Dr. Belman stepped from behind the Bel Air's trunk carrying a plastic toolbox. He'd shed his shirt and pulled on a yellow rubber obstetrical suit. He was wearing his coat over the sleeveless O.B. top, but to be able to work the coat would have to go. He found a piece of bailing twine and tied the young heifer's tail up over her back, out of the way. Johnson returned with a steaming bucket of water. Quickly washing her, Bill then splashed rinse water over the now steaming hindquarters. Opening the toolbox he'd left sitting next to the chute Bill pulled out obstetrical chains and handles. He tossed them unceremoniously into the hot water followed immediately by his already stiffening hands, wincing as ice-cold fingers contacted the hot water.

"Damn, I bet that hurts!" I said, rubbing my down-filled gloves together. "It's even painful from here."

"Be careful or I'll have you down here freezing your fingers off."

I held my hands up. "I'm cold enough in these."

Belman took no notice as he stripped off his coat and sloshed Betadine disinfectant on his arms.

"Put a little more squeeze on that heifer, she may want to go down when Bill gets inside," I said to Johnson.

"Good idea. See, you're already being helpful," Bill said as he squeezed a big handful of KY lubricant into one hand and proceeded to coat his arms with the freezing jelly.

"What do you need me to do?" Bob offered as Dr. Belman ran his right arm deep into the heifer's birth canal. Too engrossed to talk, Bill just looked over his shoulder at us, his glasses fogging up already.

"He's just checking things out, trying to figure out the puzzle," I said. The doctor groped around in the heifer for a couple of minutes, assessing the situation. Finally he started to withdraw his arm.

"He's probably got it figured out now," I said to the owner. Bill withdrew his arm part way then stopped and ducked his head away. There was an ugly grimace on his face, so my first thought was that he was straining to reposition the fetus. I was wrong; immediately on the wind I realized the true reason for his actions. An odor unlike any other assaulted Bob and me. The smell of a dead fetus, rotting in the warmth of the womb, was unmistakable. It caused me to cough and readjust my perch to minimize the stench. Bob Johnson staggered backward into the fence gagging.

"It's safe to say the calf's' dead," I said as Dr. Belman stepped away from the heifer with pinkish gray pus and liquefying tissue running off of his arm. He shook his head, fighting off the odor that was now almost strong enough to be a visible cloud.

"Head and one leg back." He said swallowing hard between each word. "I'll need the eye hooks."

I slipped off the fence and went to his toolbox. "In here?" I asked.

"Top tray." Bill fished out one chain from the bucket and threaded the hooks on it. I rapidly returned to my perch, some 20 feet away.

"He'll try to get a hook in each eye socket," I said to Bob. "This is where you wish for an extra foot or two of arm length." Johnson was inching further down the fence at every opportunity still blinking and coughing occasionally from the smell.

"Even on a warm day you can only stay inside a cow so long. The pressure they exert on your arm makes your hand go numb," I said as Belman tightened the chain, his body straightening notice-ably. "Looks like he's got his chain attached, so he'll probably need that handle in the bucket." Bob Johnson moved forward to help.

"I'll get it, Bob. You just keep some tension on this chain," Bill said. The owner obeyed and Belman attached the handle as close to the cow as he could.

"Bob, you pull down on this chain, and let's see if we can bring the head around." Belman reached back inside the cow to check on the progress. "OK, good, but you'll have to pull hard." I almost came down from my perch to help, when I heard a sucking sound and Johnson staggered backward still pulling on the chain as the head, covered in fetid pus, flew out of the heifer and landed at his feet.

"Well," I said, "that's out of the way." Bill didn't reply. Throwing the chain, hooks, and handle in the bucket he dove in again. Grimacing and straining Belman worked on for several minutes.

"Bill's trying to get the leg that's back," I said. "Right, Bill?" His reply was a curt nod.

"I've got to get it closer to the pelvis," Bill said as he reached into the bucket for his chain, this time making a loop to pass over a front foot. With the handle attached again, more pulling removed one front leg along with a new wave of noxious fumes. Bill started to look worried, and I knew his predicament. He was rapidly losing the appendages and would soon have no place to attach a chain. Compounding this problem he was facing a novice ranch owner with high expectations and the new vet as a witness to the impending failure. Belman stood with brow furrowed, staring at the heifer.

That's when I had my idea.

"Does that hydraulic squeeze work?" I asked Johnson.

"Well," Bob said, looking through the sharp crystals of blowing snow, "it would if it weren't three feet deep in snow!"

"It would work if the snow was gone?"

"Sure," he replied. "If the snow was gone."

"So, if we shoveled out the chute and the approach ally we could get her in it." I jumped from my perch and leaned into the freezing wind, pointing at the snow-covered equipment. Belman tried to rub a little steam from his glasses with his forearm to get a better look and only succeeded in smearing it around.

"I suppose we could do that, but it would be a lot of shoveling," Bob replied, scratching his head as he stared at the deep snow.

"With the three of us we could get it shoveled in under an hour," I said.

"I guess, with the three of us," Bob said turning to look at Dr. Belman. They were exchanging confused looks so I eased back to the fence and climbed up to my perch.

"Good, let's do it!" I said, hunching down again to make a smaller target for the unrelenting wind.

"Why, what would we gain?" Belman asked, his brow furrowed and a confused look on his face.

"Well," I said. "If you were working out there, I could sit here, out of the wind, and the smell wouldn't be nearly as bad!"

Bill stripped off his obstetrical sleeves. "Sometimes you're so damned close to a situation you can't see how ridiculous it is," he said unzipping his rubber suit. "I don't know if we can save this cow or not, but Clay's right this isn't the place to do it. You'll have to haul her to the hospital; then maybe we can get something done." He'd already climbed out of his obstetrical suit and was throwing the bucket and other equipment into his trunk. A few seconds later Bill was behind the steering wheel and we were headed back to Steamboat.

Chapter 6

The Health
Certificate

*I*t had been two weeks since I accompanied Dr. Belman to Yampa. He'd called after our trip to report that once the Johnson cow was hauled to the hospital for several days of treatment she had survived. The weather had warmed enabling it to snow and most of Routt County had been busy shoveling for the last week. My phone hadn't rung except for Wally calling to have lunch and Charlie Smith calling to see if I'd skidded off the road and needed help. So when Dr. Belman called I jumped at the chance to take a ride with him to Hayden.

I walked in the side door at the Westside Veterinary Hospital to find Dr. Belman and the receptionist, Lois DeLaney, in a heated discussion.

"So when can I tell Lucy she can come?" Lois asked exasperation evident in her voice.

"Never!" Bill growled back. "Can't you get it? I don't care about a newspaper article!"

Lois turned to me, "If *The Pilot* wanted to do a story on your clinic you'd let them take pictures, and accept the free advertising, right?"

"Oh sure," I laughed, thinking about the weekly newspaper, *The Steamboat Pilot*. "An' I'd smile real big for the camera, too!"

"Bull shit!" Bill exclaimed. "Let Red have all the glory. I'm not wearing a stethoscope while I smile into the camera for Lucy or anyone else."

"Listen, Dr. Belman," Lois argued. "Lucy's already taken pictures of the hospital and Dr. Sears in surgery. She just wants a good action shot of you for the article."

Bill just grunted, filling his mouth with one of the cinnamon rolls from the bakery bag I held out to him. Opening the door I'd just entered, he motioned me to follow. I tossed the bag on the counter. "Here's some doughnuts," I said as I hurried to catch up.

"Wait!" Lois yelled, running for the door. "Dr. Williams, could you try to convince my boss about the pictures?" She leaned out the door, gracing me with her biggest smile.

"Don't go putting me in the middle!" I said, jumping into Belman's Chevy. I looked back at Lois; her smile had turned to an icy glare.

"You know," Bill commented as we drove west toward Hayden, "I might cooperate if someone besides Lucy was writing the story."

"I've read a few of her stories," I said. "She makes them interesting, and they're all colorful."

"They're interesting all right. She's never let a little thing like truth get in the way of the story. She's not a reporter, she's a gossip!" We drove in silence for a couple of miles on a straight stretch of road. Passing through low, sagebrush-covered hills deep with snow, the road made a sharp left. Bill shook like a Labrador coming out of water, his face brightening.

"That's John Utterback's barn," he said, pointing to an old log barn sitting back from the road 100 yards or so. The barbed wire fence along the highway had "Keep Out" signs on nearly every post and three on the Portagee gate, with its double padlocks.

"Does Doc Utterback practice anymore?" I asked, picturing the grizzled old veterinarian.

"Only when it's election time. He's a county commissioner, you know," Bill replied, shaking his head. "Whatever clients he's got you wouldn't want anyway." We drove on skirting the river, with high sandstone bluffs to our right.

"We're headed to meet the Tipton Ranch foreman and look at a horse," Bill said. "He's just a young kid, and he's going back to New Mexico. Wife hates snow or old widow Tipton, I'm not sure which," he laughed.

"I hear the widow raises good horses," I said, immediately interested. "What are we doing for her?"

"It's not for Jill, it's the foreman...John something... he's taking a horse with him and needs a health certificate," Bill said. "I was hoping she'd be there so I could introduce you, but Lois told me this morning that she's in Denver."

"Well, at least I can see the ranch," I said, covering my disappointment.

"Not much of it, I'm afraid," Bill said, "John lives right by the highway. It's only a couple more miles, where the road skirts that big stretch of pasture along the river."

"How much of that bottom land does she own?" I asked.

"About half, maybe 400 acres," Bill said. "Then she's got another section or two of deeded ground, plus grazing on 3,000 acres of BLM land."

We crossed the railroad tracks and started across the Yampa River. In the center of the bridge Bill pointed downstream. "She owns from the middle of the river right here for three-quarters of a mile downstream and south over those low hills for a mile and a half."

We were skirting the large flat pastures of bottomland. They were under three feet of snow and blindingly white in the mid-morning sun. As the highway curved around the pastureland staying close to the bottom of the hills, I spotted the foreman's house next to the highway.

"That must be the place," I said, pointing.

"That's it," Bill replied, slowing the Belair. "This shouldn't take long." He turned in at a small white farmhouse. The drive, on the left of the house, was lined with old elm trees. The right hand line of trees made a 90-degree angle behind the house, forming the front of a large parking area that reached back to a dilapidated log shed. The driveway, made narrow by huge mounds of encroaching snow, was obviously being hand shoveled. It ended at an older blue Ford pickup. There was no room to turn around.

We were squeezing out of the Chevy with the doors pressed into the snow banks as a cowboy, his boots covered by five buckle rubber overshoes, came tromping through knee-deep snow from the equipment shed. A lined Levi jacket snapped to the neck was pulled on over a thick down vest, making him appear much heavier than he was. I guessed him to be in his early twenties, but what really caught my eye was the big bay colt tied to the largest elm behind the house. The horse was tied high in the tree with a short rope. Sweat had lathered his neck and flanks, and he pawed, moving nervously about. All the snow had been tromped from around the base of the elm, and the bark was missing to a height of three feet. The bay had bronc written all over him. Dr. Belman was busy getting out his book of blank health certificates; his stethoscope dangled from his neck.

"John, this is Dr. Williams," he said, not bothering to look up.

"Clay Williams," I said extending my hand.

"John Pratt," he replied with a firm handshake.

"Is that P-R-A-T-T, John?" Dr. Belman asked, starting to fill out the health paper. A nod from the cowboy confirmed the spelling. "Where exactly are you going in New Mexico, John?" Bill asked.

"Magdalena, at least that's the closest town," John replied with a friendly smile.

"I need a physical address." Bill said in his best professional tone.

"Sally!" John called to the house. A woman of about John's age stuck her head out the door.

"What?" she yelled, cocking her head to the side and cupping a hand behind her ear.

"Doc needs our new address!"

"I can't hear with this washer goin'!" she shouted, starting off the steps toward our car.

Belman turned to John, "Can you bring your colt over here out of the snow?"

John shook his head slightly. "I...I just tied him up," he replied.

Bill, the professional in charge, failed to understand. "We have to listen to his lungs, and I have to see him trot!" He said tapping the pad with his pen. John's mouth dropped open. He looked pleadingly at me. I just shrugged, raising an eyebrow.

"Well...all right...I'll get him," John whined, slogging through the snow toward the tree where the bay was tied.

"He means," I said to Bill, "he just tied him for the first time." Bill looked confused as John stepped into the depression where the agitated bay was tied. Instantly, the colt jumped forward; his chest and right shoulder rammed the tree trunk stopping his forward progress. In a fluid motion too rapid for the human eye the colt fired with both hind feet, striking John full in the chest. We heard a thud, like a baseball bat swung full force into tightly baled hay. "Phhhh." The air was expelled from John's lungs. His body arched skyward, his boots clearing the ground by two feet. John went down on his back, hitting like he'd fallen from a ten-story window. The bay colt danced about, lining up for another shot as John gasped for air, thrashing like a turtle flipped on its back. Blood bubbled from his nose and one corner of his mouth. I sprinted across the few yards separating us, jerking my knees up to clear the deep snow.

"Holy shit!" Belman stopped his writing and stood transfixed.

I grabbed John by the jacket collar as the colt fired again, narrowly missing the injured cowboy. I started to drag the gasping, thrashing body, my feet slipping haphazardly and throwing snow in John's face with each step. All my attention was riveted on the bronc. I tried not to allow him a target while I dragged John out of his reach. *Fractured ribs and sternum,* I thought. *He's probably got a punctured lung and bruised heart.* I ripped open his jacket and vest as John continued to gasp, trying to get a breath.

"Holy shit!" Bill repeated. "Is he OK?"

"I don't..." was all I got out before Sally interrupted.

"Of course, he's all right!" She yelled, shaking her head. "This happens all the time!"

I bent close to John's face trying to tell if he was moving any air at all. By this time, he was turning blue around the lips, but seemed to be better oriented, because he willingly laid back and stopped his thrashing. His mouth was starting to swell, and

58

I realized the blood was from a split lip and a nosebleed. John's breathing was improving; so I helped him to sit up. He rubbed his face and chest and got shakily to his feet.

"Just knocked the wind out of me," John hoarsely whispered, absently trying to wiggle an upper tooth between his thumb and forefinger.

"I thought you'd broken some ribs!" I told him. "That vest and jacket must have provided pretty good protection." I looked in Bill's direction and saw him hand the completed health certificate to Sally and start for his car. Rushing over I got in as he put the Chevy in gear.

"Good luck!" I shouted as I closed the door. John waved weakly, and I waved back. "Man, he was lucky," I said as I searched for the seat belt. Bill gave a single nod of acknowledgment as he backed down the narrow drive. The stethoscope was no longer around his neck. I detected its bulge, where he'd shoved it, deep in his back pocket.

"How'd that colt's heart sound?" I asked. We almost hit the snow bank as Bill arched himself out of the seat. Digging into his pocket, he thrust the stethoscope in my face.

"You wanna know how his heart sounded, you listen to it!" He said turning scarlet. I laughed until tears ran down my cheeks.

"I thought I'd gotten him killed!" Belman said as the redness began to leave his face. "It scared the crap out of me!"

"You suppose Sally's a nurse?" I asked. Bill turned to me looking puzzled. "Well, she's had some kind of advanced medical training." I said, "'cause she made John's diagnosis without even getting close!"

It was Bill's turn for a good laugh. "I'd sure want my wife to be more concerned, if I'd taken both feet in the chest." He said.

"Did you hear him get kicked?" I asked with a grin.

"Oh, yeah!" Bill said, shaking his head in amazement. "Hell, he was three feet in the air and those overshoes were the highest part of him."

59

"It was a short flight and the landing was pretty rough!" I chuckled.

"Man, he hit hard," Bill said piloting his car back across the railroad tracks. "That landing probably started his heart again."

"Could you believe his wife, 'Of course he's all right! It happens all the time.'" I mimicked Sally's nasal whine.

"How often you suppose he gets kicked like that?" Bill slowed for the turn at Doc Utterback's.

"Not as often as his wife thinks, or he'd be dead!" I replied.

"Jeez, the bubbles of blood from that kid's nose and mouth! When you jerked that jacket open, I thought I'd see bone sticking out of his chest," Belman said, accelerating along the straightaway into Milner. "I didn't realize how mean that bronc was... Oh no, I had to see him trot."

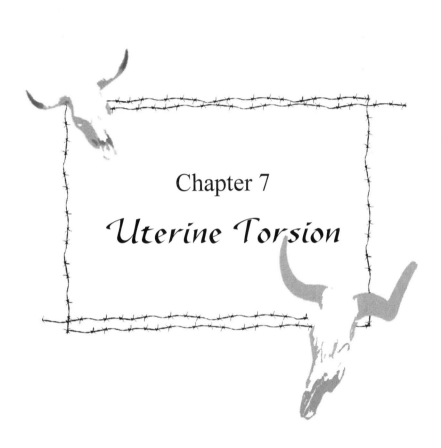

Chapter 7

Uterine Torsion

W e were still in good spirits from the entertainment John Pratt had provided when we arrived back at Bill's office. A mud-covered Ford pickup and stock trailer were parked behind the hospital next to the steel building that housed Dr. Belman's large animal treatment room.

"I forgot about Art Huddleston coming in," Bill said, scratching his head. "How busy are you? I might need a hand."

"I'm not sure I have the time," I replied, checking my watch. "I'm almost due for another cup of coffee."

"Seriously," Bill said, "could you hang around a little while? I'd appreciate it and I might even spring for lunch."

"You, buying lunch? I wouldn't miss it," I replied, climbing out of the Belair.

While Dr. Belman went to find Art, I peered through the slats on the stock trailer at a large Charolais cow.

She was big, fat and heavy with calf. She stared back, shaking her head at me in an unfriendly manner.

Bill returned jangling truck keys. "Art went to lunch. If you'll back the trailer in, I'll adjust the chute," he said, tossing me the keys. After backing the trailer into position, I watched as Dr. Belman tried to get the big Charolais moving. "There's a hot-shot in the equipment box," Bill said, pointing to the wall next to the squeeze. "Would you mind getting it for me, Clay?" I opened the heavy hinged lid, handing the battery-powered device to Bill.

"Thanks," he said, poking its long flexible shaft through the trailer bars. "Come on, girl, you don't want to make this hard."

He prodded the cow gently with the shaft. In response she shook her head, slinging slobber onto the trailer walls and floor. Bill poked her with the electric prod again, only this time his finger depressed the trigger for just a second. The cow bellowed and jumped, crashing into the side of the trailer; Bill hit her again. This time she lashed out with a hind foot and started moving toward the door. When she balked at the trailer's back gate, he touched her again with the prod sending her down the approach chute at a trot.

As she came through the squeeze, I was able to catch her behind the jaws with the scissor-like head gate that clanged together on either side of her neck. I reached over my head for the pipe lever that brought the side panels together applying the squeeze and restricting her movement. Using a piece of quarter-inch nylon cord Dr. Belman tied her tail out of the way and started washing her hindquarters with Betadine scrub.

"Art told me on the phone she'd been in labor all night," Bill said. "Interesting that she's not swollen at all." After rinsing off the soap, he opened a sterile obstetrical sleeve and examined the cow vaginally for a few seconds.

"Is she dilated?" I asked.

"Seems to cone down right at the cervix!" Bill said, withdrawing his hand, "I'd better do a rectal." The rectal exam required a little more time. "Damn, she's got a uterine torsion."

"Can you tell which direction it flipped?" I asked.

"Clockwise, I think." Bill replied. "The birth canal is closed tight. We're going to have to open her up to fix this one." Withdrawing his arm, he peeled off the sleeve. "I think the calf is positioned okay and can be born normally once we get the uterus turned back over. I'll use the right flank so I can get under the fetus. Would you mind clipping her?" I nodded as Bill motioned toward a wall-mounted cabinet. "The clippers are in there." I found them, dropped open several of the vertical bars on the right side of the chute, and started removing the hair from her rib cage back to her hind leg while Bill went over to the main hospital for instruments and supplies.

"I really appreciate the help," Belman said as he closed the steel side door. I'd swept up the hair and was putting the clippers away.

"I'll scrub her if you want to get ready," I volunteered.

"Sounds good," he said as he pulled a pair of white paper coveralls from one of the wall cabinets. I had just begun the Betadine scrub when Lois stuck her head in the door.

"Is Dr. Belman doing surgery?" she asked. I wanted to tell her, 'No, I just love to clip and scrub for no reason.' Instead, I nodded.

"Oh, good!" she said, closing the door again. When I finished, Bill, armed with a large syringe of lidocaine, began to infiltrate the local anesthetic in a vertical line midway between the cow's flank and her last rib. Then I helped him into his white paper gown and opened a disposable plastic drape, surgical gloves and his sterile instrument pack.

"Looks like we're ready," Bill said as he peeled the backing from the drape and stuck it to the cow's skin. Picking up a scalpel, Belman incised the skin through the center of the sterile drape in one swift stroke. The incision started high on her side and went straight down for 20 inches. He bluntly separated the muscle layers between their fibers following the angle of each layer until he reached the highly elastic peritoneum, which he opened with the scalpel. Several liters of hazy pinkish fluid ran from the incision. "She must have had this torsion for several days to collect this much fluid in the abdominal cavity," Belman commented, reaching through the body wall to above his elbow to palpate her uterus. The big Charolais tensed her belly dumping several more liters of fluid onto Bill's gown and coveralls, turning them a lovely pink color.

"I've got to push the bowel forward out of the way to be able to rotate the calf back counterclockwise," Bill said, thinking out loud.

"If I can help, let me know," I said relaxing against the side of the chute.

"Don't worry; if I can figure out a way for you to help, you'll be the first to know." Bill reached in again to attempt the correction.

"Come right in here," Lois called, opening the side door as she looked over her shoulder. "Here, Lucy, let me help you with the camera bag." Turning, Lois yanked a huge black bag through the door. It was still attached by a shoulder strap to Lucy Rogers.

The dumpy, middle-aged reporter was almost jerked off her feet and her camera with its big zoom lens banged against the doorframe as she made her way inside. The large, cumbersome tripod momentarily wedged crosswise in the opening. Lucy had to drop it or risk losing her arm as the steel door bounced back to slam closed.

"Bill's right in here, Lucy, and he's ready for you!" Lois gushed, smiling at Bill and giving him a little wave.

"I've got to answer the phone, but I'm sure Dr. Williams can show you the best place to stand," she said, pointing the reporter in my direction and retrieving her tripod before disappearing. Lucy stepped toward the front of the chute; dropped her bag unceremoniously on the floor and snapped two pictures in rapid succession.

At the first flash, Bill, now shoulder deep in the big Charolais, was almost jerked off his feet as the cow bellowed and lunged at the head gate. He turned toward Lucy just in time for the blinding flash of the camera's strobe on the second shot. Bill blinked, muttering under his breath. He threw his free arm over his head for protection as he tried to stay with the agitated animal banging about in the chute.

"Lucy," I said, "I'll get you standing up on this box; and then you can look right down on the action!" Dr. Belman was being tossed about like a rag doll by the struggling animal and made no comment.

"That might be a really good angle!" Lucy said, moving over by the box.

"Put your foot right up here on my knee," I said, bending down to form a step. Standing on the bin Lucy looked right over Dr. Belman's shoulder.

Bill had repositioned his arm inside the cow. The look on his face, the bend in his knees and the arch in his back told me that he was about to attempt to lift the fetus contained within a very slick uterus. It probably weighed 110 pounds. Bill needed to lift the mass above the uterine body and shove it over and to the left.

"Get ready!" I said to Lucy. "This will be a great shot."

Belman heaved on the calf elevating it clear of the vast quantity of fluid that had collected in the abdomen. As he started to push the fetus back counterclockwise, the slick organ slipped from his grasp falling back onto the abdominal floor with an audible splash. The Charolais arched her back and violently contracted all her abdominal muscles. The effect was spectacular. Eight or ten loops of bowel, distended with gas, instantly popped from the lower half of the incision, like so many long, bent circus balloons. At the same time, a gallon or more of the abdominal fluid shot from the upper half of the incision, washing over Dr. Belman's head in a flood. His glasses were knocked askew as he jerked his head to the right. Too late to avoid the liquid, he looked straight into the blinding flash of the strobe.

"Phhh...Phhh...." Bill sputtered, spitting fluid. I saw the cow tense again.

"Get ready, Lucy," I said, unable to control my laughter. "Shoot, shoot!" I urged as the cow sprayed more fluid. It was now running from Bill's hair in a constant pink stream. Belman lurched away from the cow trying to see through his glasses as he coughed and sputtered.

"Damn it, Williams, you've been dry long enough!" he growled, poking the loops of bowel back through the incision. "Get your ass down here, put on a sleeve and go in rectally. You can hold on to any progress I make with the fetus." Bill turned to the reporter. "Don't you think you've gotten enough action shots for now, Lucy?"

"I want to see how it comes out!" Lucy said bouncing up and down on the bin. "We can do a whole picture story; there are some great shots here."

"No, we cannot!" Bill shouted. "Lucy, get the hell out NOW or...or... I'll use your shirt for a towel!" Bill warned extending his pink paper arms, still dripping with fluid, toward her. I had to hold on to the chute to stay on my feet, I was laughing so hard.

66

"Okay... okay!" Lucy backed away. "Have Lois call to let me know how everything turns out!" she said as I helped her climb down from the bin.

As soon as Lucy had made her exit, Belman started in again. This time Bill was able to elevate the fetus. Working through the rectal wall I could move the calf to the left. As the uterus detorsed the blood vessels were allowed to dilate rushing fresh oxygen-containing blood to the uterus and placenta. As a result, the calf immediately became active, kicking and stretching inside the close confines.

"You feel that?" I asked, removing my arm from her rectum.

"Sure do!" Bill replied. "There's nothing like the feel of a healthy calf wanting to be born!" He stepped away from the chute, glasses bent, their lenses obscured by the drying abdominal fluid, pink paper gown melting off his arms and chest, and a big smile on his face. "As soon as I finish closing, we'll give her a shot to get labor started and while we're waiting I'll buy lunch!"

"Maybe we'll catch Art at the El Rancho," I said, already planning to relay the day's events at the local's table.

Chapter 8

Daddy Said I Could Call You

*I*awoke with a start to the loud unremitting burring of the phone; at some level I was aware that it was dawn. I shook my head to clear the cobwebs and slapped myself a couple of times. "This is Dr. Williams," I said, trying to sound wide-awake.

"Daddy said I could call you," a voice grated in my ear. I recognized Charlene Walters immediately, as much by what she said as by the whiney way she said it. The clock by my bed read 5:05.

"What seems to be the problem?" I was still blinking the sleep from my fuzzy brain as I swung my feet to the floor and stood.

"Lucy had a bay colt this morning and its kinda' weak like, so Daddy said I could call you."

"Can the colt stand?" I knew the answer but asked hoping I was wrong. Charlie would never let his daughter call if he thought the horse might survive.

"Maybe you could give it something and it would!" Charlene was her usual optimistic self.

"Get your dad to help you get the foal into the barn under a heat lamp and I'll be there as soon as I can," I said, knowing that, in late March, the main barn would have a dozen calf pens deeply bedded with straw and equipped with heat lamps.

"I'll tell him," Charlene said, sounding distant as if she knew it would do no good to ask Charlie to help.

"Charlene, it's really important to get the foal inside and warm," I said, looking at the thick frost in the corners of my bedroom windows. "If it's snowing at your place get towels and rub him down." I hung up the phone and grabbed my Wranglers, stumbling as I tried to get a foot stuffed down the pant leg.

Highway 40 was dry; the light snow wasn't sticking yet, so I made good time getting to the Walters ranch. The gray of dawn was just lighting the valley floor as I turned onto the gravel of the Lower Elk River Road. I snaked around the few turns to the ranch drive and marveled at the beauty of the valley. Wide hay meadows were flanked by cottonwoods and aspens just starting to bud. The dark green of fir and spruce stood behind them on the hillsides and meandering through the center was the Elk River, not yet flooded by the spring thaw; it sparkled in the early morning light, reminding me of the crystals hanging in my kitchen window.

"Charlie, how the hell could you own such beautiful ground?" I asked aloud as I eased through the once majestic front gate. The huge posts that held the Bar W sign had rotted years ago. The brace posts, placed to save the entranceway, now leaned at dangerous angles, too, most of their support coming from the gate itself, which was permanently jammed into the ground in a half-open position. Fortunately, the original driveway had been wide enough for two vehicles to pass so navigation through the entry was still possible. I'd been to Charlie Walter's place on several occasions so I barely noticed the junk that lined the last hundred yards of the drive. Ancient farm equipment that hadn't been operable in forty years competed for space with rusting car bodies and remnants from long forgotten building projects.

"Hey, Doc," Charlene yelled as she elbowed the screen door open while pulling on her heavy canvas coat. I waved a reply and turned right toward the huge red barn. The barn, built before 1920, was the best structure on the ranch. The steeply pitched tin roof was more than thirty feet high at the ridge where a beam at least a foot thick supported a rusting block and tackle once used to fill the hayloft.

"Hey, Charlene," I yelled back over the crowing of a rooster from the old chicken house to the right of my pickup. "Foal's in the barn, isn't he?"

My question went unanswered as Charlene trotted across the muddy parking area trying to zip her coat as she ran. A horse squealed and kicked from the inside of a dilapidated stock trailer as Charlene ran past. It caught my attention mostly because the old red WW trailer wasn't even hooked up. Two cracked concrete blocks held the tongue out of the mud and I could see Barney, Charlie's bay stud, through the slatted sides. It looked like the aging stallion had been calling the trailer home for some time; manure was packed at least eighteen inches deep in the trailer's floor. I shook my head in disgust as I picked up my stethoscope.

"Your dad in here?" I asked, sliding one of the barn doors back far enough to enter. The interior was lit with an eerie red glow from several heat lamps clamped to the tiny calf crates, and the unmistakable stink of calf diarrhea combined with the sharp ammonia smell of their urine was overpowering.

"Daddy had to go in to breakfast," Charlene said, hurrying between the crowded pens. "He said to do whatever you wanted. The colt's out here." She pushed open the rear door exposing the large pole corral.

"The foal's still outside?" I checked my watch; it had been more than an hour since we'd talked on the phone. I reached the door and noticed Lucy standing by herself looking depressed. "Where's the foal?" Charlene pointed to where a bend in the Elk River ran through the pen providing drinking water for the corralled livestock. I could see the outline of a newborn foal lying on broken ice at the edge of the stream, hindquarters still in the water. I ran over and pulled the remains of the amniotic sac from the foal's chest before I gathered him up and rushed to the barn.

"Daddy said not to move him or we'd kill him for sure!" Charlene screamed, her eyes wild with fear as she stood rooted to the ground.

"So we just let him freeze to death?" I elbowed open the barn's back door wide enough to get the foal through and stumbled inside dumping him unceremoniously on the floor.

"I thought you'd give him something first," she whimpered, still unable to move.

"Charlene, I need one of those heat lamps and some gunny sacks. Now!" I quickly checked the comatose foal's heart rate and raised his lip, noting the pale blue color of his gums. "As soon as you get a heat lamp on him start rubbing him down with a gunny sack," I said dragging the limp body close to a calf pen so that

Charlene would have a place to clamp a heat lamp. She was moving into action now and I took one of the rough burlap feed sacks from her and started rubbing the foal's chest trying to stimulate a little life from the inert body while she got the lamp operational.

"Is that too close?" Charlene asked clamping a heat lamp in place.

"No, that'll be fine. Rub on him while I get some drugs," I stood up, rubbing my already painful knees. "You might want to drag one of those over to kneel on. It'll save your legs," I said motioning toward some sacks still full of grain leaning against the wall.

I hurried to the truck and started to rapidly assemble drugs and supplies. I didn't want to forget things, so I made a mental picture of the procedure I would use. I grabbed everything I might need filling a plastic carrying tray with various bottles, bags, syringes and needles. Last of all I tossed in a roll of white adhesive tape and a tube of super glue. I heard the screen door slam as I was returning to my patient and I knew Charlie would be with us momentarily.

"Let's see if we can get another source of light," I said, trotting back into the barn. "Something that's not red. I need to be able to see a vein."

"I don't know if Daddy..." Charlene began, but I interrupted.

"If I can't see a vein I can't treat the foal! I need light, Charlene." My urgency sent Charlene scurrying to a set of shelves near the door and I dragged a feed sack over by the foal to preserve my knees.

"Oh, there's a bulb over here," she said rummaging through bags and boxes. "I'll see if it...there's two more here, too; one of them is bound to work." She waved the bulbs in the air, a smile across her narrow face, and then moved over to replace the heat lamp bulb from a holder in the empty pen to my right.

"Daddy won't like us using that on the floor!" she said, a horrified look crossing her face as she saw my grain bag stool for the first time.

"This will make his vein easier to see," I said, ignoring her comment and pulling the comatose foal up on the bag so that his head, neck and shoulder arched over the fat rounded sack of oats. "Now put your thumb right here." I pushed Charlene's thumb against the foal's neck to occlude the jugular vein. "It would be easier if you'd kneel on this grain," I said, looking at how Charlene was hunched over.

"I'm okay," she said, looking toward the front door as she strained to remain standing. I shook my head and waited for the vein to distend enough for me to identify it.

"This little guy is so shocky he doesn't have enough blood pressure to fill his vein," I said with the seconds dragging by. When his vein had partially filled I slipped a four-inch catheter gently into the jugular and threaded it to the hub, affixing adhesive tape and gluing it in place with my Superglue. I attached a liter of Ringer's lactate and opened the stopcock allowing the fluid to run as fast as possible. "Hold this bag for me," I said handing Charlene the Ringer's. "Keep it up about eye level so it will run as fast as possible." I was already mixing a vial of Soludeltacortef, a rapid onset form of cortisone, and I administered it in a bolus into the intravenous tubing. Spotting a loose nail I hung the fluid bag. "Run these to the house and put them in your microwave for four minutes," I said, handing Charlene two more bags of fluids. "I'll find a blanket to warm this guy up."

"Should I put them both in at the same time?" Charlene asked taking the Ringers Lactate.

"Yes. Just get them warm for me, please," I said, already hunting for a blanket to cover the foal. Charlene nodded and started for the house as her father stomped into the barn.

"What do you think, Doc? He gonna make it?" Charlie Walters asked as he leaned on one of the calf crates with his gloved hands pushed deep into the pockets of his down parka.

"I doubt it. You're probably right as usual, Charlie," I said, covering the foal's hindquarters, which weren't in the heat lamp's beam, with a lined horse blanket. "Maybe if we can reverse the shock we'll have a chance though."

"I told Charlene to knock him in the head, but she had to call." Charlie shook his head and moved over closer to the heat lamp.

"Was that before or after you decided to leave him in the river?" I asked, trying hard to be civil.

"I didn't want to warm him up too fast;'fraid it might kill him," Charlie said, placing one boot directly under the red lamp's glow. "He was shaking real bad and couldn't stand anyway," he added as the little horse began to shiver showing the first sign of life since I'd arrived. "You know he's out of my best mare; I just love that mare, and this one was supposed to be my replacement stallion for old Barney. Nothin's too good for him, Doc. Do whatever you have to do."

"Oh, good, he's waking up," Charlene said as she arrived with the warm bags of fluids clutched against her chest.

"I believe he's thinking about dying," I said as I raised his lip again and saw that the blue color had deepened. The foal tried to raise himself, shaking uncontrollably, and flopped off the grain sack jerking loose the intravenous line. I picked him up under the chest and dragged him back to the warmth of the heat lamp.

"See, he wants to stand up," Charlene said, reaching out to stroke his chest. The foal continued to paddle with his front legs, making it difficult to keep him under the lamp. His eyes were rolled back in his head and he was opening and closing his mouth in a completely uncoordinated manner.

"We're just too damned late to get his shock reversed." I sat down heavily on the grain sack pulling the foal up onto my lap to keep him from beating himself up banging into the crates and the floor as his thrashing became more violent. With a final shudder the little body went limp and his eyes immediately took on a lifeless glassy stare.

"I told you it was a waste of time to get Doc out of bed," Charlie said, pulling the foal off of me by its hind legs. I stood, shook my head and tossed the intravenous set and the unused fluid bags in my plastic container. Charlie continued to drag the carcass toward the front of the barn and I slowly followed to my truck preferring not to watch as the dead foal's head thumped across the drive. The old man stopped to catch his breath and straightened up stretching out his back. "At least you'll be in time for fresh coffee at the El Rancho," Charlie said, bending over to grab the dead foal again. "Soon as I get him taken care of I'll follow you in and buy you a cup."

"I think I'll pass," I said, closing up the tailgate on my vet box. "I need to stop by the house and shave." I walked around to the cab wondering what Charlie would have to say to the boys at the El Rancho.

"Could you back your truck up a little bit, Doc?" Charlie asked, standing on the passenger side of my cab.

"No problem." I eased behind the steering wheel and backed down the drive a few yards. Charlie opened a narrow gate and dragged the colt through by the hind legs. He had to jerk on the foal a few times when the elbows hung up on the gatepost, and the foal's head bounced up the steps as he pulled the carcass into the small shack beyond. *What's going on?* I wondered. Then I saw Charlie coming back down the steps.

"No use in letting that foal go to waste," Charlie said as he dragged the skeleton of a calf out the door. "Those hens clean everything up right down to the bone," he said, holding up the remains by a hind leg.

The chicken house. I was too shocked to even wave a goodbye as I backed down past Barney's trailer to turn and make my way out the drive. *Only at Charlie Walter's,* I thought as I slipped my pickup through the half opened gate.

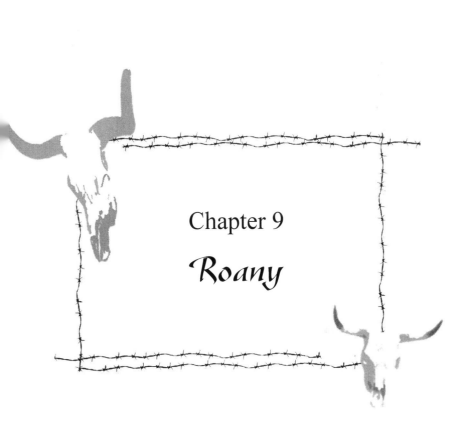

Chapter 9

Roany

*I*t was late April, spring in most parts of the state, only in the Colorado mountains we don't call it spring. When the melt is in full swing, it's mud season. I arrived at my veterinary clinic just before eight and had to hurry to unlock the door. The phone was already ringing.

"This is Dr. Williams," I answered.

"Hi, Clay, it's Bill Belman," came the reply. I smiled to myself. I hadn't heard from Bill in a week or two, and I pictured his round face and the small round lenses of his glasses. Dr. Belman was an inch or so taller than I am at five-foot-nine. He was in his mid-fifties and developing a paunch. He always wore a dark blue wool cap, in the style of a train engineer, to cover his nearly bald head.

"To what do I owe the honor of your call?" I asked, unable to keep from smiling as I pictured Bill's discomfort. Getting Belman to make a phone call was like asking a cat to go for a swim.

"If you've got a minute today, maybe you could stop by," Bill said. "I want to give you a heads up on a case I'm sending your way."

"I'm headed to Hayden in an hour or so. Would that work?" My interest was already aroused.

"I'll be in the hospital all morning, so any time will do," he said. "I'll talk to you then."

"Okay, I'll see..." I started, but the line had already gone dead.

I guess I was lucky to get that much out of silent Bill, I thought, remaining in the good mood that a call from my closest competitor had engendered. I thought of the Dr. Bill story I'd heard last week and smiled.

I'd gone to the El Rancho for lunch on Thursday. The usual crew was there, sitting at the big table near the kitchen, the table reserved for locals. It would seat a dozen men and remained at least half full from six in the morning till around three in the afternoon when anyone still present moved into the bar. All day men would come and go. They would be talking and eating or just having a cup of coffee and a visit. It was an unwritten rule that no women sat at the big table, so a local coming to lunch with his wife ate in the main part of the restaurant. These couples weren't outcasts though; half the men at The Table would carry their coffee over to chat.

The special each Thursday was roast beef with mashed potatoes and a vegetable. Larry had been cooking at the El Rancho for years, and roast beef was his specialty; cooking beef and drinking. Short and scrawny with a ruddy complexion that was most apparent in his bulbous nose, Larry seemed to go weeks without combing his thinning sandy hair. When the flask in his right hip pocket grew empty it signaled a break. He'd take a trip to his pickup for a smoke and a refill. Disheveled and dirty, Larry knew how to season a roast, and the potatoes were the real thing, so at least one Thursday a month I had to get by the El Rancho. This particular day The Table was in high spirits.

"What gives with all the cheer?" I asked. "The ski mountain's been closed for weeks, so it can't be the departure of the tourists!"

"It's your colleague, Doc," Tim Shelton, a local rancher, replied. "Jess had Dr. B. out last week and ... Well, you tell him, Jess."

I turned to Jess Mackey, a large man in bib overalls. His flaming red hair was only a shade brighter than his complexion. He had chubby cheeks, a double chin and a high-pitched, scratchy voice. Jess ran a few mother cows and worked full time at one of the local mines where he pushed coal around with a huge Cat. He was extremely talkative. The times I'd gone out to look at one or the other of his horses I could hardly get a word in edgewise. "Yeah, Jess," I encouraged. "Let's hear it!"

"Wa...well," Jess stammered. "Bill,... er... Doctor Belman, came by last week. My good red cow was down. You remember the one, Doc?" I smiled and nodded my assurance, although I had no recollection of any of his cows.

"Just tell Clay the story!" Tim said.

"Well, he knows Roany," Jess said his voice raising an octave. "Anyway, she'd been down for a few days and I'd tried to get her up with the tractor. I'd used the loader. I used it real gentle-like, Doc. I sure didn't want to hurt her worse."

"I'm sure you didn't do any damage," I said in my most professional tone. Although I did wonder exactly what Jess did with the loader? Moving him along, I added, "So then you called Bill?"

"Well, no, not right off. First I called Fred Smitt... lives down the road. Fred's got a cow lifter thing from when he had a dairy in Iowa. Fred brought it over, but it was missing one of the parts that goes over the hip. Fred said it didn't matter though 'cause she was so sick she couldn't stand even if we could get her up." Jess looked around the table for approval. Several of the ranchers nodded indicating that they would have made the vet call a last resort, too.

"That's when I called Dr. Belman!" Jess exclaimed triumphantly. "He got there in a hurry too, came that same day!"

I envisioned Bill rolling in with his Chevy Belair, several buckets of medication in the back seat. He carried a bucket for each call he was making. I remembered asking him if he didn't forget to bring medicine and things practicing out of his car that way. I told him I wasn't that well organized; I needed my truck with the storage box on the back. Bill's answer was classic. "Well," he said. "I've been in practice so long there's only three drugs I know how to use. I put all three in every bucket."

"Dr. Belman drove right up to me and rolled down the window," Jess continued. "I told him all about how I'd found Roany down three or four days before. How I'd brought her feed, which she wouldn't eat, and water, which she wouldn't drink. How I'd called the feed store for advice and picked up the Dr. Bell's Tonic that didn't work, and how Fred had come to help."

"Belman just looked at me through those funny glasses of his and didn't say a word," Mackey complained in a whine. "I said my wife even came out to the barn and slogged through the mud just to shake her head. Roany looked bad."

"Still Dr. Bill didn't say a word. I led him out through the corral," Jess said, getting more nervous with every sentence. "I told him I probably should have just shot her. That was Fred's advice. I said I probably should have listened to Fred. I bet I should have shot her, I told him. He just looked at Roany and got out his stethoscope. He listened and poked and looked and prodded, but he didn't say a thing to me." Jess stopped to take a swallow of coffee and look around the table for reassurance.

"Anyway," he continued, "Dr. Belman stood up and started back to his car. I figured he was going for medicine. So I told him I guessed I was glad I didn't borrow Fred's gun." Jess seemed pleased with that thought.

"Funniest thing, though," Jess said, shaking his head. "Dr. Belman got into that Chevy of his, started her up and rolled down the window. He looked me right in the eye and said, 'Shoot her,' then he drove away."

Jess was staring straight into my face, expecting... what? An explanation? I couldn't help but smile. "Ya know, Jess," I said, "Bill Belman is the best cow vet I've ever seen." There were nods of agreement from all the cattlemen in attendance. "Maybe," I added, "if you'd called two or three days sooner..."

"Oh, no!" Jess interrupted "She looked pretty good then. I wouldn't have wanted to shoot her without giving her a chance!"

Several of us at the table had to look away and cover our laughter with coughs and a lot of throat clearing. Not a soul embarrassed Jess Mackey with a heartless comment; the damage was done, Roany was gone. Several men told Jess how sorry they were about his loss and they meant it. Locals stick together in these parts.

Chapter 10

The Cryptorchid Colt

I gathered up a few items that I didn't normally keep in my truck, preparing to run down to the Fields ranch in Hayden. Locking the clinic I stepped down to the doughnut shop.

"How's it going this morning, Ken?"

"Not bad, Doc. What can I get for you?"

I was already helping myself to a large cup of coffee. "I'll have a glazed French and take four of those cinnamon rolls with me," I answered, adding a second heaping spoonful of sugar to the cup as I looked around for the cream.

"It's still in the carton," Ken said motioning toward the refrigerator as he continued to bag the rolls. "You must be stopping at Dr. Belman's." He held up a cinnamon roll.

"Bill's got a case he wants to talk about, wouldn't say what it was on the phone."

"Sounds mysterious."

"No, I don't think so, just Bill's aversion to phones. It's probably a horse owner with a question. The only thing he dislikes more than a horse is a horse owner. I think it's because horse people ask a lot of questions. He told me once that horse owners drive him crazy. He said bouncing along on a horse loosens their tongues and blurs their minds." I picked up the glazed cruller from its napkin on the counter and took a bite. The sweet glaze melted on my tongue and I tasted both the butter and the eggs prominent in Ken's French doughnuts. I followed the bite with a swallow of dark rich coffee inhaling the aroma. "You did yourself proud again this morning!"

"I'll put these on your tab," Ken said as he handed me the cinnamon rolls.

"Be sure you do!" I said giving him a look.

"Hey, listen, it was Belman who told me to put any cinnamon rolls you get on his bill. The only way I can stay out of trouble is to charge you both every time. On second thought that's not such a bad idea."

"You live in here, Doc?" Sheriff's deputy Nate Trogler asked as he entered through Ken's screen door; the little bell at the top jangling merrily.

"The only way you'd know that is because you check every day," I said, gathering up my bag of goodies.

"I'm just getting a few for the office," Nate said, reaching for a coffee cup. "Looks like you're stocking up though." He eyed my bag.

"They're cinnamon rolls," Ken said.

"Going somewhere with Belman?"

"Boy this is a small town!" I growled. "Anything else you want to know about my business?"

"Just whose wife you're seeing. That way if we get a shooting call we'll know if it's you." Nate replied, unruffled.

"I've had enough of this abuse!" I headed out the door.

"Must have hit a raw nerve, huh, Ken?" Nate continued, still trying to get a rise out of me. As I closed the door I heard his parting shot. "Probably Belman's office help. That DeLaney chick is a fox."

A few minutes later, pulling into Bill's hospital, I grinned at Trogler's last remark. Lois DeLaney was pretty all right, and rumor had it that Nate's girlfriend was longing for the big city. I wondered if Nate was already looking around. Parking, I slipped in the back door. Before the door was half open the unmistakable smell of antiseptic mixed with lemon air freshener accosted me. *Why,* I wondered, *did all receptionists have to try and cover the antiseptic odor with too much air freshener?* I gently closed the door, but Lois appeared out of nowhere, surprising me as I tried to locate Bill by peering into his office.

"Dr. Belman is with a client," Lois said in the hard tone she used when I came in the back, a tactic that we both knew was designed to eliminate her interference in my BS sessions with her boss. Ever the receptionist, Lois tried to keep Bill on task, and anyone coming in the back door tended to interfere with the work schedule she had planned. I waved the bag of cinnamon rolls, hoping to appease her, and set them on the tray next to the coffee pot. She was tempted momentarily as evidenced by a slight lick of her lips, before she turned up her nose. Straightening her blouse, Lois turned on her heel.

"Dr. Belman has another client in the waiting room," she said. And, since my departure wasn't immediate, she added, "He has a very full schedule."

"I'm kinda' in a hurry myself," I lied. "I only came in because he called and asked me to stop this morning, but maybe I can find time later in the week."

Realizing I was here at her boss's request, Lois's demeanor instantly changed. "Why don't you have a cup of coffee and I'll see if he's finished. I'm sure it won't be a minute," she purred.

I laughed and Lois's jaw tightened; her eyes seemed to emit sparks as her face turned a flaming red. She exhaled audibly as she hurried to the small animal exam room. I knew Bill would be out as soon as possible. It was hard on him to be cooped up in a small room with a client expecting some sort of conversation.

Barely a minute elapsed before Belman came striding up the hall. His blue cap was pushed way back exposing his baldhead. He had a quizzical look as he stared at the blood tube held in front of his face and he scratched his temple with his free hand.

"I wish I knew something about small animal medicine," he said, still eyeing the blood. "I'm sure I should know what's wrong with this dog! I've seen this before and I don't have the slightest idea when or where." He shook his head and laid the blood sample on his desk.

"Wish I could help." Bill was infinitely more qualified than I to diagnose internal medical problems in dogs. "You know me. If there's a chance to cut there's a chance to cure. If it's a dog and not a surgical case I'm no damned use, so I won't even ask."

"We both know that's not true," he said, still staring at the sample. "Anyway, that's not why I called. I want to send you a case that's right down your ally."

"Why do I get a nervous stomach when you have a case 'right down my ally'?"

"This is on the level, Clay. Mary Hinthorn has a yearling filly with an umbilical hernia, and it looks like a candidate for your safety pin repair."

"Why don't I describe the procedure to you and you can have all the glory!" I said, knowing it was of no avail. I'd tried to interest Bill in this, as well as several other surgical techniques, but he was quite happy to let me do all the horse work in the county.

"I've already told Mary you'd be doing the surgery, and I thought if you had time in the next day or so I could go along and treat a calf at the same time. If you don't have time this week, no problem, the hernia can wait."

"Either tomorrow or the next day will work fine. How soon do you need to see the calf?"

"Tomorrow would be good. If we go mid-morning I'll buy lunch when we're done."

"Sounds good. What's going on with the calf?"

"Tom and Mary dehorned about twenty head with a saw," he replied coming around his desk.

"How many ended up with saw dust in a sinus?" I asked, heading for the door.

"Almost all twenty. I've been battling sinus infections for a few weeks and I'm down to one calf." Bill said turning toward the small animal waiting room. "See you about ten and thanks for the rolls."

The sun was warm on my arm as I headed toward Hayden, and the rich smell of freshly turned earth was in the air. I reviewed the surgery I was about to perform.

I'll need Richard to bring four bales of straw over to the front lawn, I thought, remembering the spot I'd chosen for my operation. *Then I'll sedate the colt with Rompun. When it's taken effect, I'll anesthetize him with ketamine. That'll keep him down long enough to place a catheter in his jugular vein and get the triple drip running.*

Richard Fields' ranch was north of the Yampa River just across the Hayden Bridge. The headquarters occupied twenty acres of gently sloping ground separated from the hay meadows that lay along the river's edge by seventy feet of cliff. As I drove under the Fields Ranch sign I noticed that the cherry trees were all in bloom. They lined the circle drive in front of the main house, and their scent mixed with the aroma of the freshly mown lawn in the center. As I climbed out of my pickup I heard Richard yell a greeting from the house. I waved back, noticing that he had already brought the hay bales to the lawn and begun to assemble the paraphernalia I needed for the pasture surgery. I was still getting things together when Richard and his son, Jarred, arrived with the horse.

"Let's get his head facing uphill. Right there to the left where the ground is nearly level," I said. "That way when he starts down he won't stagger backward." I administered the sedative and, as it was taking effect, I readied a cotton rope around the colt's chest and hind legs. Then I dosed the young horse with ketamine. I rested Cruiser's head on my shoulder and gently pushed back on his chest. The colt wobbled a step backward, jerked slightly and sat down for a second before lying over on his side. "Let's get him tied down, then I'll place a catheter in his jugular for the remaining anesthetic."

In a very few minutes I'd finished scrubbing the inguinal area, covered the horse with sterile drapes and was feeling through surgical gloves for the location of the inguinal canal. The colt was on his back with bales of straw on either side to keep him from falling over. I was behind him on my knees, leaning forward between his flexed hind legs, which were secured with the cotton rope. I probed firmly for the familiar feel of the canal. Once I'd located it I incised the skin and bluntly opened the tissue with the fingers of my right hand.

Using a curved sponge forceps I made a grab for the testicle, gently attempting to pull it through the internal inguinal ring. "Damn. I thought I had it!" I cursed as the forceps came out empty. "This is the tricky part, to get that baby through the internal ring without making a huge hole that we have to suture."

I aligned the forceps for another try but stopped to smile; there I was performing major surgery in the world's most beautiful surgical suite: the intense green of the lawn merging into the delicate pink of the cherry blossoms with the Yampa River sparkling below and air so clean it almost hurt my nose. However, after three or four more attempts I was sweating profusely and had to have one or the other of my helpers wipe my brow at regular intervals. Rocking back on my heels I looked around hoping for some kind of divine intervention as I tried to keep my cool. Another fifteen minutes of extreme frustration and the testicle slid through the internal ring as if it had never caused a problem.

The feeling of relief at finding the testicle was like a huge weight had been removed from my back.

Quickly placing the emasculators and closing them with a crunch I freed the testicle from its cord, holding the trophy high I grinned from ear to ear. Incising the scrotum over the normal testicle I stripped back the tunics and easily removed it as well.

"Look at the difference in size," I said, laying the two testicles side by side. "Even though the retained one is smaller, it was producing enough testosterone to make this guy meaner than a gang member on steroids." As I spoke I was untying the leg ropes, then we moved the straw back out of the way.

As I laid out the lead in front, Richard was tying a second rope to Cruiser's tail. We each found a bale of hay to sit on and waited quietly, allowing the horse a stress-free environment.

"How long do you think?" Jarred whispered.

"Slip up here with me and we'll have a look at his eye," I said as I eased behind his head. Jarred joined me. "See anything funny?"

"Gees, his eyeball's darting back and forth!" Jarred exclaimed loudly, the sound causing the colt to jerk and tilt his nose into the ground.

That worried me so I headed for the truck and more sedation.

"Cruiser may be a tough colt bent on standing before he's ready, so he's going to get another shot. That way he won't get anxious while the anesthetic wears off." I had the sedative in a syringe and was headed back to the colt.

"Look at him now!" Jarred said as the colt jammed his head under his shoulder and started to paddle again, this time with much more vigor.

"Grab that rope and pull his head straight!" I yelled, racing for the colt. Jarred pulled his head and I landed kneeling on Cruiser's neck to administer the sedative. I tried momentarily to find the catheter in his jugular vein. The colt almost threw me off, flopping like a trout thrown up on the bank, so I opted for an intramuscular site and stabbed him in the neck. By this time Richard had the tail rope and didn't need to be told what to do. Cruiser redoubled his efforts and flipped me off his neck without much more effort than he would have needed to remove a fly. I landed on my back and rolled out of the way, coming to my feet in time to see Jarred lose his as the colt rolled onto his belly and wildly threw his head.

"Let his head go!" I yelled, an order that must have seemed confusing since not three seconds before I'd wanted him to pull on the rope. As the horse fought to his feet stumbling forward, Jarred realized his predicament. He scampered out of the way and I joined Richard on the tail rope. Pulling with all our combined strength we halted the colt's forward progress briefly and he tried to steady himself. The spinning world was too much for Cruiser.

He staggered left, then crumpled on his front legs and performed an almost perfect somersault, jerking Richard and me forward into his thrashing hind feet. Throwing his arms up to protect his head, Richard took a shot to the forearm that sent him reeling backwards. I spun to my right as a hoof whistled past my ear. The colt swung his head ever more wildly, splitting his lip on the ground, and rolled onto his sternum again. This time nobody had a rope to try and help, and he came up and over in another somersault throwing large chunks of sod into the air and tangling both ropes about his legs and body. He continued rolling and twisting, splattering blood in a wide arc. Making three lunges and narrowly missing a cherry tree he crashed into one of the bales, exploding it and sending straw ten feet in the air. Rolling away Cruiser regained his feet, rocked back and, crouching on his hind legs, he spun 360 degrees to fall again. This time the lead from his halter wrapped around a hind leg just above his hoof and trailed off over his back. I grabbed the rope and pulled hard, bringing his upper hind foot within inches of his nose. The colt continued to flail with his front feet, but I kneeled on his withers and pulled on the rope and prevented him from getting up. The horse was breathing hard and covered in a sweaty lather. He had a few rope burns on his lower legs and a lacerated lip, and his right eye was beginning to swell. One lost bale, a badly bruised forearm and surgical instruments scattered about were the only other casualties. Cruiser stopped his struggles as his eye movement subsided. I eased the tension on his leg rope, and he seemed content to rest.

Richard was appraising the situation at the same time. His relief was evident and when our eyes met he grinned.

"You do that just to make sure his guts would stay in, Doc?" He asked rubbing his arm.

"Things were going so well I thought we needed a little excitement!" I said, gently laying out the leadrope in front of the horse again.

"I've n..n..never seen anything l..like that!" Jarred said as he dropped onto one of the remaining straw bales. His hands were trembling, and his face had become three or four shades whiter.

"Well, you never can tell which of these colts are going to be tough, but it sure is good to have help as good as you two when things start to get a bit Western. You did a great job, Jarred."

"I just tried to st...st...stay out of the way." He stammered his face turning red.

"That was exactly the right thing to do! Sometimes staying out of the way is the best course of action." While we talked Cruiser rolled up on his sternum and looked around as if nothing had happened. He remembered the other horses, whinnied and stood easily.

"Must be lunch time at school," Richard said pointing down the drive as a red pickup roared into view throwing up dust and gravel. Three teen-aged boys were in the cab and two more were in the bed. They were all waving wildly to Jarred.

"How'd it go!" The driver yelled sliding to a stop and eyeing Cruiser.

"It got a little Western, but we handled it, no problem." Jarred replied, leading the colt toward the barn.

As I drove back to the clinic I thought about the anesthesia wondering how long it would be until better products were available for field surgery. My thoughts changed to tomorrow's surgery as I passed Dr. Belman's hospital. I always enjoyed working with Bill.

Chapter 11

The Over Boots

*D*r. Belman's parking lot wasn't crowded when I pulled in a few minutes before ten the next morning. A stiff breeze was blowing and little wispy clouds chased across the deep blue. The temperature was in the low 40s, making it a chilly April day.

"Care for a cinnamon roll?" Bill asked as I came in the back door. He was helping himself from the bag next to the coffee pot.

"Don't mind if I do. Looks like somebody has been to see Ken already today."

"Oh, no, they're the ones you brought by yesterday," Belman said, taking a bite. "Holding up pretty well though," he added as he brushed away the crumbling icing on his chin. "I sure appreciate your helping me out by fixing this colt. Pour yourself a cup while I get ready." Dr. Belman stepped into his pharmacy, returning almost immediately carrying a plastic pail. "How about we take your truck since I've got everything I need right here?" He swung the red plastic bucket for me to see.

"That's fine," I replied, stirring sugar into the coffee I'd poured. I found a plastic lid and snapped it on the paper coffee cup, hurrying to catch up as Bill headed out the door.

"Hope you don't mind if we make a small detour by Allen's. I need to pick up some overboots."

"No, I don't mind. I need a pair of five buckles myself," I answered, already driving toward Bob Allen's Men's Wear downtown. It was no problem to make a u-turn right in the middle of the block on Main Street, a feat that two weeks ago, with the mountain open and the skiers in town, would have been impossible. I pulled up and parked right at the store's front door.

"I'll only be a minute!" Belman exclaimed over his shoulder as he bounded from my truck.

"No hurry," I replied, getting out and slamming the cab door. I followed Bill into the store, not bothering to feed the parking meter. Ski season was over, and for the few weeks until the summer tourists started to arrive there was an undeclared moratorium on parking violations.

As I entered Allen's, the aroma of new clothes and leather hit me. It gave me an immediate sense of peace like the smell of steak on the grill when you're hungry. The overboots were lined up along the left wall, beneath shelves filled with jeans and western boots, shelves that stretched the length of the store. The overboots were in pairs by size. Four- and five-buckle, round- and pointed-toed. I started down the line looking for the nines, nines with pointed toes and five buckles. There were several pairs and I picked the first ones, inspecting them for blemishes as I carried them to the register.

"I've got yours in the back," Bob Allen said to Belman, starting around the counter toward the rear of his store. "I wouldn't want someone to get them by mistake," he added, giving me a wink and a grin as if I should know some joke. I smiled and nodded although I had no idea why.

Bob was thin to a fault, which made him appear taller than his five-foot-ten-inch stature. He had a long, pencil-thin nose and high cheekbones and always wore a sports coat over a soft cotton shirt. He headed for the storeroom at a trot, coattails flapping against boney hips. Returning a moment later with a pair of round-toed five buckles, he placed them on the sales counter for Belman. Bill didn't wait for any conversation. He took the boots, ducked his head and headed for the door making a rapid exit.

"I'll take these," I said, swinging the pair I'd picked out onto the counter.

"You didn't get a pair like Belman's, did you?" Bob Allen asked, laughing.

"Mine are pointed-toed instead of round, if that's what you mean."

"Doc hasn't told you yet?" Allen asked in wide-eyed surprise.

"Told me? No, I guess not."

"Bill will have to tell you, but be sure to check out his pair!"

As we drove to the Hinthorn ranch I waited somewhat impatiently to be included in the boot tale. I was glancing around trying to get a look at Bill's boots.

"I put them out of sight behind the seat," Belman said, knowing what I was looking for.

"Bob said I should check out your boots," I commented. I was approaching a stop sign and Bill didn't reply right away. As we stopped he opened his door.

"Lean forward," he ordered. Levering the seatback so that it would tilt, he removed the boots and set them between us. "There, that make you happy?"

"I don't see what the fuss.... Oh, hell, they're both left boots!" I was even more bewildered. "I still don't get it," I said.

"A year ago last fall I was headed to Yampa. It was late November with about two feet of snow on the ground. I was in a hurry and needed some over boots. I ran in to Allen's and grabbed the first pair of elevens along the wall. Bob was with another customer so I just held them up and asked him to put them on my bill. When I got to Yampa they were both right boots. I needed 'em, so I wore 'em and called Bob to let him know. I told him to charge me for two pair. He never did and I went for two winters never getting by to pick them up. He called last week when he was cleaning out the storeroom, said if I'd pick them up he wouldn't even charge me."

"I can see why he thinks it's funny, but that's an easy mistake to make the way he lines them up. And besides, maybe some kid had mixed them up. I've seen enough of them playing around the store."

"I just didn't want any questions from Bob Allen," Belman replied. "I've worn holes in the right ones."

We drove the remaining few miles in silence. I was enjoying the drive and the quiet companionship. I turned off on the

Hinthorns' driveway, bouncing along the washboard of gravel as we followed the dirt track. We were heading for the pole corrals and old barn with its peeling red paint and patched siding.

"Let's get your hernia out of the way first," Bill said. "That way if there's a problem we'll have time to fix it. If I have to come back for the calf, that won't be a problem."

"That's fine. You're the boss. I'm just here for a little safety pin job." I stopped the truck in front of a large lodge pole pine gate that led into the main corral. An approach chute and squeeze formed one end, and the long wall of the old red barn formed the corral's other end, with a twelve-foot door right in the center. I started getting the drugs and supplies for my hernia repair out of the truck, while Bill opened the gate for Mary who was making her way across the muddy corral.

"I just got the colt penned up in the barn," Mary said in a voice an octave or two below mine. "Little son of a bitch didn't want to follow his mama, and that old mare tried to tromp all over me. No ground manners. No wonder the little snot is such a bastard to deal with." I looked up in time to see Mary spit a stream of tobacco juice right in front of her Australian Shepherd pup, stopping him in his tracks. She half-heartedly kicked in his direction. "Jasper, git the hell out of here!" she shouted, sending the dog scuttling under the gate to crouch just out of reach.

I didn't know Mary Hinthorn well, but I did know she gave no quarter and took no prisoners. "Tough old bird" was the phrase I'd heard most often used to describe her. Mary looked to be in her mid-seventies, wiry, with a large hawkish beak and skin like saddle leather. She'd raised three boys. They all drove heavy equipment and worked for one or another of the coal mines in the area. The smallest tipped the scales at 240. It was said that Ma could twist an ear off any of the three and wouldn't hesitate to do it anywhere, any time.

"Good morning, Mary." I said grinning.

"What's so damn good about it?" Mary retorted as she came through the gate and stopped to stamp the slimy corral mud off her boots on the gravel of the parking area. "You haven't been here long, have you?" She asked squinting intently at me. "I know 'cause Doc don't have you broke in yet. You're damn near on time. He'll have you over an hour late when you're fully trained," she added before I had time to answer.

"So far Dr. Belman's better at being on time than any veterinarian I've worked with," I said, picking up my new boots and stepping away from my truck.

"Two possibilities," Mary growled spitting again, this time in my direction. "One, you're a little kissass kid, or two, you ain't worked with many vets."

Realizing too late just how overmatched I was I looked to Belman for help. When I tried to catch his eye I could see he was about to split a gut, grinning ear to ear. He ducked his head and looked the other way and I knew that I was on my own.

"Well, I've never been accused of it, but I did kiss an ass or two in vet school; anything to graduate," I admitted, trying hard to end the conflict.

"Mary, why don't we have Clay do the colt's hernia first?" Bill asked, figuring I'd had enough at that point.

"Okay, sure," Mary said, all sweetness and light. She'd made her point. We all knew who was in charge. "Come right this way, Dr. Williams. It is Williams, isn't it?"

"Williams is right, but Clay's fine. The 'Doctor' thing makes me nervous," I answered, trying to reinforce the truce. I was slow again. Mary had to get in one more salvo.

"Make you nervous 'cause you figure you don't deserve the 'Doctor'?" she asked, slyly peering over her bifocals. Her look was one of deep satisfaction, and I wondered if the glasses were just for effect.

I was in over my head, so I waited meekly with my tail clamped firmly between my legs. Belman and I pulled on our overboots, and the three of us slogged through the muddy corral toward the barn. After the Hinthorn dehorning went poorly the nursing cows were kept in the large corral so that their calves could receive daily treatment. The result was thin slick mud, now ankle deep. Thankfully, all the pairs save one were back out on pasture.

"There's that last calf," Mary commented, pointing to the far corner of the corral as she wiped tobacco juice from her chin with the back of her hand.

"He looks like he's stopped losing weight," Belman remarked. "Maybe today will be his last treatment." We stepped up on a high concrete block in front of the barn door, then through the door onto rough burlap sacks thrown just inside. Mary took the lead, stamping her feet and wiping her boots on the bags.

"You want to use the stall the colt's already in, Clay?" Bill asked, although it was more of an observation than a question.

"The stall will probably work well." I said. "He shouldn't be down more than a few minutes."

We cleaned off as best we could and moved down the aisle to a large stall well bedded with clean wheat straw. A big roan mare watched intently from the back corner and in the dim light I could just make out her colt. She'd already positioned herself in front of him, probably expecting the worst.

"She won't take you; she's all show," Mary said as she slid open the stall door with the mare snorting and throwing her head menacingly.

"Sure could've fooled me!" Bill exclaimed, easing into the stall as Mary quietly haltered the broodmare.

I set my little tray just inside the door and picked up the syringe of sedative I'd laid out. "Let's get a hold of him and push him against the wall in the corner there," I said, stepping around the mare in front of the colt. Bill closed in from the other end and as he grabbed the foal's tail I caught him with an arm around his shoulders. I used my body to push him against the wall, keeping my knee pressed firmly under him behind his front legs. As he felt the wall against his right side the colt squealed and leapt a few times trying to break free. Both Belman and I kept him firmly squeezed in place, and when Bill picked up on his tail the colt stopped struggling. I reached over the baby's back and around his neck with my right arm, occluding the left jugular vein with my fingers. The vein distended rapidly and in a second I was able to thread the hypodermic needle into the vessel and send the calming fluid coursing through his young body. I withdrew the needle and both Bill and I released the animal, stepping away and allowing the sedative to take effect.

"Damn, that crap works fast!" Mary said, as the foal's head immediately began to droop.

"It's pretty fast," I agreed. "You can let the mare stay close unless she wants to eat one of us."

"I think she'll be okay," Mary said. "She don't know vetinaries like I do."

Dr. Belman and I watched closely for a minute or more, getting a feel for the amount of anesthetic that would be needed. As the little horse began to wobble, his head almost touching the floor, I easily administered the general anesthetic. A few moments later we were easing him onto his side. "Let's roll him straight onto his back," I suggested. "Mary, if you would straddle his neck standing over him and keeping the front legs straight up." I held him while she got in position. Bill was already controlling the hind legs, keeping our patient on his back. The colt had a mass bigger than an apple protruding from where his umbilicus should have been. I dropped to my knees and gently messaged the hernia. Almost immediately the entrapped intestine slid back into the abdomen.

"The sack is large, but I can only get two fingers through the hole in the belly wall, so it's not a big hole," I said, probing the hernial ring. I picked up a large safety pin and pushed it through the skin at the base of the empty sac. "I use at least two of these big blanket pins and try to catch the very edge of the ring. Then I tape the safety pin lock with a little adhesive tape to keep it closed."

I completed the procedure almost as fast as I talked, spreading the heavy, round rubber Elastorator band and slipping it over the sac and pins.

"That band is just like the one we use to do the lambs' tails," Mary said, as I released the band allowing it to constrict the empty sac of skin, cutting off the blood supply. "The whole damn thing falls off in a week or so, right?"

"That's right, Mary, but I would like you to check on the progress every day. I don't want the skin to drop off too early, before the belly wall has sealed across the opening," I said as I took the front legs from Mary and laid the foal on its side.

"So what the hell am I supposed to do when I come out tomorrow and the skin's already dropped off?" She asked, giving me her meanest look yet. "I suppose you're gonna tell me to call you. Hell, the little son of a bitch will already be playin' jump rope with his guts!" she said, throwing her arms in the air. "Then you can come out, act real surprised like and kill him for me. On top of that you'll probably send a bigger bill than the one for today!" she added, continuing to stare me down.

"I see you've read my book," I said with a big smile that hid my discomfort.

"No, I've just dealt with you vetinaries for damn near fifty years. Don't nothin' ever change. You boys is as predictable as a rat in a grain room."

"Well, I'm glad to see I'm not alone," I said still trying to smile. "So far I've had almost no trouble with this procedure. The only complication I've seen was once when the elastrator band broke and I had to get another over the sac."

"If something bad happens, it'll happen to me," Mary said, shaking her head and appearing resigned to whatever outcome was in store.

"I know we're all having fun here, but can we get the calf treated while the colt wakes up?" Belman asked, entering the fray for the first time.

"Good idea." I replied, all too ready to relinquish center stage. Mary only grunted an acknowledgment.

"The hardest part of this whole thing will be getting the calf caught," Belman commented as he started for the barn door carrying his bucket with its syringe and hydrogen peroxide. We waded through the muddy corral setting the gates to be able to get the calf into the chute.

"Let's try to get the cow in first. We can let her into the squeeze and close her off in there, keeping the calf behind in the approach chute. Then, Clay, if you'll get behind him and push him up tight, I'll get his head and flush his sinus." Bill was already moving the cow and calf toward the opening. I fell in behind the pair and sloshed across the pen.

"Now I remember why I do horse work," I laughed, only half joking. "Cattle work is always sloppy, and the beasts have no respect for my body," I added as I pushed the cow into the approach and stepped in behind her calf. Dr. Belman deftly controlled the levers of the squeeze, easily separating the cow and holding her still with a light pressure on the chute sides. I shoved the calf tight against the end gate of the squeeze grabbing his tail and twisting it up over his back. "I wish God had mounted these fly swatters off to the side. It would keep my hands cleaner."

"There you go being a horse practitioner again," Bill said as he climbed over the approach chute descending just in front of the animals shoulder. Belman used his knee to push the calf against the side of the chute. "This will just take a minute," he said, pulling the big 60 cc syringe filled with hydrogen peroxide from his pocket. "Hold on, little fella. I'll have you fixed up in no time." He pushed the syringe through the small opening in the calf's head and, depressing the plunger, filled the sinus with the medication. The hydrogen peroxide released its extra oxygen on contact and the gas foamed up out of the hole, squirting into the air in a high-pressure stream. "That ought to clean you out, little guy," Bill said as he released the calf and climbed out of the chute.

I was about to turn loose of the tail hold and follow Dr. Belman when I felt the calf sag. Knees buckling, the animal dropped as if he'd been shot. I'd been in practice long enough to know a dead animal when I saw one. There was no doubt in my mind; I was looking at one now. Hoping I was wrong, I stepped over the still carcass and checked for an eye reflex by placing a finger gently on his cornea. There was no blink, only an eye already loosing its brightness staring back at me.

"What the hell?" I asked.

Bill had already jumped to the ground when the calf went down and was staring through the boards slack jawed and pale.

"What do you suppose happened?" I asked. Belman, now a deathly white, just shook his head.

"Son of a bitch!" Mary screamed, with a glare directed straight at Dr. Belman. "I knew the minute you stepped out of the truck I never should have let you touch that calf!" I was stunned first by the calf's death and now by this tirade. I abandoned any thought of either leaving or examining the calf further and just backed against the chute's side with my mind reeling.

Mary continued unabated. "I knew it, I knew it, son of a bitch, I should have thrown you off the place!" I looked at Bill and noticed that he'd backed into the chute getting as far from his attacker as possible without actually turning to run. He was shaking uncontrollably now.

"Anybody with two left feet!" she shouted, pointing to Bill's overboots. Bill looked down bewildered. I remembered the boots and started to laugh as Mary continued to point and shake her head. Finally she was unable to contain herself and began to laugh with me. We were howling, with tears running down our faces while Bill stared at the overboots. His pallor was gradually replaced with redness.

"By God, I've wanted to get you for years," Mary said. Then turning to me she howled again dragging me along until my sides hurt from the laughter.

103

"Well, it was worth the wait, wasn't it?" I asked looking toward Dr. Belman and starting to laugh all over again.

"Bill is always sooo professional," Mary said, placing both hands by her mouth to stretch out the *o*'s. "I've just had this urge to get his goat for years, and if I had to lose a calf to do it, then he died for a good cause." She brushed the tears away and slapped Bill on the shoulder.

"No hard feelings there, Doctor?" she asked. Belman, still red faced, could only grin a very sheepish grin and raise one left foot.

As things came back into a normal perspective, we moved the calf into the barn to examine him on the dry floor. We found that the long-standing infection had weakened the skull, and the pressure of the foaming liquid had pushed the underlying bone into the poor creature's brain. His death was both instantaneous and painless.

We packed up and I got behind the steering wheel. Mary was smiling broadly when she walked up to my driver's side window. "Anybody with two left feet!" I repeated chuckling.

"It'll be your turn next time," she said, looking me in the eye. Then she winked and we both laughed again.

Chapter 12

Joyce Sailor

"I think I'll pull over... see if we're headed right," I said as Linda Hilton and I bumped along the gravel road north of Savory. We'd vibrated along the washboard for miles, and the rancher feeding his cattle was the first sign of life since leaving Baggs, Wyoming, almost an hour earlier.

"What'd he say?" Linda asked as I closed the pickup door.

"We're okay," I shifted into gear and continued to bounce north. "We're getting' close, a few more miles. He said we can't miss it." I held the steering wheel in a death grip trying to keep my truck on the road and not bounce up and crack my head on the roof of the cab. "I hope this is worth the trouble."

"She said she had at least a dozen to sell when I talked to her last night," Linda said, keeping one hand braced against the headliner. "Most of them are out of an Irish Thoroughbred."

I shook my head. "How did she get an Irish horse clear out here?"

"Joyce sounded like quite a character on the phone, but my friend in Denver swears she's legitimate," Linda's voice sounded as if she was sitting on a massage chair turned to the highest setting.

The county road ended. "We'll know soon enough," I said. A right angle brought us onto a narrow lane that crossed the Savory River on a one-lane bridge. Trees and brush crowded over the bridge scraping the sides of my truck. We followed the track as it skirted a bluff a couple of hundred feet high with a talus slope running right up to the edge of the drive. On our left a meadow was positioned between the bluff and the river encompassing fifty acres or more. Several of those acres were filled with ancient, dilapidated equipment of every size and shape. Tractors, pickups, plows, bailers, harrows, trailers, implements of every shape and size were dissolving into the soil from unrelenting rust. Much of the debris appeared as mounds overgrown with grass. A herd of about twenty horses grazed peacefully in and around the old junk taking no interest in our passage.

106

"Is that what I think it is?" Linda pointed to a flat area surrounded by a high chain link fence. The surface was covered to ankle depth with aspen leaves. Two white posts poked out of the debris several yards from either side fence.

"Hard to believe, but yes, I think there's a tennis court under there," I said, making the left hand turn that brought us past the court and in front of the ranch house.

"There must be a dozen bedrooms in there," Linda said, gesturing toward the three-story home. "Why would you board it up?"

"Maybe they close it up for the winter because it's too hard to heat," I guessed as we eased past the massive log structure. The old house sported a covered porch that must have been twelve feet wide running completely around the building. The shutters and doors were trimmed in a dark forest green, and, huge as it was, it was dwarfed by the grove of pine and spruce in which it stood.

"Maybe you're right, and it's just closed for the winter. Joyce did say to keep going 'til we couldn't drive any farther." Linda peered out the window as the rutted drive curved to the left past an old sod roofed cabin ending in front of a dilapidated barn.

"This must be the place." I pointed out the window at a small frame house with tarpaper peeling off the roof to reveal the rough sawn boards beneath. The little house, once painted white, was literally falling into the Savory River. One room at the far end was hanging out over the eroded riverbank.

"I'll see if we can look at some horses." Linda started toward the house while I waited by the rickety picket gate a few yards away, trying to guess the age of an old blue Plymouth parked beside the fence.

"Good morning. May I help you?" an elderly lady asked, opening the door to Linda's knock.

"I'm looking for Joyce Sailor." Linda stepped back and glanced in my direction.

"I'm Joyce Sailor. What can I do for you?" Mrs. Sailor asked, stepping outside. She was dressed in loose fitting sweatpants and a sweater. The clothes, combined with pink fluffy house shoes, made it appear that we were unexpected.

"I'm Linda Hilton. We spoke last night...You, ahh, you gave me directions over the phone. We're here to look at horses." Linda gestured toward the pasture and then checked her watch.

"I didn't know you meant today, dear," Joyce said loudly, glancing back inside. "But, since you're here..." She leaned around the door into the house and said something, but I could only make out the name Jim.

"Let me get my coat," she said, pulling an old black trench coat from inside the door. She stepped from her fluffy slippers into knee-high rubber irrigation boots, grabbed a six-foot long lounge whip and trudged toward the picket fence with Linda following behind.

"Good morning," I said, smiling and holding open the wobbly gate. Mrs. Sailor looked me up and down and then turned to Linda.

"Thought we'd start with these," she said, gesturing toward the herd grazing amongst the junk. "If you don't see what you want here, there's more I put in the round pen over by the big house." She waved her whip, carving a large circle in the air.

Why did she bring the horses in if she didn't know..., my thought was interrupted by the banging of the door as a bow-legged cowboy trotted out of the house still tucking in his shirt. White hair peeked under the sweat-stained Stetson he'd pulled so low the brim almost touched his hawk-like nose. His ankles wobbled in high, riding-heeled boots, and his spurs clanked together with a high-pitched ring at every step. We stopped to watch as he came by head down. Mrs. Sailor hooked his arm as he hurried past. Spinning him around she knocked his hat off revealing a mop of disheveled hair and planted a big kiss on his lips, smearing bright red lipstick over a wide area. Stepping back she smiled, a distinct twinkle in her eyes.

"Now, Jim, you just come on back any time," she said bending over easily to retrieve his hat.

"I'll see you," he mumbled as he smushed his hair down trying to reset the Stetson on a forehead that was rapidly reddening to match the lipstick. He hurried on toward the Plymouth without a backward glance.

"That was sure fun, honey," Mrs. Sailor waved. "I'll call you." She turned and started through the gate. Looking me in the eye she spoke quietly, "I just love that old man."

The Wyoming wind and sun had done their best to weather her face to a mass of wrinkles and liver spots, but they couldn't disguise the beauty of her younger years or remove the sparkle from her eyes. Even in irrigation boots there was a grace to her movements as she turned to take Linda's arm and I caught the fragrance of roses as she passed. .

"Now, sweetie, exactly what is it you're looking for?" Mrs. Sailor asked, her full attention on Linda as they wound their way toward the open pasture.

"I'm looking for prospects to start as jumpers and a dressage horse or two, horses that I can resell after a few months of training."

I fell in behind, staying within earshot as the two women chatted amiably about the horses. As we approached the herd began moving out into the open meadow. Two younger looking mares trotted past enjoying the morning sun. Mrs. Sailor pointed to one of them making slashing motions with her whip that sent both mares into a gallop.

"See that mare there?" She aimed the lounge whip at the retreating bay. "She can do dressage and all that crap. The other'n ain't no slouch, either." She stepped in front of Linda. "You otta take 'em both. Make you a good price on the pair."

On my right, between a pickup with all four wheels and the windshield missing and an even older and rustier tractor, I noticed a chestnut mare; she appeared to be scratching her face on her front ankle. Her foal loafed nearby; his lusterless hair coat and big belly said parasites as plainly as if he'd had a neon sign on his back. What caught my attention was fresh blood around the mare's mouth when she raised her head. *She's not scratching her face, she's chewing her leg,* I thought, moving in her direction. *Probably eating on the granulation tissue of an old wound.* I eased in close enough for a good look at her. Blood squirted from a fresh laceration on the back of her leg just above the hoof. The pastern wound appeared to have severed the digital artery and vein and probably involved the deep flexor tendon controlling her foot. Looking around I realized that Mrs. Sailor and Linda had drifted off into the open pasture so I hurried over with the news.

"Mrs. Sailor!" I caught up to them as they leaned on an old bailer, talking price. "You've got a mare cut up pretty badly over here." I pointed toward the mare and foal. The old woman wheeled around at my interruption, a scowl on her face.

"You a vet?" She spit the words at me, hands on her hips, glaring with her face twisted as if she'd swallowed chewing tobacco.

I stiffened in surprise. "Yes, ma'am, I am," I said, slightly embarrassed.

"Oh, you are?" She smiled, batting her eyes, and I noticed her long dark lashes, resplendent with just the right amount of mascara. Taking my elbow in her left hand her right arm around my waist she turned me around, Linda completely forgotten. "Now Doctor, maybe you could show me the poor mare. And please, call me Joyce."

"She's there, ah… Joyce, just next to the red Ford," I pointed toward the mare and foal.

"Would you mind taking a look with me?" Joyce asked, patting me on the back. "I get so busy sometimes I don't notice little scrapes."

"This looks fresh," I said approaching the mare. "It probably happened last night or this morning."

"Oh, my," Joyce said seeing the leg. "I'm sure she wasn't cut like that when Jim and I ran them off the hill last night." She waved toward the bluff still staring at the blood as it pumped from the mare's wound. I stepped up to try and see around behind the limb, but the mare backed away, looking around as if to leave the area.

"Maybe we could catch her up and have a closer look at that." I looked for a rope or a halter, but could not see either close by.

"Yes, fine, let's do that," Joyce still hadn't moved a muscle.

"Is she broke enough to catch with a halter, or do we need to run her in someplace?"

"She's easy," Joyce mumbled shaking her head. "Halter..., yes, a halter. I'll catch her for you, Doctor." I stood back as Joyce made a trip to the barn and then caught the mare. On examination the laceration was about what I'd guessed. She'd caught the leg and pulled back, slashing the back of her pastern just above the hoof. The digital artery and vein were opened and the cartilage above her heels was exposed. Her tendon, though abraded, appeared to be in tact.

"It could have been a lot worse," I said, setting her hoof back on the ground, blood dripping from both my hands. "Let's get the bleeding stopped." I turned toward my truck thinking of the materials I'd need. "Bring her over here, please, Joyce; it'll be easier close to my truck."

"Goodness me," Joyce said leading the mare over. "I must be getting senile. I didn't even notice your vet truck when I came past."

"My truck sort of blends in when it needs to be washed; I don't think your mind's going," I said, thinking of the sales pitch she'd been giving Linda.

"Aren't you the sweetest thing?" Joyce said as she sidled over to pat me on the arm.

"The wound's located right where there's lots of movement," I said, lifting the bucket I'd just filled with water and disinfectant.

"So the only way sutures will hold is if we put her in a cast, and I have two problems with that. First, I have no cast material on the truck, and second she'd need to be stalled in a dry stall for two weeks."

"I could stall her in the barn," Joyce said, pointing to the ramshackle structure. "How dry does it need to be?"

I looked toward the old building noting that it was filled with manure at least two feet deep. The manure had bowed the sidewall out enough that many of the boards had popped loose at the bottom and I wondered if there was enough headroom left for a horse to stand comfortably. "Let's get the bleeding stopped and a bandage on and then we can talk about our options," I said bending over to my work.

"You're the doctor," Joyce said, holding the mare while I began to inject local anesthetic around the nerves at the mare's ankle, deadening the lacerated area.

It didn't take too long to shave the area, clean and disinfect the wound and compress the edges into near apposition with a bandage. "I believe this wound will heal if we keep it clean, and bandaging is our best option for that. It can be sutured and cast in a day or two if you would like. Suturing would reduce the healing time and we'd end up with less scaring," I said in my most professional manner.

"Well, she is one of my best brood mares," Joyce said scratching her head. "On the other hand," Joyce waved at the machinery, "she'll not be the first one around here to have a scar and I'd hate to confine her colt to a stall."

"I think whatever we do we'll have a sound mare, barring some sort of unforeseen complication, of course," I said, pulling up a large dose of thick white penicillin in a syringe. "To keep the bandage on we will have to confine her for a few weeks, maybe a small pen instead of a stall."

"We can put her in the round pen as soon as we turn those horses out, and I'll bring her some water," Joyce said, leading the mare toward the nearest tree and tying her there. "Now, Linda, what else have you seen that you like?" Retrieving her lounge whip she started pointing out other prospects.

"Joyce," I called, "when was her last tetanus vaccination?"

"I'm sure she was vaccinated on the track," she said over her shoulder, taking Linda by the arm and guiding her toward a group of geldings farther out in the meadow.

"When was that?" I shouted.

"Only a few years ago," Joyce turned to yell her reply and then resumed her conversation.

I looked at the mare. "A few years... You haven't been vaccinated in a few years. Well, girl, there'll be at least one horse on the place boostered for sleeping sickness and flu as well as tetanus."

A few hours later I'd examined six head; Linda and Joyce had made a deal on four of them. My personal favorite, a big two-year-old Thoroughbred gelding, chestnut with four socks and a nearly perfect blaze ending just above his nostrils, had been passed up because of a draining tract on the outside of his left front foot just above the hoof. "That tract could be from a piece of dead collateral cartilage that needs to be removed," I said, carefully pressing on the area. "Quittor surgery isn't without its risks."

I gave Joyce penicillin and bandage material for the mare with written instructions, along with a bill that she promised to pay when she delivered Linda's horses in a few days.

"I'll see you Tuesday or Wednesday," Joyce said, waving as we pulled out. "I might bring a colt or two to castrate, if I have room in the trailer, and I'll be sure to settle up on the cut." Joyce was smiling and there was a twinkle in her eyes.

"I wonder what she's planning," Linda said looking at me with a wrinkled brow as we drove away.

"You had that feeling, too?" I shook my head and chuckled. "That old horse trader might try anything."

113

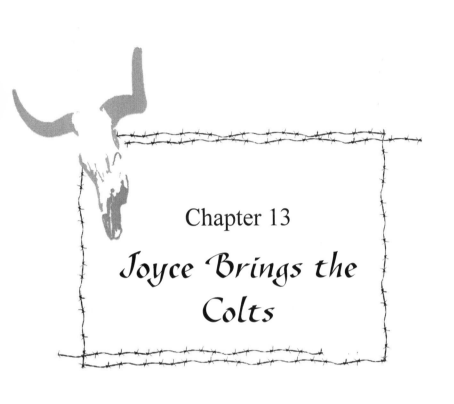

Chapter 13

Joyce Brings the Colts

*T*he first thing Monday morning I answered a call from Linda Hilton. "Clay," she said, "I just spoke with Joyce Sailor and she plans on bringing my horses on Wednesday. She wants to bring three colts for you to castrate as well."

"I think that will work," I said, "as long as she's here in the morning so we can let the colts stand around after the surgery. They'll need a couple of hours before they ride home. I could meet her at the rodeo grounds and do the surgery there."

"Maybe you should give her a call, because her plan is to drop the horses and the trailer here around six-thirty on her way to Denver, picking the geldings up on the return trip in the afternoon."

"How does that suit you?" I asked. "I could cut the colts just as easily at your place. Maybe get started around nine?"

"My problem," Linda said, "is that I can't be here on Wednesday. I don't mind you using the stalls or arena; there just won't be any help available."

"I'm sure, after seeing Joyce's setup, that the colts won't be broke. I better find someone to bring along," I said, already planning the con job I would use on Wally Watkins. "Do I need to contact Joyce?"

The phone was silent for long enough that I was about to ask if Linda was still on the line. "I can call her… I guess. I'll let her know that will work," Linda said. "I need to explain to her where to put my new horses anyway."

Wally and I arrived just before nine Wednesday morning prepared to castrate the colts. We found them in the first stall of Linda's barn. There were two notes on the stall door. Linda's said that the other horses were in the last two stalls. The second, written in perfect flowing script read:

Dear Dr. Williams.

I only brought two colts since I had no room for more. As you suggested, I brought the mare so you could put her in a cast. I'm sure you'll want to keep her until she's all healed up. Feel free to move her to the most convenient location. The good sorrel colt with the bad foot is here too. I can leave him with you as long as you like. He's no problem, gentle as a kitten. We've even had a halter on him once. We should be back from Denver around six; Jim has his surgery this morning. Joyce

"It would have been nice for Joyce to let me know about the other horses," I said removing the note. "We can castrate these colts and then go back to the clinic for another sterile set of instruments and cast material."

"I'm wondering about the kitten that's been haltered once," Wally said. "Is that why Jim, whoever he is, needed surgery today?"

I started down the barn. "I think Jim's title is probably boyfriend. I don't know about his surgery; he looked pretty healthy the last time I saw him." I reached the first horse and opened the stall door. "Let's have a look at the kitten. He'll be a nice horse if we can get his foot fixed," I said.

We took a quick look at the gelding and let ourselves in with the mare and her foal. I briefly checked out the mare's bandage and then we started on the castrations. The young colts were scared in their new surroundings making them easy to handle. Taking a lariat we slipped a loop around their necks and turned the rope into a war bridle. The confinement of the stall allowed me to get a needle into them and, after administering a sedative, they were content to stand without further encouragement. The first colt was numbed with local anesthetic and the standing castration completed in a matter of minutes. The next one was a different story.

"I thought that first colt was just too easy," I said, unable to touch the second horse on his side. "Maybe if we can get a twitch on him, I can get him blocked." That failed, so in addition we used a blindfold. It impaired his accuracy, but it did nothing to discourage him from kicking each time he felt my presence. "There's a soft cotton rope in the truck," I said. "Just hang onto the twitch a while longer."

117

"Roger that, he's okay as long as you're not around," Wally said.

I returned with the rope and looped one end loosely around his neck tying it with a bowline. "We'll get his hind leg up off the ground and stop some of this foolishness," I said, flipping the line under his right hind leg to rest just above the hoof. I brought the rope back along his side and through the neck loop. Pulling on the free end brought his hind foot forward and elevated it toward the loop which was snug against his chest. "That should stop him from kicking me," I said, rubbing him on the side and watching him as he realized that he couldn't reach me with a blow. Then I went back around to his left side and, because he was forced to keep his left hind leg on the ground, I was able to inject him with local anesthetic and complete the castration. "We're making good time," I said, looking at my watch. "Let's get my surgical pack and stop for coffee on our way back."

By ten-thirty we'd completed the round trip and were ready to deal with the mare's laceration. "We'll put her in Linda's wash rack," I said. "The floor mats will make the work a lot cleaner." Sedated and blocked with local anesthetic, the wound was easily cleaned.

"I didn't think you could suture a wound that's several days old," Wally said as I threaded a needle with suture material.

"I'll freshen the edges by trimming off a tiny margin," I said. "Creating a fresh wound will allow a few stitches to bring the skin together. Immobilizing it in a cast will enable healing in two weeks instead of six or eight."

We chatted as I sutured, bandaged and applied the cast encasing the leg from the bottom of the hoof to the fetlock in plaster. "This new waterproof Zoroc is great stuff," I said as I rubbed the last roll of plaster smooth. "Now we just need her to stay perfectly still for another ten minutes while the cast hardens, then we can cover the bottom with rubber so she won't wear thru the plaster." I stood and stretched my back.

118

"She'll need to be stalled right? Where you gonna put her?" Wally asked.

"From the note she left I'm sure Joyce hasn't figured out a dry, clean place at her ranch so I'll see if Linda has room and wants to make a little board money. Hopefully I can leave her here." I tapped on the plaster with a fingernail. "This is dry. Let's get the gelding done; I'm getting hungry for lunch already."

Wally unbuckled the mare's halter and let it fall away. "What kind of problem are we looking at with the gelding's foot?" he asked.

"It's hard to say until we follow that draining tract to its source," I said, opening the sorrel gelding's stall door. "The toughest part may be getting a halter on this big bronc." I reached back, took the halter from Wally and eased in alongside the gelding. Reaching out I rubbed him on the shoulder until he calmed and I was able to slip the lead over his neck. "Easy, buddy," I said. "We're not gonna hurt each other now, are we?" I let the big horse feel the rope's pressure around his neck. Once he was comfortable with that I stepped up and slowly slipped the halter over his nose, bringing the loose strap behind his ears and buckling it.

"That wasn't so bad," I said. "Joyce must have had a halter on this guy more than once." I stepped away to give the sorrel some space and pulled the loose end of the lead rope over his neck. As the rope slid off his neck the horse wheeled away from me to his right, heading for the back corner of the stall. I pulled hard throwing my weight into the lead, jerking him back around to face me.

He came straight toward me and went up, rearing to paw with both front feet. Narrowly missing my head his right foot ripped my shirt pocket off as if he had a pair of scissors. I jumped away shocked by the colt's speed. Wally grabbed my belt. "Whoa, Clay, you okay?" he asked as he yanked me out the stall door. I caught my heel on the door frame as I staggered backward and went down on my back in the aisle. Wally leaped over me to block the opening as the colt wheeled away to stand shaking at the back of his stall. I rolled out of the way and sat up.

"Yeah, he missed me," I said examining my ruined shirt. "I just got a little careless there for a minute. Did you see where my syringe of sedative ended up; I had it in my shirt pocket."

Bending down near the door Wally ran his hands through the shavings. "Something hit the wall here by the door," he said as he came up with the little syringe.

I spent the next few minutes getting up to the colt again. With Rompun and ketamine coursing through his veins, it took less than a minute to achieve anesthesia. As soon as the gelding hit the ground I injected Lidocaine into his digital nerves to numb the foot and started an intravenous drip to extend the general anesthesia time. "The local's just in case he decides to wake up before I'm finished," I said. Wally had helped me on several different occasions and we were starting to be a pretty good team. He hung the IV bag from a rafter while I shaved the surgical site.

"I'm sure you want the leg raised," Wally said as he slid a five gallon plastic container under the colt's cannon bone to elevate the foot. The rest of the preparations were completed in a very few minutes.

"I see we're using a sticky drape," Wally said, removing the wrapper from the sterile plastic.

"I want it contoured to stick tightly over the hoof wall, the bulbs of his heels and around behind his pastern," I said as we removed the backing. Once the plastic was in place over the incision site, we used standard cloth drapes around the leg to prevent accidental contamination and I made an incision just above the coronary band extending from the heel half way to the toe. I excised the collateral cartilage and removed the infected tissue surrounding it. "I think I'll drill a hole about here," I said, marking a spot on the hoof wall. "That should provide drainage for my surgical site."

"I'll bet Linda has an electric drill either in the tack room or the shop," Wally said. "How big a hole do you want to make?"

"I won't need that," I said. "The hole only needs to be large enough to run a little plastic tubing through. I can make the hole with a bone pin. There's one in my surgical pack." Placing the latex drain and closing the skin incision required only a few minutes. I shut off the intravenous drip while we waited for the cast to dry, and his recovery from anesthesia was uneventful. I made out an invoice and wrote a note to Joyce asking her to call me while Wally gathered up all the paraphernalia and returned it to the truck.

"I seem to remember something about you buying lunch," Wally said as he made the last trip to the truck.

"Just name your poison," I said tacking up the invoice and note with a push pin.

"What do you suppose the special is at the El Rancho?" Wally asked.

We were already in my truck when I answered. "It's Wednesday, not Thursday, so it won't be Larry's roast beef if that's what you're salivating for. My bet for Wednesday is something fried, chicken or maybe chicken fried steak."

"You're probably right; let's make it the Holiday Inn. I'd gag if he made chicken fried steak."

"Just because it's the special doesn't mean you have to eat it," I said, turning left onto Highway 40. "You can order off the menu, you know."

"Someone at The Table would have to try it, and they'd undoubtedly be sitting next to me. The Holiday Inn will be just fine."

"I had no idea you hated chicken fried steak; I thought that was a Texas specialty you'd grown up eating."

"I don't hate chicken fried steak, I hate Larry's excuse for chicken fried steak," Wally said as a tremor passed through his body. "In fact, I don't think I've had a decent chicken fried steak anywhere in Colorado."

"The Holiday it is then, but you've got me craving a chicken fried steak right now. I just don't remember if they serve it," I said, trying to picture the menu.

After a lunch of hot pastrami sandwiches and potato salad, I dropped Wally off at his shop and returned to the clinic. Joyce phoned about four-thirty.

"I picked up the colts, Doc," she said. "I figgered you'd want to hang onto the other two."

"I'm still at my office," I said thinking of the check she'd promised to bring. "Are you stopping by?"

"I was runnin' late so I've already passed your clinic; then I had to get some gas so that's why I'm calling," Joyce said. "I thought I'd bring the rest of the castrations on Friday when I go down to pick up Jim."

"Speaking of Jim," I said, "what kind of surgery did he have?"

"Oh, the silly old man, he busted his leg and needed plates an' screws an' things," Joyce said. "We were bringing a herd of horses off the hill. Jim busted off the edge like he was in the Kentucky Derby an' hit a little ole' boulder. Somersaulted my good bay gelding an' got the gelding an' my saddle all scratched up. Jim went flyin' an' smacked a rock; busted that big bone above his knee. Couldn't even get back on his horse. I had to lead the bay down and corral the horses by myself. Jim took most of an hour to hobble down."

"Is he going to be okay?" I asked. "At his age a fracture can be pretty serious."

"I told him. I said, 'Honey...' He likes me to call him honey. 'You can't bust off down through those boulders like that. You're not seventy any more. You gotta' be more careful.' But it's like pouring out a canteen in the Sahara Desert; it does no good. He doesn't listen. My dime's about used up an' my truck's full, so I'll see you Friday."

"I thought you were bringing a check today," I said, but I was talking to myself, Joyce had already hung up.

Linda continued to keep my surgery cases stalled, and I called her on the next Thursday to see if she had any news. "I haven't been able to get Mrs. Sailor on the phone," I said, "and I was wondering if you've talked to her?"

"She sent me a nice thank you note for keeping her colts on Wednesday, but made no mention of being back before next week when she's due to pick up her mare," Linda said.

"Let me know if you hear from her," I said. "I'm trying to plan my day tomorrow and I don't know if it will include castrations for her or not."

"I'll be sure to call if I hear anything or if she shows up with the colts," Linda said.

"I need to check the casts tomorrow anyway, so I'll just bring castration equipment and stop by first thing in the morning."

"I'm planning on being here all day if you need any help," Linda said.

"Thanks, Linda, I'll see you in the morning," I said, hanging up the phone. *Odd that Joyce didn't mention the sorrel gelding in her thank you note,* I thought, scratching my head.

The casts were fine, but Joyce remained unavailable throughout the next week. Friday morning I sedated both horses and removed the plaster. They had healed nicely and, after removing the sutures, I lightly bandaged both of them to prevent any reflex swelling. Since there was no contacting Joyce I went on about my day. Around ten o'clock I returned to the clinic and found that Linda had left a message; Joyce was waiting at her place. I hurried to meet them.

"I see you finally made it; I wasn't sure how long to wait," Joyce said as I climbed out of the pickup. "We couldn't reach you." She looked at Linda and nodded tapping her foot.

"Darn phones, sometimes they're a real nuisance," I said shaking my head.

"Well, you're here now," Joyce said. "Are there any instructions before I haul the mare home?"

"Just remove the bandage tomorrow," I said. "She healed well. The gelding looks good, too, but leave his bandage for a couple of days so the hole in the hoof can fill in with granulation tissue."

Joyce smiled her biggest smile and the twinkle was back in her eyes. "I know how much you like the gelding, Clay, so I've decided to make him a present to you."

I was shocked and it must have shown because Joyce and Linda both laughed. "A present, just like that," I said.

"Just like that," Joyce said pulling his papers, a bill of sale and another page from a briefcase I hadn't noticed. "Here's the bill of sale and his papers, I've already signed them."

"Thanks... I didn't see that coming." I took the paper work and noticed the sale price of 'one dollar and other consideration' neatly written in. I hesitatedd rereading the sentence and Joyce slipped the third page on top. It was my invoice for the previous work. I only thought about it for a second. "Okay, you've got a deal," I said tearing the invoice in half.

"I did bring three more colts to castrate," Joyce said waving toward the trailer.

"When I finish with these colts, the gelding's paid for in full," I said, looking her in the eye. She made no reply; just batted her long lashes at me and smiled her best smile.

Joyce waved goodbye as she pulled out of the ranch heading back to Wyoming. "I'll bet she didn't pay you for board," I said turning to Linda. "That makes the gelding worth a little more. I'll write you a check for both him and the mare."

Linda laughed again. "She did pay their board and said she didn't want you to have any surprises. I didn't understand it at the time."

"Joyce definitely is a horse trader," I said, looking at the gelding's papers to make sure she was even listed as the owner. "Two Dead Flies, why would anyone name a horse Two Dead Flies?"

"More to the point," Linda said. "Why would anyone buy a horse named Two Dead Flies?"

Chapter 14

Mending Fences

"Sorry, Doc, I didn't see you," I said as I almost knocked John Utterback off his feet. He was coming out of Boggs Hardware, head down, muttering to himself. I just had time to grab Doc's arm and keep him upright. A short man and slightly built, he couldn't have weighed more than one-thirty-five. I'd had a chance to meet John Utterback on several occasions, usually at the El Rancho. It was his favorite hangout when he was in town.

"Who the hell are you, anyway?" Utterback asked, squinting at me through rheumy eyes. Doc desperately needed bifocals and only wore them occasionally, mostly when he wanted to look distinguished. Well past eighty, he still drove his horses in the chariot race every February during winter carnival.

"Doc, it's Clay Williams," I said, shaking the proffered hand. Doc had practiced veterinary medicine longer than anyone in town, at least anyone I'd talked to, could remember.

"Well, Clay Williams, you live around here?" Doc asked, taking a step back and squinting even harder.

"Just south of town," I said, not bothering to add that he'd stopped by about two weeks earlier to campaign. Doc was a county commissioner, had been for forty years. Though he was always unopposed, he campaigned hard at each election. During his campaign he'd meet all the newcomers and visit with all the ranchers in the county. At each stop he'd offer to provide any veterinary services that were needed and ask for support in the upcoming election.

"Too much snow south of town. I live in Milner. Much better weather in Milner. If you're thinking of moving I'm a realtor. Know a lot of good property down there," Doc waved his arms, vaguely pointing west toward Milner.

"I didn't know you were a realtor," I said.

"Oh yeah, on the side. What is it you do?" He asked still squinting.

"I'm a veterinarian," I said. It was something I'd repeated each time we'd met.

"Veterinarian, huh? I used to be the only vet in these parts, but with all the people movin' in, I can't git to everybody, so I just concentrate on the horses. I do all the horse work around here." He waved his arms, gesturing in all directions, the movement causing him to lose his balance. I caught his arm for the second time. "You ought to think about moving up here. Bet you'd be busy ... if you're any good."

"I'll consider that," I said, shaking my head.

"What is this, a veterinary convention?" Nate Trogler had come out of the courthouse and was passing by in his uniform. Nate was over six feet but didn't appear that tall because his shoulders were so massive. He gently patted Utterback on top of his baseball cap. "Don't work too hard, Doc," he said as he stepped around the old man.

"Who the hell was that?" Utterback asked, turning to peer at Nate as he walked away. "Was that the sheriff?"

"Yeah, Doc, that was a deputy, Nate Trogler." I said shaking my head again. Nate had lived his whole life on a ranch just about a mile from Utterback's place.

"Trogler... sounds familiar. A Trogler had a place down near me in Milner as I recall."

"That would be Nate's dad, Pat. They still have the ranch. In fact, Nate still lives on the place," I said, as I eased around Utterback to get closer to the hardware store door.

"Ya s'pose they want to sell it?" Doc was searching his pockets for a pen. He'd already gotten out his pad.

"I doubt it," I said.

"Ya never can tell," Doc mumbled. "It don't hurt to ask, an' speakin' of ranches I better git on down to mine." He gave me a wink and a sly smile. "Spent the night in town. New girlfriend." I acknowledged his comment with raised eyebrows and a nod. "I give ya a card?" he asked, placing one in my palm. "I'm running for county commissioner. If ya do decide to move up here I'd like your vote."

"Thanks, Doc, I'll be sure to do that." I turned again, starting for the door.

"Where the hell'd I park?" Doc was leaning, hunched over at the edge of the curb squinting up and down the street.

"Just across there by the hotel," I said, pointing toward the Harbor House with its pale green stucco. I'd spotted Utterback's aged Ford, easily recognizable by the dents and scrapes on all four corners, the bent tailgate that hadn't closed in several years and the Australian Shepherd sitting in the back that was nearly as old as Doc.

"Well, thanks, young feller, thanks for the help." Doc was shaking his head as he lurched from the sidewalk heading for his truck with short shuffling steps. "How the hell did he know where my truck was?" he mumbled, shooting a glance in my direction.

I smiled at his comment while opening the heavy glass door to Boggs Hardware. I was looking for light bulbs for the clinic. The old hardwood floor squeaked as I moved down the left hand aisle to the back of the store. In the dim light a large bear wearing an oversized tee-shirt hunched over the sale table. The bear was John Baker. I hadn't seen John in a few months, not since I'd traded in my dirt bike for a larger model. "Honda John" had owned the motorcycle dealership for several years. Recently he'd acquired the Ford store and become the auto baron of Routt County.

"How's your truck running, Clay?" John asked, his moustache twitching where it ended below his chin. He was pawing through the discounted light fixtures.

"Couldn't be better. I haven't had a problem since you talked me into the Ford," I said, picking out a box of bulbs for the recessed lights in the clinic waiting room. "How've you been?"

"Well, truth is, I've been well until last night. You don't happen to know a Greg Jones, do you?" He asked, rubbing his rather large, crooked nose thoughtfully.

130

"I don't think I do. Where does he live?" I pulled a bulb from the box and checked it for an intact filament as if I were candling an egg looking for an embryo.

"He told me he lives in Milner. I let him try out a big Harley yesterday afternoon and he hasn't brought it back. I'm gonna' call the sheriff if he's not back by lunch time."

"Why wait? If they find him and he's just late returning it, no problem. If he's skipped at least you'll have a couple of hours' head start," I said. "Did he leave wheels at your place?"

"He left an old truck that doesn't even have any plates! I'm beginning to wonder if I'm getting ripped off, and talking to you isn't helping," John said fidgeting nervously.

"I'm probably over-reacting," I said, taking my bulbs and heading for the register. "I've got to go to Milner this afternoon. I'll keep an eye out for a new Harley."

"Thanks, Doc. It's big and black with old style leather saddle bags," John called down the aisle, waving halfheartedly in my direction.

I finished the Milner call, an uneventful colt castration just south of the Yampa River, and was heading back to Steamboat when I remembered my promise to John. I made a slight detour through the Milner trailer park but didn't see any motorcycles at all. As I came back onto the highway I realized how thirsty I was and stopped at the Milner store.

"Hi, Sandy!" I said as I tromped over the dirty tile on my way to the cooler in the rear of the grocery.

"Doc Williams, I haven't seen you in a while. You need directions, or is this strictly a social call?" Sandy stopped sweeping, leaned her large frame on the broom and ran pudgy fingers through matted blond curls, catching her breath in the process.

"I'm not lost today, Sandy, no directions this time. Mostly it's a refreshment break." I opened the cooler and picked out an RC. "Although I did tell Honda John I'd look around for a missing Harley."

"John Baker lost one of his bikes?" Sandy put her broom aside and waddled my direction, her unlaced Keds slapping the linoleum.

"Seems so. Let a guy test drive one and he hasn't returned it. He told John he lived down here." I popped the tab on the RC and let a large swallow slide down my throat.

"We've got a lot of miners and construction workers in the trailer park; it could be someone from here," she said, picking a soda from the case and opening it. "I haven't heard anything about it though." Taking a long drink, she let out a loud belch and grinned in my direction.

"What do you have in the way of snacks?" I asked, ignoring Sandy's display and starting toward the counter.

"I got anything you want, as long as it's fattenin'," she cackled. "Chips, nuts, junk like that. Next aisle over, candy's there, too." She said starting toward her cash register. I took my time picking out some pretzels and still won the race to the register. "Them pretzels ain't fattenin'. You need somethin' greasy to fill you out." She pulled her tee-shirt down over her ample belly and hitched up the orange sweat pants that were her habitual uniform.

"You may be right, but this will have to do." I tore open the bag, taking a swig of RC before starting to munch the salty snack.

I was counting my change and preparing to leave as a car pulled into the gravel parking area. Peering through the screen door I spotted Nate Trogler getting out of his patrol car, a black and white Ford Bronco with Routt County Sheriff emblazoned on the door. Trogler was always entertaining so I decided to chat a while longer. Nate hitched up his pants and adjusted his holster as he climbed the store's steps.

"Hey, Sandy, put your hands in the air and step away from the counter, this ain't no social call! And you, Williams, hit the floor and spread 'em. I know you two are up to no good." Nate laughed as he jerked open the screen door straining the hinges.

"This is sexual harassment, you ass hole! I'll have your badge for this. You can't throw your weight around and give that kind of shit to a lady!" Sandy lurched around the counter, her hands still in the air, the fat folds under her arms jiggling at every step. She flopped her massive frame against Nate. Throwing her arms around his neck she dragged his head down to her level and planted a big slobbery kiss on his face. Trogler had just enough time to turn his head; coming away with his entire cheek smeared bright red with lipstick. "Take that, you bastard," she said, stepping back to admire her work.

"You sure know how to treat a man. How in the world could it be that you're still single?" Nate said, wiping the lipstick off with a paper towel from the store's counter.

"Divorce ain't final for another two months, honey. Then I'm all yours." Sandy duck walked back around the counter. "If I were only ten years older," Nate said with a sigh, swatting Sandy's backside as she passed.

"You've always been a smart ass, started soon as you were old enough to talk." Sandy reached across the counter and pinched Nate's cheek.

"I've seen enough of this love affair," I said, pretending to gag as I headed for the door.

"Now hold on, Doc, this really is official business. I'm down here looking for a motorcycle thief." Nate straightened up and tried to look official. Betrayed by his baby face, he couldn't quite pull it off, even in uniform.

"Damn, with the whole county lookin' for him, the poor son of a bitch doesn't have as much chance as a seed at a watermelon eatin' contest," Sandy said, finishing her soda and crushing the can in one easy motion.

"More people been by lookin' for this guy?" Nate asked, immediately interested.

"Me, for one. John told me about it this morning," I said, taking a pretzel and offering the bag to Trogler. Nate looked at the pretzels and shook his head.

"Thanks, but no, I just had lunch. Do either of you know anything about this guy?" Nate looked from one to the other as we both shook our heads. "Well then I'll drive through the trailer park and go over and check the rental cabins at the Johnson place." Nate said, already starting for the door.

I followed and was halfway to my truck when John Utterback roared onto the gravel parking lot. He lurched to a stop in his old Ford, its tailgate flapping and banging. Doc was able to open the driver's side door on the third try. He really put his shoulder into it and almost fell out when the door popped open. Hanging onto the window frame he crawled down and came around the pickup holding onto the bed for support. He squinted at the two of us, finally picking out the uniform on Nate.

"You the sheriff?" Doc said, pointing a gnarled finger at Trogler.

"I guess I am today, Doc." Nate walked in Utterback's direction. It didn't seem to help though, Doc just squinted harder.

"You gonna' fix my fence?" Doc glared at the officer.

"Well, I don't know for sure, but I kind of doubt it. What's wrong with the fence?"

"The damn thing's down. What the hell did you think was wrong with it?" Doc advanced on the deputy. "If you ain't gonna' fix it, who the hell is?" He shook his fist in Nate's face. "Does he have a brother?" The screen door banged as Sandy came out to join the fun.

"Are you talking about me, Doc? I've got a little brother. You probably remember Tom. He helped you race your chariot last year." Nate looked at both Sandy and me shrugging his shoulders as he scratched his head.

"No, you idiot, the motorcycle guy. Does he have a brother?" Utterback was starting to get really angry now.

"I don't know, Doc. What does he have to do with your fence?" Nate said, looking perplexed.

"He's the one that tore my fence down, you moron. Why else would I give a damn about him?" he said, pulling a pouch of Red Man out of his back pocket. Doc stuffed a large chew in his mouth.

"So, you've seen the motorcycle rider. Doc, is this the same guy who was test driving a bike from Honda John in Steamboat?" Nate was looking more interested by the second.

"How in the hell should I know?" Utterback said, sliding his baseball cap back and scratching his head. "You still haven't said if he has a brother."

"I don't know if he has a brother or not, Doc. Just forget the brother thing for a minute. When did he tear down your fence, anyway?" It was Nate's turn to scratch his head.

"How the hell should I know? I wasn't there. It must have been yesterday er last night sometime." Doc Utterback spit a dark brown stream at his feet. "I don't give a damn when it happened. I just need the fence put back up. So, who's gonna' do it? You ... you gonna' fix it?"

"Now, Doc, if you weren't there, are you sure a motorcycle knocked your fence down? Wouldn't it make more sense if one of your cows knocked it down?"

"Of course it would, you big dumb jerk, but then there wouldn't be a motorcycle tangled in the fence, would there?" Doc said shaking his head. "Jesus, it's like talking to a damn baby." Doc looked at Sandy, "Must be the sheriff! They always hire the simple ones." He spit again, making a direct hit on the toe of his own right boot.

"It's there? The motorcycle is there?" It was Nate's turn to scratch his head.

"'Course it's there. How the hell else would I know it was a motorcycle tore my fence down? Do I need to write this down for ya, boy?" Utterback said as he scrounged in his shirt pocket. Coming up with the stub of a pencil, he shook it in Nate's face.

"I'm beginning to catch on now, Doc," Nate said with a grin for Sandy and me. "When the guy hits your fence he takes off. Is that right?"

"You're catching on now, Sonny. He hit my fence and took off into the rocks." Utterback was nodding and grinning for the first time.

"So you don't need this guy's brother. We just need to find the rider and have him do a little fence repair." Trogler started to herd Doc toward his truck. "Let's go have a look at this fence of yours and see if we can find this Greg Jones character."

"Listen ass hole, we have to find his brother 'cause the scum bag went into the rocks," Doc said starting to lose his temper again.

"I'm a pretty good tracker and this fella's on foot, we'll catch him," Nate said rubbing his hands together and smiling broadly.

"Ain't you heard a dang thing I've been sayin'? He went into the rocks! Busted the helmet in half, too," Doc said, holding his arms out as if he were flying.

"You mean he's still lying out there?" Nate started for his pickup on the run. "Damn, Doc, you could have said he was injured," Trogler jerked open his driver's side door. "Follow me, Clay. We might need your truck!" The excitement was infectious and I trotted for my pickup.

"Hold on, he ain't injured, and he ain't goin' nowhere." Doc had to spit again and then sidled up to Nate once more. "That's why we need to find his brother to fix my fence. That boy's dead!"

"Dead, you mean like ... d .. dead? He's out at your place dead?" Nate's jaw dropped, he stood slumped forward staring at the old man. I stopped and spun around. Sandy and I looked at each other in disbelief.

"Dead? ... sure is! Helmet split open, blood everywhere, ugly." Doc replied with a twinkle in his eye. He waved his arms like an umpire calling a base runner safe.

"I've got to ca ... call the highway patrol and the coroner!" Nate said to no one in particular as he danced from one foot to the other and waved his arms about. "Clay, would you bring your truck anyway, just in case?" He started for Doc's truck taking Utterback by the elbow.

"Just in case what?" Utterback asked stopping dead in his tracks. "You think I don't know dead? I've been a vetinary since way before you were born. I know dead and this boy's sure as hell dead." Doc jerked his arm away from Trogler's grasp.

"No, Doc, it's not like that. I'm sure you know a lot about dead," Nate said, trying to regain control of the old man's arm.

"Just what the hell is it like then?" Utterback wasn't moving an inch.

"Uh .. maybe he's just unconscious, or something," Nate said with a halfhearted wave.

"Oh, he's unconscious all right...with his brains splattered all over my rocks."

Trogler opened the door of the green Ford and pushed Utterback toward the seat. "Where are your keys, Doc? I don't see them here." Nate nervously looked around the cab.

"You think I'm daft? Leave the keys in the cab and you're askin' for some scum bag to steal it. Probably go for a joy ride an' end up runnin' through my fence." The old man laughed. "No, sir, I keep my keys on me." Utterback checked his pants pockets as he spoke.

"There they are," Nate said pointing to the large ring of keys. "Right on the seat cleverly hidden under that stack of newspapers." He winked at me and shook his head. Then he started for his vehicle but had to turn back to close Doc's door after the old man slammed it for the third time to no avail.

"Wait! ... Wait, for me, I have to lock the door!" Sandy squealed in falsetto as she lumbered up the steps reaching for the screen door. I'd started my truck, but I waved Nate on.

"Go ahead. I'll give Sandy a lift." I pulled around the parking lot lining up to head west and waited for Sandy to heave herself into cab, panting hard.

Doc's place was on the right less than a mile from the store. The highway veered left skirting a long rock outcropping that stood fifty feet or more above the highway forming a narrow grassy plateau. A talus slope littered with broken sandstone stretched from the base of the cliff to the highway. Thick stands of scrub oak were interspersed among the boulders reaching right to the highway's edge obscuring the ranch's boundary fence. The deputy had stopped in the borrow ditch just past the drive while Doc left his pickup halfway on the highway with the driver's side door hanging open.

I pulled in the driveway, staying on the gravel. As I made my way through the oak brush I could see that the fence had been ripped from several posts just to the left of the Portagee entry gate. Tangled in the wire was a new black Harley and twenty feet beyond was the driver's body. I didn't need to get any closer to see that he'd flown headlong into a pile of large boulders. The largest rock was half the size of my pickup. Greg Jones' helmet had indeed split in half on impact and his skull hadn't faired one bit better. Nate had already clambered through the twisted wire of the fence and reached the body. My curiosity satisfied, I wasn't overly anxious to get a closer look.

"Oh shit, oh shit! I really do need the coroner!" Nate yelled as he raced back to his pickup. Yanking open the door, Trogler jerked the microphone from its clip on the dash.

"Patsy, get Ted Lane and the highway patrol out to Doc's quick!" Waiting for a response, he stepped into the vehicle and closed the door. I could see through the window that the deputy was having quite a discussion. Nate was bouncing up and down waving his arms, his face becoming redder by the second. Finally he threw the microphone across the cab and it bounced off the passenger door. "Jesus, you can't get simple orders followed without a dozen questions." Nate said as he climbed back out of the Bronco.

"I hope you told them to send an ambulance and a body bag," I said as I prepared to leave. I had gotten close enough to see the extent of the injuries. "Come on, Sandy, I'll take you back to the store on my way to Steamboat."

"The hell you will! I ain't leavin' till the excitement dies down," Sandy said, climbing through the fence for a closer inspection of the deceased. "Well shit, Greg, you did it this time. Looks like you were cruisin' just a little too fast." She spread her arms and spun around with her eyes crossed and her tongue out the side of her mouth. I had to look away and she laughed heartily. "Hey, look, the Doc's a little queasy. Too much for you, Williams?"

"I just think he deserves a little respect," I replied, blood rising in my face.

"Well, maybe you better take a closer look over here 'cause this guy don't deserve nothin' but a hole in the ground," Sandy said, laughing as she looked around at Trogler. Nate was checking out the sod in front of his boots. "You guys, go screw yourselves!" She stomped off toward my truck but stopped when a siren sounded as one of the emergency vehicles topped the hill east of Milner. "Hey, Nate, you think Collins, that cute state cop, is on duty?" Sandy hitched up her sweat pants again and started to tug on her tee-shirt.

Nate shrugged and gave her a "How the hell should I know?" look as he thumbed through forms in a plastic file box. I was about to try backing out onto the highway when the Bell ambulance crew rolled in with lights flashing and siren blaring to stop right behind my truck. Then sirens seemed to come from all directions and the ambulance was followed closely by the first of two state police vehicles. Then another sheriff's car raced up. Finally Jim Hicks, the game warden arrived. At about the same time, a volunteer fireman from Hayden came sliding up.

Everyone was talking at once and checking out the wreck. About all I could get out of the confusion was that the next move was to wait on the coroner, Ted Lane. Lane owned the local funeral home and was rumored to have become the coroner so that no stiffs could bypass his mortuary. Trogler had asked his dispatcher to let John Baker know the situation and he came with a trailer to haul away the mangled Harley.

Doc Utterback strutted back and forth and explained to whomever would listen that he had found the body and it was on his property. If there were to be a picture in the weekly newspaper, *The Steamboat Pilot*, he, as the property owner and county commissioner, should be prominently featured, perhaps directing the officers to the body.

"Trogler,_call in and see what's taking Lane so long to get here, will you?" Patrolman Collins asked, as he walked about with Sandy, salivating, close on his heels.

"Sure thing, Bill. I was just about to do that." Nate reached through his open window to key the mike. Then he leaned inside to hear the reply. A few moments later his head came out of the vehicle. "He says he'll be here in a little while. He had a viewing scheduled."

"Are you kidding me? He had a viewing scheduled." Collins started over to Nate's Bronco. "Let me see that mike." He took the microphone from Nate and stuck his head in the window. Nate backed away turning to the rest of the gathering.

"I'll bet Ted'll be here inside of ten minutes with lights and siren when Bill gets through with him!" Nate said, braking out in a large grin.

I checked my watch and settled in to wait. Meanwhile Doc Utterback was trying to be the good host and offered us Cokes or lemonade from a refrigerator he kept in the barn. It was closer to fifteen minutes, but we were treated to the siren and flashing light bar as the coroner arrived. It took Ted Lane all of two minutes to make his investigation and pronounce Greg dead at the scene. Jumping back in his hearse, Lane fled, throwing dirt and gravel.

"Probably has another viewing," Sandy giggled, poking Bill Collins in the ribs.

The State Troopers had finished with their chalk and measurements and it only took a few minutes for them to finish the necessary forms. Packing up quickly, they decided on the El Rancho for coffee, and Bill Collins roared off in the lead. The ambulance crew lost no time in shoving the corpse into a body bag and gently tossing it onto the gurney for the ride back to Steamboat, their only complaint being that they had to drop Greg off and might miss out on the first cup of coffee.

"Don't worry boys," Trogler said as he hitched up his pants again, "The news won't be out for another twenty minutes. You'll get to tell this story thirty more times today."

"Can we do the lights and siren thing, too?" Sandy said as Trogler bundled her into his Bronco. Nate made a u-turn and I started to pull out behind him when Utterback placed two fingers in his mouth and let out an ear piercing whistle.

"Hey ... HEY ... Hang on ... Wait a minute!" He yelled as he waved his cap wildly. "Who's gonna' fix my fence!"

Chapter 15

Kicked

I started my day that Thursday with breakfast at the El Rancho, mostly to hear about the motorcycle wreck. The story had grown overnight and was being told and retold each time with further embellishment by folks who hadn't even been present. Listening to it for the third time my pager buzzed. It was John McHugh, a retired Denver fireman who lived up the Elk River. His mare Molly had cut her leg and John thought she needed stitches. I rearranged my schedule and drove up the Elk River, turning onto the gravel just past Glen Eden Resort at nine-fifteen. A short mile later I pulled up to the chicken wire fence that protected John's garden from marauding deer.

"Doc, I'm glad you could make it so fast. We've been really worried about Molly," John said walking over to my truck. .

"If we're gonna suture her wound it needs to be done as soon as possible," I said stepping out of the cab.

"She seems a little better now, but she couldn't even stand on the leg when it happened," John frowned and shook his head.

"It's good to finally meet you," I said extending a hand. "We've talked on the phone so many times." My hand was immediately engulfed and almost crushed by a huge paw. I had a vision of being six years old and matching hands with my dad as I looked up at the six-foot-six fireman. John's hair, now limited to a ring around his ears, was only a shade lighter than his badly sunburned head, and his eyes seemed to swim behind thick bifocals.

"How bad is you're mare's cut?" I asked, my eyes fixed on John's enormous hands.

"I'm sure it needs stitching. You can see the muscle in her arm!" John said, looking a little pale. He swallowed as he looked at the bay mare tied to a nearby post.

"Let's take a look," I said, starting over to the horse. The big, jug-headed mare glared at me through little pig eyes and tossed her head at my approach. I untied her lead and eased around to her left examining all four legs. I repeated the procedure on the right side and was about to ask where she was cut when, stooping down, I saw the wound. It was an inch-long vertical slice on the inside of her left forearm halfway between her knee and elbow. The tiny cut was barely through the skin. My first reaction was to spray something, anything, on it and drive away. McHugh, on the other hand, was concerned. He was probably wondering whether his lovely mare would be sound or even survive. I made sure this was her only wound and put on my best bedside manner. "This isn't as severe as I had imagined."

"Oh, good. Nancy's been really worried," John glanced toward the house. "Nancy! Doc says she's gonna be all right!" He shouted, sliding his bifocals back up his nose and waving for her to join us. "When it happened a few hours ago Molly didn't want to put her leg down and, well, we thought it might be broken. Nancy was sure we'd have to put her to sleep."

"No, no, she'll be just fine," I said, squatting down to the level of the scratch. "There are a couple of ways we can handle this. We can spray a little Wound Coat on it every day for a week or so and it will be just fine, or we can spend some money and suture it. If we heal it open it probably won't even leave a scar. If we suture it, we'll have to remove the stitches in two weeks. That will mean another trip out." I turned to John.

"I sure don't want to be a bother," John said, pushing his hands into his pockets. "But if it wouldn't be too much trouble, I know Nancy would like it sewn up. Besides we're going down to Denver in a few days and won't be here to put on the medicine." He looked toward his wife with a weak smile as she approached. Short and round, Nancy was wearing a gingham dress and apron befitting her grandmotherly status. She was smiling, her cheeks rosy below large round glasses.

"It's definitely not a bother; I try to make a living doin' this sort of thing." I'd already tied the mare back to the fence and was on my way to the truck for local anesthetic and suture material. I filled a small syringe with Lidocaine and switched to a tiny 25-gauge needle. "I'll just slip this under the skin and she won't feel a thing," I said, holding up the syringe for McHugh to see. "Then I'll shave the wound and close it with a couple of stitches."

I left the mare tied and bent down to inject around the wound. The needle hadn't even touched her when she shied and started pulling back. I made a grab for the end of the lead hoping to get her untied before she could break John's post. Molly was snorting, her neck was bowed and she had a look in her eye that said,"I'm not scared, but you'd better be." I jerked the rope as hard as I could and the knot gave, letting Molly run backward. The rope burned through my hand before I could let it go, popping my hand open as the knot passed through it. I had to catch the lead again to prevent the mare from running off. As she tried to wheel I pulled hard jerking her to face me. When I glanced at John it was obvious he'd never seen anything like this.

"Maybe we'd better take the edge off her. I'll mix up a little cocktail," I said, stepping away and handing the mare to the fireman. I returned with the sedative and eased up beside her neck. "Stay on my side of her and if she wants to run backwards we'll go with her. She'll stop in a few yards. Just keep her head over our way so she can't throw her shoulder into us."

"No problem, Doc. She's real gentle." John was rubbing Molly on the side of the head and I thought I'd misjudged him; he looked as if he understood the mare. I had the syringe in my left hand and reached out with my right to stroke Molly's neck. I touched her and she bowed away trying to run backwards. Surprised, John threw all of his considerable weight against her, bracing and almost sitting down. Instantly the mare felt the pull and reared straight up. She jerked John off his feet. Shocked by her speed and power, John turned the rope loose. Molly bolted veering away. I seized the lead and was barely able to hang on spinning her around to face me as she careened sideways. I gave ground and she stopped a few feet from the fence snorting and blowing.

"I think we've upset Molly a little," I said, making my third run to the truck and returning with a twitch.

146

"What the hell is that?" John asked with a deer-in-the-head-lights look.

"We're gonna' need a little persuasion to get a needle into her," I said, holding up the chrome chain attached to a three-foot oak handle. "Just let me have her." Holding the lead just below the snap with my right hand, I slid my left hand down her nose and grabbed her upper lip. Most horses jerk back a little when you grab the lip and I had anticipated the reaction and went with Molly. I had, however, misjudged her intensity. She went up in the air again. Jerking her head away she pulled me in front of her. Striking with both front feet she ripped the left pocket off my shirt, barely missing my head and chest. I was jerked off my feet, real-izing as I left the ground that I'd badly underestimated the mare. I still had the lead in my right hand and I shanked her a time or two with sharp jerks on the rope and was able to regain control.

"Maybe we could put her in the trailer or something. I don't want you getting' hurt," John said, backing away from the fracas.

"She'll be okay," I said as I positioned the twitch over my hand again, but I was beginning to wonder why I hadn't pushed harder for the wound spray option. "When I get an ear on her and have her nose you twist on the twitch handle, just be sure to stay off to the side."

"Sure, Doc, I'll do whatever," John said, coming up on the balls of his feet like a prizefighter.

"I'll quiet her down a little first," I said rubbing her neck with my right hand, before I slid it up over the top of her head and grabbed her left ear. "Crank that handle 'til she squints," I said, squeezing her nose as hard as I could. This time Molly just stretched her neck out and squealed quietly. I dilated her jugular vein and slipped in the sedative. As I stepped away from the mare, John relaxed some of the pressure on the twitch. Instantly Molly whipped her head to the right, simultaneously striking at the twitch with her left front foot as she reared. Steel struck oak with a resounding crack as her shoe hit the handle. Her hoof ricocheted off the twitch handle and hit McHugh squarely in the left fore-arm. The twitch windmilled off into space narrowly missing his jaw. John's arm spasmed; his wrist flexed and his fingers cramped into a claw. He crouched, half bent over, holding his left arm as a goose-egg bruise formed on the underside of his elbow.

"Damn," John muttered between clinched teeth. "She's quick." He was rapidly turning white and weaving slightly. I wrapped an arm around the big man and pushed him toward my pickup. He leaned heavily on the side of the truck until I could get the passenger side door open and sit him down on the edge of the floor. Gingerly rubbing his arm, McHugh slowly regained his color. "Gees, Doc, I don't know how you do it. She could just as easily have hit me in the head." A tremor passed through him. "If she had, I'd be dead!" John's hands trembled as he tried to straighten his cramped fingers, pulling on them with his right hand.

"John, are you okay?" Nancy called. "You be careful, you know you don't know anything about horses."

"I'm fine, honey," John waved her away with his good arm.

"I'm sorry I distracted you when I stepped away from Molly. She's a tough old bird and she'll put the hurt on us when she gets an opportunity," I turned back to the mare. She was standing, eyes half closed, head down, swaying slightly. The sedation was taking full effect. "I think we've got her now. I'll slip that local anesthetic in and get her sewn up."

"I've still got one good arm; maybe you'd be safer if we twitched her again," John got to his feet and straightened to his full height.

"That might not be a bad idea," I said as I twisted on the oak handle again. "I'm using absorbable suture so we won't need to take the stitches out. They'll dissolve over time and in a little wound like this there's not much chance they'll get infected." It took all of two minutes to finish and I pulled the halter off the still-sedated mare. I was cleaning up when it occurred to me that if there were ever a cut that was going to get infected this would

148

be the one. Then, sure as hell, I'd have to come back and deal with her again. "I'll give her a little shot of long-acting penicillin," I said, filling a syringe with the thick white antibiotic.

Molly was still dozing peacefully when I threw my arm over her neck. I squirted alcohol on the injection site from my flat plastic bottle and shoved it in my hip pocket. Then I stabbed her in the left side of the neck to give her the shot. Molly wheeled away, alert and awake, but she couldn't get coordinated for any forward movement; she just spun in a circle to the right. Laughing, I picked up my feet and let her carry me for several revolutions as I injected the penicillin. Pulling the needle out, Molly instantly returned to her stupor as if you'd flipped off a light switch. Still laughing, I carelessly walked away, heading for the fence where John's wife stood.

"That mare's tough as they come," I said to Nancy standing on the other side of the chicken wire fence.

"I don't know about horses, Dr. Williams, I'll take your word for it." She fidgeted from one foot to the other. "I have cookies and lemonade on the porch if you'd like." Nancy pointed toward the house. I was still ten feet from the fence and I could see the lemonade sitting on the picnic table, beads of sweat carving trails as they ran down the ice-cold pitcher.

"That would be wond..." My head snapped back and my world went black. When I opened my eyes I felt intense pain in my right hip. Something wet was running down my leg and I couldn't move or speak. Was I shot? The taste of dirt and blood filled my mouth. I was trying to figure out where I was when I heard voices.

"Oh, my God, she's kicked him and broken his back!" Nancy screamed. "John did you hear that crack? I'm sure his back's broken! I'm going to call for the helicopter." She was already fleeing for the house, holding her dress up and running with little baby steps. It was at that point that I realized Nancy was talking about me.

"No, no helicopter...I'm okay!" I said, but even to my ears it sounded garbled and cryptic, more like "Nahh, nn... heytrr... m...ay."

"What?" Nancy slowed, dropping her skirt she cupped her hand behind one ear. "What'd he say?"

"I'm okay," I tried again, spitting out mud and blood. I scooped the dirt from under my upper lip with a finger. "No hel..i..cop.. ter," I repeated more slowly, trying to make myself understood. "My back's not broke." The sharp pain in my neck and hip made me nauseous and light headed.

"Oh, good," Nancy sounded relieved and started to come through the little gate to where I lay two or three feet from the fence. "Then get up, Doctor." She bent to take my arm and I tried to raise myself but immediately became dizzy.

"Gees, lady, give me a minute. I can't get up, but I'm sure my back's not broken." I was still spitting blood and mud and intense pain was shooting through my hip."

"Molly sure kicked the crap out of you!" John said, bending over to get to my eye level.

"Yeah, almost literally....Damn, it hurts to laugh." I tried to stop, but the whole mess was just too comical.

"I knew we should have sprayed Wound Coat on that cut, but no, you had to go and stitch it up!" John said laughing and holding his bruised arm with tears running down both cheeks. "Let's see if we can get you to the house." McHugh bent over and tried to help me up, but we had to abandon the idea because we both broke out laughing again.

"I don't see anything funny," Nancy said shaking her head.

"I guess you had to be there," John replied, still shaking with laughter.

I finally made it to all fours and John got me up. With a little help I hobbled to the house. Bending over the kitchen sink I rinsed and re-rinsed my mouth. My lip had only a small tear. My gums and the inside of my upper lip were raw from contact with Mother Earth, but what really hurt was my rump.

"I thought for a minute there you'd peed your pants," John said gesturing to the wide muddy streak down my leg. "When that bottle exploded it sure sounded like your back was broke."

"I felt that alcohol running down my leg and thought I'd been shot and was bleeding to death." I started to laugh all over again and had to grab onto the sink because my hip hurt so badly.

"That flask is still in your pocket. Want me to get it out? It might give you're hip a little more room." John gently took hold of the plastic bottle's neck and tried to pull it out.

"Wait, wait!" I yelled, the pain making me dizzy again. "Maybe I should drop my drawers first." I unbuckled my belt and dropped my pants enabling John to remove the flask.

"Wheeoo," John whistled. "Would you look at that … blew the whole side out of that bottle." He showed me where the entire seam on one side had split. "That thing in your hip pocket probably saved you from a broken back. Nancy, look at this!" John carried the flattened bottle in for his wife to see. I gently checked the point of impact and could easily feel the imprint of a hoof. "Hey, Doc, don't pull those pants up yet; I want to take a look at ground zero."

"Ground zero was pretty well distroyed," I said, hanging on to my belt awaiting McHugh's inspection. Just pulling on the elastic band of my undies hurt like hell.

"Holy shit! You've got a perfect black horseshoe with all the possible shades of blue around it. You've got a bruise big as a dinner plate." John stood there pulling on my shorts. "Nancy, come look at this!"

"That's okay," I said, ripping the elastic from John's hand and gingerly pulling up my pants. McHugh went to the cupboard and returned with two fingers of amber liquid in a small tumbler.

"I think you need this, Doc," he said handing me the glass. "A little Wild Turkey for its medicinal value."

The bourbon burned my lip and gums enough I didn't even notice the fire as it ran down my throat and hit my stomach. Immediately I began to feel better, losing the clammy feeling, which must have been from a mild case of shock. I stood still, holding on to the counter, as the ache in my hip began to subside.

"You know," I said, laughing at the thought. "If she'd kicked me any harder I'd have landed right in your chicken wire fence."

"Excuse me?" John's mouth fell open. "Come over here." He put an arm around my shoulder, helped me into the living room and turned me toward the wall. "Have a look, Doc," he said.

I looked in the wall mirror at raised red marks. They formed a distinctive octagon pattern covering my forehead, the left side of my face and my neck.

"How'd you think that dirt got packed under your upper lip? You were still a foot off the ground when you hit the chicken wire. Heck, you didn't connect with Mother Earth until the return trip." John was crouching to my level and smiling at me in the mirror. "I'll show you the dent in the fence. A little harder and you'd have gone right through it." McHugh straightened up, slapped his thigh with his good arm and laughed. "Molly came out the best of all," he said.

Chapter 16

The Lipizzaner Mare

I stayed at John McHugh's for the better part of an hour loosening up my hip and waiting for the aspirins to take effect. Then I headed back to Steamboat. Turning onto US 40 from the Elk River Road I spotted Dr. Belman's blue Chevy disappearing behind his veterinary hospital. Beating the oncoming traffic I followed him.

"Hey, Dr. B, I got word you wanted to see me. What's up?" I said, gingerly climbing from the cab of my pickup and limping over to where Belman was unloading his car.

"What the hell happened to you?" he asked.

I rubbed my hip. "Just got a little careless," I said, eagerly reaching out to shake hands with my good friend and colleague.

Belman returned my handshake. "Kicked by one of your patients, I'll bet," he said shaking his head.

"The mare is a bit of a pain, but I'll take responsibility for being stupid," I said, continuing to rub the leg. "I didn't stop just to get sympathy. Lois left a message that you had something to talk to me about."

Bill assumed his favorite pose. He leaned back against his car, crossing one leg and resting the toe of his work boot on the ground. Pausing and drawing out the moment as he peered through his round wire framed glasses; he seemed about to make an important announcement.

"Well," he said raising the bill of his blue wool cap to scratch his balding head, "I do have something to talk to you about… but I'll be damned if I can remember what it is. Seems like it was kind of important though." He shook his head and started for the clinic's back door. "Come on in. Maybe Lois will remember." Bill opened the door already calling for the receptionist. I followed behind, struck by the aroma from the coffee pot. The ever-present plate of doughnuts beckoned, adding chocolate and cinnamon smells to the warm air.

"You needed me?" Lois asked, leaning her head around the corner.

154

"Do you remember what I needed to talk to Clay about?" Belman asked, picking up the last cinnamon roll.

"I believe you wanted to speak with Dr. Williams about the Nichols mare," Lois said, giving me a hard stare.

"That's right, thanks, Lois." Bill said, waving her away.

"Your eleven o'clock, Mrs. Stanley, is in room one," she said, awaiting a response. Belman just smiled and turned to me.

"Come on to my house, Clay," he said, heading into his private office without so much as a backward glance. He shut the door. "Lois can get a little pushy. I've got to put her in her place about twice a day, or I'll end up working for her. She can entertain Mrs. Stanley a little bit longer." He sat, checking his watch.

"The Nichols mare… is that Jim and Kathy Nichols?" I asked, removing a stack of magazines from the only available chair.

"Ahh, yes! Our resident psychologists are now in the horse business. They bought a mare and she has a couple of those small cutaneous lumps on her thorax. They didn't like my advice, which was to leave them alone, so I suggested they call you," Belman said taking a bite of his roll.

"I've never met them, but I'd be happy to help you out with a second opinion. Will they be calling, or should I give them a ring?"

"I'm not interested in you helping out. I want you to get those people out of my hair. They've only had this horse a week and I've had to talk to them three times. You're their new veterinarian," Bill said, placing both hands on his desk to stand.

"That sounds pretty final," I said, trying to keep the grin off my face.

"You're damned right, it's final. They're your headache. Horse people... I don't know how you do it." Bill shook his head and started for the door and his eleven o'clock appointment.

"I'll just wait for them to call then," I said with a laugh. "You probably haven't seen the last of them yet."

155

"Lois has strict instructions; I'm unavailable for the next year," Bill growled, as he rounded the corner into the small animal half of the hospital.

I didn't have to wait long. Mrs. Nichols had called twice before I returned to the clinic. I made the appointment for the next morning. The Nicholses lived in an exclusive subdivision of large lots and expensive homes between the ski mountain and town. I found the address. A very unattractive, seven-foot-high chain link fence surrounded the entire property. All they needed was a large pile of gravel to make it look like a highway department maintenance yard. *How did the home owners' association allow that?* I wondered.

Both the Nicholses met me at the gate. It was a big double gate made of wrought iron, and they opened it with a flourish. A four stall-barn had already been completed on the left of the drive; its pitched steel roof was only a few feet from the new fence on one side and a small hay barn on the other. *They've never seen much snow,* I thought.

"Good afternoon, Dr. Williams," Mrs. Nichols said, extending her hand as I climbed from the cab of my pickup. In her mid-forties, she stood tall and straight. Her blond hair, noticeably graying, was pulled into a tight bun, and heavily-rimmed glasses hung from a chain around her neck. She was dressed in riding pants and English riding boots, as was her husband.

"Hi," I said. "Please, call me Clay." I stepped away from the truck and shook Kathy's hand.

"Yes, well...Doctor, I'm Kathleen and this is my husband, Dr. James Nichols." Her motion toward James was almost a curtsy.

"Doctor, it's nice to meet you," I said, reaching out to shake a lifeless hand. James was even taller than his wife, well over six feet. He was thin to a fault. Even his stretchy riding pants hung limply about his thighs and formed a loose pouch below his rump. His riding gloves were folded neatly over the braided leather whip tucked under his arm. A closely shaved head and starched white shirt, buttoned at the throat, gave him the appearance of an officer in the Third Reich straight from a 1960s movie. I wanted to click my heels together and bow slightly as I held the limp fingers.

"We've been hearing quite a bit about you," Dr. Nichols said as he turned, striding toward the barn.

"You can't believe everything you hear," I said. *Could that be a German accent?* I wondered, following along. I had to make a conscious effort not to march with a goose step.

James ignored my comment as he opened the big barn door. The solid oak door was bound in brass and must have weighed four hundred pounds. It slid easily on highly greased tracks. A brass "N," two feet high in flowing script, decorated the door's center. *This monstrosity will be frozen in place six months out of the year,* I thought, stopping to gawk at the monster.

"You like the door, I see," James said. "Mrs. Nichols designed it. It came out quite beautiful, don't you think?" He gave his wife a knowing smile.

"Oh yes, it's lovely," I said, with a big smile. Husband and wife linked arms and proceeded to the first of their four stalls.

"Mrs. Nichols and I have acquired a very valuable registered Lipizzaner mare. We are concerned about some nodules and wish for you to examine them." James pulled on his riding gloves before removing a well-oiled halter from its brass, horse-head shaped, hook beside the stall door. He marched into the stall holding the crop vertically in front of his face. "Amorosa! Stand!" The grey mare jumped back and stood quivering against the side of the stall, as Nichols snapped the crop back under his arm and clumsily haltered her. I started into the stall, but Nichols held up his hand like an officer directing traffic. "I shall remove her from her place of safety prior to the examination," he said, brushing me aside.

"Oh, I see, we wouldn't want to stress her with an exam in her 'place of safety,'" I said stepping back out of the way. *Let's get her out here in the aisle where she can drag you around,* I thought.

"That is correct, Doctor. One must never create stress in the place of safety," Kathleen smiled. I wasn't sure if she was happy that I was so perceptive or if she was smiling at her husband's ability to teach someone of my limited intellect.

"Cute mare," I said, admiring the little grey horse. She was correct and balanced, but what really caught my eye was the abundance of long flowing mane and tail. She definitely wasn't carrying any Appaloosa blood.

"Amorosa is very beautiful. She marked the highest of all the mares at her inspection," Kathleen said, as she placed her hands on her hips, eyes flashing.

"I'm sure she did," I said. "She is really a cute mare."

"Cute is not the word I would use to describe her beauty," James said, puffing out his cheeks.

I thought it best not to respond, so I stepped up to the near side of the mare and rubbed her neck, watching her eye soften as she relaxed.

"The nodules are on this side, Doctor!" Nichols rolled his eyes at his wife. I ran my hand along the mare's rib cage and kept it on her rump as I stepped behind her. Two small lumps were visible half way up her side. They were firm, located subcutaneously and adhered to the skin. Amorosa showed no sensitivity when I squeezed the bumps.

"Undoubtedly eosinophilic collagen necrosis," I said, scratching my chin. "How long have they been present?"

"At least four or five weeks, I should think," James said, looking to Kathleen as she nodded her agreement. "She acquired them at the trainer's farm in Denver."

"We're probably too late for intralesional cortisone to be much benefit," I said shaking my head. "We could try that, but I wouldn't get my hopes up; they appear to already have calcified."

"What about removing them surgically?" James asked, moving closer to get a better look.

"The skin's pretty tight over those ribs and if the wound edges separate we may very well have an ugly scar," I said, pulling on the skin to check the tension.

"I just hate seeing them," Kathleen said. "There must be something we can do."

"Come over here, Mrs. Nichols," I said, moving to the left side of the mare. Kathleen obediently moved around beside me.

"Yes, Doctor?" she said, as she watched me run my hand over the gray's ribs.

"You see how smooth her thorax is over here?"

She moved in close to run her hand along the mare's chest. "Yes, I can see that," she said.

"Well," I said, stepping back. "It's my opinion that since injecting them isn't likely to help, and removing them will probably make a bigger mess, the best thing you can do is to always look at her left side." James took a step back folding his arms across his chest and Kathleen wrinkled her brow looking quite bewildered.

"Excuse me, Doctor, I didn't quite understand that," Kathleen said, blinking rapidly.

"He's making a joke, dear," James said, smiling politely. "I'm sure the doctor sees the importance of removing these unsightly blemishes."

"Oh, I understand now," Kathleen, laughed. "That's a good one, Dr. Williams!" She smiled and nodded to her husband.

"Perhaps that was an attempt at humor," I said, stepping over to lean against the stall. "Still, the lesions are strictly blemishes. We can inject them and give them a couple of weeks. If there is no change, we can cut them off at that time. My advice, however, is not to open that can of worms." I turned to get some injectable Triamcinalone from my truck.

"I will be riding Amorosa and I don't wish to produce sores," James said, handing the lead to his wife and following me. "These nodules are directly under my saddle!"

"We'll try injecting them," I said, pulling up 3 cc of the corticosteroid into a syringe. I switched to a tiny 25-gauge needle, returned to the mare and carefully infused the drug into both lesions. "These areas of collagen degeneration are the most common skin lesions I encounter. They're almost always located on the back and I have yet to see one cause a saddle sore. So, if this technique fails to reduce them, we can cut them off. That is, if you still want that done." I started back to the truck.

"I believe that will suffice for today," James replied. "We will require you to reexamine Amorosa's lesions in two weeks. Perhaps our new stallion will have arrived at that time."

"Just give me a call," I said, getting into my truck. The short drive back to my clinic involved a lot of head shaking. *Maybe Bill's right about horse owners; maybe they're all a bit strange. That pair needs a stallion like I need a fifty-foot sailboat,* I thought.

I could hardly wait to give Dr. Belman a call and, as it turned out, it wasn't necessary. Bill's empty Chevy was parked in front of my clinic. The lack of a driver meant the good doctor was undoubtedly having coffee with Ken at his doughnut shop. I hadn't even closed the door on my truck when I heard my name called.

"Hey, yourself, Ken!" I replied.

"Your competition, or should I say colleague, is over here gracing my establishment with his presence," Ken said, glancing over his shoulder with a head jerk to summons me. The sweet aroma of fresh doughnuts filled my nostrils as I followed Ken inside. I waved a greeting to Bill Belman and helped myself to a glazed French cruller and coffee before going to sit with my friend at one of the four tiny tables.

"Just the man I wanted to see," I said sitting down. "You won't believe where I've just been." I washed a delicious bite of cruller down with a sip of scalding hot coffee and waited for Bill's reply.

"I'm not into gambling, but I could probably win one of those lunches you're always trying to bet me. I'd say you've been to see our favorite psychologists, at least that's where Lois told me you'd be," Bill said, a big stupid looking grin across his face.

"How the hell does your receptionist know every damn thing that goes on in this town?" I asked, shaking my head.

"I think it's more like the county; she knows all the gossip countywide," Belman said. "So, what did you think, are those lumps terminal?"

"I don't think I made too many points when I told them to always stand on her left so they couldn't see them," I said taking another sip of coffee.

"Not much of a sense of humor there; probably from New York," Belman said.

"I did let James talk me into injecting them, but I think it's way too late to do any good."

"Maybe you'll get lucky," Bill said. "It's something to try. I didn't think of it or I might have tried it myself. How did you like the stallion fence they've built?"

"Is that what the fence is for? I thought they'd built it to protect their garden from a marauding buck. How did the neighbors let them get away with that? I thought their exclusive development had all sorts of regulations!"

"Actually the home owners' association is responsible for that fence," Bill said, pushing back from the table, stretching out his legs and crossing one big-laced boot over the other. "They didn't want any stallions up there, but they have easements for bridle paths and specific language encouraging horses in their bylaws, so they were stuck. It was quite a fight. The homeowners' association thought that their fencing requirement would dissuade the Nicholses from getting a stallion. Obviously, they were wrong; so now they can all look at the beautiful, stallion-proof fence." Dr. Belman shook his head and chuckled.

"What's the deal with these folks; the first horse they get is a mare that may be too much horse for them to handle, so they buy a stallion?" I scratched my head. "What am I missing here; why Lipizzaners?"

"I know why," Bill said smiling broadly. "The great rumor monger, Lois, supplied the answer."

I brought over the coffee pot for refills. "I can hardly wait," I said. Returning the pot, I leaned past the partition and called to Ken banging around in the back. "You better get in here. Dr. B. is about to lay a good story on us!" Ken dropped what he was doing and followed me over to the table, drying his hands on his apron as he walked.

"More doughnuts?" he asked, "They're on me." We both quickly shook our heads.

"No, thanks!" I responded immediately, knowing if I had time to think about it I could come up with at least one reason why another doughnut would be okay.

"Remember last summer, when the Lipizzaner show came through and set up at the fairgrounds?" Belman leaned forward conspiratorially. "Lois says our psychologists went to that show." Bill sat back, smiling as if he'd solved one of the great mysteries of the universe.

"And so?" I asked, furrowing my brow.

"The announcer said that the Lipizzaner is the world's smartest horse, and since the Nicholses are the world's smartest people they just had to have some!" Bill stood and laughed, a twinkle in his eye. "You can close your mouth now, Clay."

"Well, it makes a good story," I said, taking a sip of coffee.

"You just met them. We'll see what you think after you answer their calls for a few more days," Bill said, taking his cup and plate over to Ken's counter.

Ken took the dishes and dumped the cup and saucer in the sink. "I haven't had those folks in yet, I guess," he said.

Bill stopped at the door. "I don't think you'll have to worry. If you're not serving granola with unprocessed sugar and organic milk the Nicholses won't be stopping by."

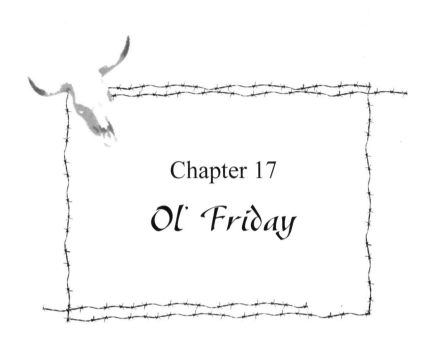

Chapter 17

Ol' Friday

*S*teamboat's psychologists didn't enter my mind on Saturday as I drove west headed for Craig. It was beautiful, warm and sunny with a thousand shades of green covering the hills and meadows.

"Doc, hi," Donny Hardy yelled, jumping up and down and flapping his arms before I even came to a stop in his drive. His little brother Bobby gave me a tentative wave as he peeked out from behind Donny's hip.

"Hi, guys," I said leaning out of my pickup window. "What do you think? Where should I park?" The two Hardy boys with their wild mops of red hair stood at attention; huge grins lit their round pale faces. Both their arms were covered in freckles and I wondered whether Franklin Dixon had these Hardy boys in mind when he wrote his books.

"Dad says in the pasture." Donny ran to open the big double gate, Bobby close on his heels. I pulled through and then turned down the fence to leave room in the pasture for the trucks and trailers that would be coming to the 4-H horse-worming clinic. I was about to stop when I spotted the end of a garden hose sticking through the fence another twenty feet ahead so I pulled on down beside it. "Dad said you'd need water," Donny said, nodding in my direction as he elbowed his brother in the ribs.

"Ouch," Bobby squealed punching Donny in the arm. "Oh, yeah, the water," he said, running to turn on the hose. The first truck and trailer pulled through the gate before I'd even gotten the rear door of my veterinary unit open. They made a big sweeping turn in the pasture and lined up near the end fence. I waved to the driver and continued to gather up my supplies. Coiling the long plastic stomach tube, I placed it in my stainless steel bucket.

"How many horses do you think we'll have today?" I asked, and as I looked to the boys for an answer I noticed Bobby pulling on his brother's shirt for attention and throwing glances my direction.

"Mom counted forty-three if everyone comes," Donny said, shaking off his little brother's grip. "Okay, okay, but you have to ask him!" He whispered to the younger boy. "Bobby wants to ask you somethin', Dr. Williams," Donny said, pushing his little brother out from behind his hip.

"No problem," I tried to put on my friendliest face for the boy. "What is it you want to ask, Bobby?" I got down on one knee to be on the six-year-old's level.

"Umm…I uh…I'm not in 4-H," Bobby said looking at the toe of his cowboy boot as it drew lazy circles in the dirt.

"It's only cause he's too young," Donny offered putting a hand in the middle of his brothers back to stop the slow retreat the little boy was making.

"Yeah, that's why," Bobby, said with a big smile.

"Okay…I'm not sure why I need to know that," I said, changing to a squatting position and rocking back on my heels as I pushed my Stetson back to scratch my head. I sat for a couple of seconds awaiting an answer.

"Well, it…it…it's about Ol' Friday," Bobby said after Donny shook him by the shoulder. "Could you worm Ol' Friday, too?" Bobby stuck his chin out toward me with the question and his eyes lit up appearing twice their size. I couldn't help but laugh.

"Sure, we'll take care of Ol' Friday," I said nodding my head, "but he'll have to be last since you're not a member yet and this is a special clinic for the 4-H club."

"All right! I'll go tell mom," Bobby said, bouncing on his toes before he sprinted for the house.

"Oh, did you think this was just gonna be our club? Mom called all the clubs in the county, any of them with a horse project," Donny said standing a little straighter with his hands on his hips.

"That's fine," I said filling the bucket with water and pouring in disinfectant until the Nolvasan turned it a very pale blue. "You just keep them coming, and I'll keep killing those worms."

I reached out and tousled Donny's red curls before starting to fill my measuring cup with the wormers.

"Cool, I'll get 'em lined up; mom has a list of all the horses. She even went to the bank so she could make change just like at the bake sale," Donny said waving his arms every which way. "What is that, anyway?" He pointed to my measuring cup as I added the second of the chemicals.

"Well, the pink stuff," I said tapping the gallon jug of Omnizole, "is for blood worms and all their relatives, but it won't kill bots. So for the stomach bots we add this clear stuff." I picked up the gallon glass jug of Combot and turned it so Donny could read the red and white label. "You had a horse project in 4-H last year, didn't you?" Donny nodded, squinting at the Combot label. "Well, then you know all about the worms and bots horses get." I dipped the end of my large dose syringe into the mixture in the measuring cup and pulled back the plunger tipping the cup to get the last few drops as my syringe made the familiar sucking sound like a straw in a Coke cup with only the ice left in the bottom.

"I know there's blood worms and round worms and a bunch of small string style worms and that the yellow specks on their legs are bots. I learned that much," Donny said, hiking up his Levi's with both hands.

"That's really good, Donny," I said, dipping some of the water from my bucket into the cup and swirling it around to suspend any wormer that had stuck to the sides. "The string style parasites are actually called small strongyles with the blood worms being the large strongyles and the yellow specks are bot eggs that those bee-like flies stick to your horse's hair. After they hatch the bot larva spend the winter in your horse's stomach," I said, setting the cup next to the syringe on my tailgate and picking up my nose clamp. "Now, let's see if you can get those folks to bring a horse over."

"Hey, Charlie, bring Comanche on over," Donny yelled, waving wildly toward the recent arrivals who were busy unloading a couple of horses and failed to hear the boy. "Cha.r.liee, bring

Comanche over," Donny jumped up and down as he yelled swinging both arms over his head.

"Donny...go over and tell them, son!" Bob Hardy was just coming through the gate. "Go on over and ask them to bring their horses and do it nicely."

"Okay, dad," Donny stopped mid-wave and started to run toward his friends' trailer. "I'll get them for ya."

"Morning, Clay, you sure you're ready for this?" Bob asked walking up with an outstretched hand as two more families arrived with trailers in tow. "Helen's got things pretty well organized. She'll be down in just a few minutes, as soon as the last batch of cookies comes out of the oven." Bob stepped back and waved the last pickup forward to a stop. "I'll run back up and bring Helen's table down, then I can help you out."

"I think Donny and I can handle it until you get back. Worse case scenario, we sit on our hands 'til help arrives," I said, patting him lightly on the back as he turned to go.

I'd finished with the Smiths' two horses before Bob and Helen arrived with cookies and a huge thermos of coffee. Tom Smith helped Bob get the table steadied and the metal chairs unfolded as Helen spread her red-checked cloth under the big tray of cookies I was lucky enough to hold. All thought of worming horses vanished until the thermos of coffee was operational and Bobby arrived with the cream and sugar.

"Bobby, run back up to the kitchen, look on the table and get the cash box and the clip board that's under it and bring them back down here," Helen said, holding her youngest by the shoulder. "You can go and play with the boys as soon as you get that for me," she added, turning her son around and pointing him toward the house. Bobby took off at a run, arms pumping, making the 'Brrr...' sound of an engine revving up. The sound changed as Bobby down shifted for the slight incline that took him to the back door. "That boy, I swear, if he can't ride he drives everywhere he goes."

"He's already asked about Ol' Friday," I said, pouring up more wormer for the next horse. "I told him he'd have to be last, but we can put Friday in anytime. Just let me know when you want to do him."

"We've got to be here for all the horses so putting him last will be fine; it might teach Bobby a little patience," Helen said as she filled another paper cup with coffee for one of the new arrivals.

"I'd better get back to it," I said, looking at the pasture fast filling up with kids and horses. I carefully set the coffee cup on my tailgate and looked around for the next victim. "Are you next?" I asked a skinny girl of about twelve. Her ponytail bounced up and down as she nodded her head and handed me a lead rope attached to a big rangy sorrel. "Do you call him Blaze?" I asked as the gelding turned to look at me.

"Chester, but I didn't name him," she said, stepping back to give me room to work.

"Okay, Chester, let's see how you're gonna' like this," I said, rubbing the horse on the side of his face. Chester snorted and leaned back as I slipped a finger into his left nostril. "I think we'll need a twitch for you," I said, rubbing him again with my right hand as I reached in my back pocket for the aluminum clamp. Hinged with a pin at one end the two eighteen-inch aluminum rods it created an effective vise for clamping an upper lip. A piece of nylon cord with a snap on the end was passed through holes drilled in the other end of the rods so that when they were squeezed the cord could be wrapped around them both and snapped to the halter keeping the nose clamp tight.

"I thought a twitch was made out of an ax handle," the girl said staring at my nose clamp.

"I like this nose clamp when I need to be able to twitch a horse without any help. It works well on good, gentle horses like your sorrel." Quickly grabbing Chester's nose I slipped on the clamp and tightened it down. The horse jerked back momentarily then dropped his head extending his nose and squinting both eyes.

168

"When they squint like that I figure we've gotten their attention," I said, looking at Chester's young owner. The girl was squinting almost as much as her horse and her upper lip was raised to expose a huge set of braces. "Now, if Chester will be good for just a little while we'll get his worms killed and he won't get a bloody nose in the process." I held his left nostril open with my right thumb as I passed the long nasogastric tube. "Watch right here," I said, pointing to the left side of his neck, "and you'll see the tube in his esophagus... see that?" I blew into the tube in order to dilate the esophagus and ease its passage, then moved it slowly back and forth a few times for the girl to see before quickly finishing the job and flushing the wormer from the tube with a dose syringe full of water. After removing the clamp I took the time to rub the gelding's nose until he relaxed and the look in his eye softened. "That's it for Chester." I turned back to my truck for another sip of Helen's coffee before refilling my measuring cup for the next horse.

"Unless the Daniels show up soon I think we're done, Doc," Helen said just over two hours later.

"That went pretty well, everyone survived and we only had one bloody nose," I said, tipping the third thermos of coffee up to get the last drops. "That colt wanted to start a fight right off and I couldn't get him to stop shaking his head. I'm a little surprised he didn't have a worse nose bleed than he did." I swallowed the last bit of coffee and tossed the well-used paper cup in the trash. The cookies were just a memory and my stomach was starting to growl, probably as much from the wormer I'd ingested blowing on the stomach tube as from the fact that it was nearing noon.

"That was Stan Benson's colt, and he told me they'd just started halter breaking him last week," Tom said, folding the tablecloth and starting up to the house with an armload of stuff. "I left that envelope you wanted, Helen," he said, looking back and nodding toward the table.

"Thanks, honey, I need it for the cash and checks to give Doc," she said, opening the cash box and checking her list. I cleaned up and put things away and by the time I'd finished Helen had laid the large manila envelope on my seat. "Thanks a lot for doing this, Dr. Williams; come up to the house for a sandwich if you want."

"Thanks, Helen, but I'd better get back to Steamboat. I've still got a few things to get done today. It did go really well though and I appreciate how well you had it organized. I'd be happy to do it again sometime," I said, getting into my truck. Helen started for the house and I turned my truck around and pulled through the pasture gate.

"You don't need to close it," Helen called as she reached the house. I waved, but I stopped to shut the gate anyway knowing my dad wouldn't be happy unless I left the gate the way I'd found it. I was just climbing back in the truck when I heard a door slam at the house.

"Doc, Doc...wait...what about Ol' Friday?" Bobby was sprinting down the drive waving both arms.

"Gosh, I almost got out of here without getting the most important patient wormed," I said, hanging out the side of my pickup. "You get Friday and I'll come up to the house." Sliding behind the wheel I backed along the asphalt drive. By the time I'd pulled everything back out and measured up the wormer Bobby had his horse haltered and waiting behind my truck.

"Here's Ol' Friday." Bobby hugged the aged gelding's head, rubbing him around his ears. "You won't hurt him, will you?"

"Heck, no," I said getting my nose clamp and hanging it over my left arm. "I guess we'd better put this on just in case he wants to shake his head."

"We wouldn't want Ol' Friday to get a nose bleed like Mr. Benson's horse, would we?" Bobby said as he continued to rub the gelding's head.

"That's right, Bobby we wouldn't," I said, taking the lead rope and herding Bobby over to the back of my truck. "I'll just

170

move Friday over here away from the truck in case he tries to go somewhere," I said, laying the stomach tube over my neck and leading the old horse onto the grass beside the drive.

"He'll be good, won't you, Friday?" Bobby said, looking fondly at his mount.

"I'm sure he will," I said, squeezing Friday's nose with my left hand and moving the aluminum twitch into place with my right. Friday didn't even flinch as I pinched his lip.

"You'll be all right, Friday. This won't hurt you, boy," Bobby said as I compressed the old horse's nose with the rods using my left hand, then with my right I wrapped the nylon cord and snapped it to his halter. Friday watched totally at ease with the procedure.

"You can watch his neck and tell me when you see the end of the hose moving down it. We don't want to get this stuff in his lungs," I said, looking at Bobby as I passed the end of the naso-gastric tube into the old sorrel horse's left nostril.

"Good boy," Bobby said smiling at his trusted friend. I grinned remembering Pepper, the bay who was my best friend at Bobby's age.

"When I was about your age I had a little gelding I rode every day," I said, watching Bobby as I continued to pass the tube.

"How old was he, Dr. Williams?" Bobby asked, moving closer to the action.

"Well...," I said trying to remember. "Ahh...Shi...oot," I screamed, pain shooting up my left arm. I swiveled my head just in time to see the stomach tube fly down the drive. My left arm was rigid and my wrist was fully flexed with my fingers extended, stiff and quivering uncontrollably. In that split second I realized that Friday had struck me with a front foot. I shoved his nose away from me with my right hand hoping to avoid a hoof in the face and the old gelding struck again with a well-aimed shoe striking my right forearm causing an identical spasm in that appendage. Without the use of either arm I was at a definite disadvantage, so I stepped away to regroup. Friday was completely calm as he quickly fired a third time blasting the nose clamp, breaking its snap and sending it high in the air to clatter on the asphalt thirty feet away. I assumed the old kid's horse was finished until Friday barred his teeth and made a run at me. What was I to do? I wheeled away and fled as fast as I could with two spastic arms flailing uselessly. I could hear hoof beats on the asphalt above the sound of snapping teeth as I raced away.

"Don't hurt Ol' Friday!" Bobby yelled as I reached the street; only then realizing that the gelding had given up the chase and was calmly munching grass beside the black top. I bent down rubbing my forearms on my thighs as hard as I could to restore some life into at least one of them. "Are you okay, Friday?" Bobby asked his buddy, rubbing him on the neck. "He didn't hurt you, did he boy?"

"I think Ol' Friday is going to be just fine," I said as the numbness started to subside leaving a throbbing pain where bruises were already starting to form in the middle of both forearms. I stood to walk back up the drive as the back door slammed. Looking toward the house I saw Tom through the living room window as Helen rounded the corner behind my truck. Tom was doubled over holding onto the couch for support and though I was too far away to hear it, I knew his laughter filled the house.

"Doc, are you okay?" Helen asked as she hurried down the drive past my truck.

"Yeah, I'm fine," I said shaking my head, "or at least I will be in a few weeks. I just got a little careless." I was still rubbing my arms as I gathered up the hose and the remains of my nose clamp. "I'll just be a little more respectful of Bobby's bronc this time." I rubbed Ol' Friday's forehead before slipping the tube in his nostril and easily completing the worming.

Chapter 18

The Short
Branch Saloon

A few weeks later summer was in full swing and I remembered what Charlie Smith had told me in those first cold weeks of February. On this particular Friday I was stuck in the office hoping the phone would ring because I had promised myself that I would catch up on my reading. I was half way through a boring article detailing the numbers and kinds of bacteria found in the reproductive tracts of a population of barren mares when I heard someone stamping the mud off their boots on my front door mat. I looked up in time to see Wally Watkins come through my door wearing his ever present smile.

"What are you grinnin' about this mornin', Watkins?" I asked.

"I'm not grinning today, Doc," Wally said. "I cut my new filly's head loading her a few minutes ago. I was just gonna' take her over to the rodeo grounds for some exercise and she got cut loading in the trailer."

"Let's have a look at her," I said, following him outside.

It was easy to see the laceration. The cut formed a V that started in the center of her forehead just above her eyes. Each side of the V was six to eight inches long extending over her poll. Blood continued to seep from the wound making an irregular track down her face. I gently took hold of her forelock and raised the flap of skin exposing the glistening white skull underneath. One quick slash with a pocketknife would have completed the scalping. The filly shook her head as if she were shaking off a fly and I let the skin flop back into place.

"I'll bet she's still got a headache," I said, noting the dazed look in her eyes.

"She probably does. She sure hit that roof hard," Wally said, shaking his head.

"Let me get a few things together and then we'll do a little sewing." I was already heading into my office for the necessary equipment and drugs. Returning I sedated the horse and allowed the sedative a couple of minutes to take effect. Then I attempted to numb the area with Lidocaine, but the filly flinched and shook her head, jerking the needle out. I tried to insert the little needle again, but every time I'd try she'd toss her head making it impossible to infuse the anesthetic. I played her game for a minute or two trying to improve my chances by covering her eye, but the filly wasn't having any of it. Anytime she sensed my attempts she'd throw her head, and she was getting wilder with each round despite the sedation. "I'll get a twitch and we'll see if we can keep her from throwing her head." I pulled out my nose clamp, two three-eights-inch aluminum rods about a foot long hinged together at one end.

"Let me see if I can get this on her," I said as I placed the clamp over my left arm and approached the filly's near side shoulder. Gently taking hold of her halter with my right hand I eased my left hand over the filly's head just below her eyes, sliding gently down her muzzle and off the end of her nose. As my hand came over her upper lip I grabbed it with a death grip between my thumb and middle finger. She jerked back. After the initial jerk she stretched her head out and stood transfixed. I slid the clamp over my hand onto her lip and squeezed the rods together.

"If you could squeeze on this, I think we can get her blocked." I said, stepping back far enough for Watkins to take hold of the twitch

"I'll see what I can do," Wally said, taking the clamp. I noticed him begin playing with the pressure to judge the filly's reaction as I infused the anesthetic without further incident.

"I think you can take the twitch off now, but be sure to rub her nose when you do. It'll make twitching her a lot easier next time," I said as I finished shaving the skin edges and cleaning the wound.

"I wouldn't let you do that a second time if it was me," Wally said, shaking his head as he vigorously rubbed his horse's nose.

"If she never gets away from you as you put the twitch on, you can do it every day for a month and she'll be just as easy on day thirty as day one," I said, washing the wound with surgical soap.

"You mentioned the rodeo grounds; you know anyone that lost a horse over there?" I asked as I finished the sutures.

"Nope, but I seldom see any of the people who board there. I usually take my horses over in the morning for exercise…it's a nice big arena."

"Just wondering because I was out on Twenty Mile at the Torrez ranch yesterday and they showed me a Paint gelding that just wandered in a week or two ago. The Torrez place backs on Howelson Hill so I thought maybe the Paint came over the hill from the rodeo grounds."

"No, can't say as I've heard of a missing gelding," Wally said, as he examined my sewing job.

"I think that looks pretty good. I'll give her some antibiotics and a tetanus shot, and we'll be about done," I said slipping a needle into her neck.

"That looks great," Watkins said looking at his watch. "Just in time for lunch, too. I'm buying if you have the time."

"I'll make time. I never turn down a free lunch." I helped Wally get his filly back into the trailer.

"Why don't you follow me?" he said, checking the trailer hitch. "I was thinking maybe the Short Branch Saloon."

We pulled out onto US 40 turning left into town. I was already thinking of the sandwich I would order. Ronny, the cook, was a ski bum turned cowboy, and he made the best hot corned beef sandwich in northern Colorado.

The Short Branch was the brainchild of Lou Timson. Lou had been involved in all sorts of endeavors. I knew he had been a builder, clothing storeowner and Indian trader. It was common knowledge around town that he'd been bankrupt almost as many times as he'd been a millionaire. Wally pulled over down the block from the saloon where there was enough room to park his truck and trailer along the curb. I eased in behind him and we walked the half block to the 'Branch'.

"Lou sure hit the jackpot with the Short Branch," Wally said, peering in the big plate glass window. "It's crowded every night."

176

"He's definitely got the Midas touch," I agreed. Opening the big pine door, we stepped into the Old West. The saloon sported the longest brass-railed bar in Colorado, and the Bar Back was right out of a John Wayne movie, all walnut and mirrors with a copper counter top and copper sinks. The beer and whiskey glasses were lined up for yards, and the lighting made them sparkle like sequins on a dancer's dress. Vintage rifles hung on the old red brick walls between his collection of mounted game and Navajo rugs. Deer, elk, bear and lion stared down at us while rugs from Ganado and Two Grey Hills accented the room and served to dampen the restaurant noise.

"I just love coming here," Wally said as he pulled out one of the big walnut chairs. It made a pleasurable grating sound on the polished pine floor. "I expect to see Glenn Ford having a shoot out every time I come in."

"I know what you mean," I agreed, nodding as I sat down. "Lou doesn't miss a trick either. Ronny told me that Timson supplies all the employees' clothes. That's how they carry off the atmosphere."

"I'd never noticed, but now that you mention it all the help look like they're right out of Tombstone," Wally said, cracking open a peanut from the bowl on the table.

Looking around I noticed some deep gouges in the floor. "Did you happen to be in here last summer over the fourth when Gimpy got drunk after the rodeo and he and Billy rode in here horseback?"

"No, I missed it, but I hear the place was packed," he said. "It's a wonder nobody was killed."

"I guess a couple of tourists got banged up, and Lou was afraid he'd be sued, but they thought it was the most exciting Fourth of July they'd ever had. Lou says he still gets tourists in who want to know what time the horses come through," I said, waving the waitress over so we could order.

"You can't buy that kind of advertising," Wally said, quickly checking the menu.

The waitress was a little too slow for Ronny. He leaned his skinny frame across the bar and yelled, "What are you two having, Doc, the corned beef?"

"For sure, but I'm not speaking for Mr. Watkins here," I said waving to Ronny. "He's old enough to order for himself."

"I think I'll have the Steamboat burger, rare, with Jack cheese," Wally said.

"You want fries or rings with that?" Ronny asked pulling the pencil from behind his ear and scribbling down the order.

"Fries will do just fine. Oh, and a Coke."

"Likewise for me," I said, pointing at Ronny to be sure he heard me. The place was just starting to fill up for lunch; a couple toward the back already had their sandwiches. There were two more tables of locals I recognized and a table against the wall occupied by three rowdy guys who, it seemed, had been there since the bar opened. From the looks of them the pitcher of beer on the table wasn't their first.

Watson had noticed them, too. "Looks like we've already got some hunters and the season is still months away," he said, motioning toward them with his chin.

We let the beer drinkers entertain us while we waited for our food. The waitress flirted with the ever more boisterous table. They were starting to get looks from the other customers, and the arriving lunchtime patrons were picking tables as far away from the noisy trio as possible. Lou Timson pulled out a chair at our table surprising me. He eased himself down.

"Doc, Wally, how are you?" he asked. Lou was talking to us, but his eyes never strayed from the men across the room.

"Think you might have a problem?" I asked, nodding in their direction.

"I don't want to take the chance. They've already broken a pitcher, and the big guy almost broke a chair falling in the spilled beer. Now that it's getting toward lunch I need to move them along. I've got the constables already in route," Lou said. "If they'll just stay quiet until the cavalry arrives we won't have a scene." Timson seemed equally at ease with either possibility. I noticed he kept his chair back away from the table and his feet under him, obviously ready to spring into action.

"Kate!" Ronny yelled, "We've got an order up!" The waitress spun around as if to argue when she let out a squeal and whirled back to the table drawing back her right arm.

"You son of a bitch!" she hissed as she unleashed a resounding slap to the nearest drunk's face. "You don't pinch me!" Instantaneously the bar fell silent and in that brief moment I noticed Lou check the street. My eyes followed his and I saw two uniformed patrolmen crossing half a block away.

The drunk almost turned his chair over as he shoved it back to jump unsteadily to his feet. "Why you dirty li'l...," he slurred, making a grab for the waitress and sloshing half his mug of beer down his pants. Kate sidestepped, easily avoiding the clumsy drunk. His buddies were already pulling him back into his chair, laughing raucously.

"You asked for that, Bill!" the oldest said, still hanging onto his arm.

"I'll show that li'l bitch when she comes back!" Bill growled, slamming his mug on the table, spittle running down his chin.

Kate had already turned again and was headed to pick up the order, which happened to be a corned beef sandwich and a burger destined for our table. I hadn't noticed Lou when he stood up and sauntered toward the rowdy's table, but I saw him motion for the boys to leave.

"I'm sorry," Lou said in a quiet voice, "but you boys will have to take your party outside. The local law would have my license for continuing to serve you fellas. You know how it is; my hands are tied. Come on, Bill, let's make this easy on both of us."

Bill was shaking his head, and when Lou reached across the table gesturing toward the door, Bill became obstinate. Timson moved to help the man up, but Bill grabbed the sides of his chair

179

with both hands as if to say, "You"ll have to carry me out." Lou must have been waiting for just such a gesture, and he acted in an instant. He reached right in Bill's face and came away with his upper lip pinched firmly between his thumb and forefinger in a perfect twitch.

"Ahhhhh...," Bill screamed as his arms flew straight out. His eyes began to water and his fingers fluttered limply. When he tried to reach for Lou's hand I saw the muscles in Lou's forearm tense, and Bill quickly extended his arms again.

"Now you other boys rest easy. Bill and I'll follow you outside before those two patrolmen come in here and arrest all of you," Lou said, nodding toward the door and never losing his quiet calm. The eyes of every customer looked out to see the officers approaching the saloon door. Chairs slid back, and Timson raised Bill up on his tiptoes. Backing carefully toward the door so as not to disturb the other customers, Lou Timson led a docile drunk out the entrance behind his unsteady friends. The bar erupted in laughter as the door closed.

"Who is that man?"

"He must be the bouncer, did you see that?"

"Man, that guy's nose must hurt!"

It seemed everyone had a comment to make, and a few minutes later Lou returned to cheers and applause.

"Just a little noon-time entertainment," Lou said, raising his arms, his fingers extended in a victory salute reminiscent of Nixon. "Tell your friends, I'll be here all week!" Laughing good naturedly, Timson made the rounds of his patrons gratefully accepting their accolades.

"The guy's amazing," Wally, said, shaking his head "He just got a lot more advertising you couldn't buy."

"Here we are with Marshall Dillon," I laughed. "No wonder this is the main tourist attraction in town. Lou keeps it up and this place will draw more people than the ski mountain."

"What's the matter, Doc, you don't like my corned beef?" Ronny asked, coming around the bar in our direction. It was then I noticed the sandwiches we'd been served a few minutes earlier.

"Lou puts on such a good show I forgot why I was here," I told him. "I'm about to regain my appetite though."

"So what do you think, sandwich good?" Ronny asked standing over me. I took a bite, as he laid the check on our table.

"Great," I said, wiping my mouth. "The beef's really lean," I added, hoping that was what a cook would want to hear. Ronny just stood looking down at me through eyes that seemed to be sunken half way to the back of his skull, so I thought I'd try again.

"How's the cowboy program coming along? I saw your truck and the gun rack. Have you found a Blue Heeler to ride in the back?" I asked.

"No, and I'm not getting one either. I like Border Collies better," Ronny said, rubbing his scraggly black beard. "I have a line on some pups, good working stock, too!"

"Dare I ask, are you getting a cow for the ranch?" I asked, trying hard to keep a straight face.

"I was saving my money for a horse trailer first," Ronny said, making a helpless gesture, "but now I'm not sure what to do."

"What do you mean?" I asked.

"After the thing with my horse," Ronny said dejectedly, "I'm not interested anymore."

"You're not making sense to me," I said. "Do you have a horse?" I was pretty sure Ronny lived in a condo with several roommates.

"Had a horse, past tense," Ronny corrected. "He was stolen by those traveling saddle salesmen that came through a few weeks back."

"They stole your horse and you can't find them?" I asked. "I can't remember exactly, but I do know those guys had an itinerary. I think they were going to Salt Lake with a few stops along the way. Did you call the sheriff?"

"The sheriff's office caught up with them before they reached Salt Lake, but they didn't have Comanche. They probably sold him before that!"

"I didn't even know you had a horse," I said, bringing up the point for the second time.

"Oh, yeah, a good gelding; I was boarding him over at the rodeo grounds at Howelson Hill." Wally's head went up, and he started to speak. I cut him off with a quick shake of my head and a stern look.

"With a name like Comanche, I'll bet he was a Paint," I said.

"Yeah, he was a Paint, sorrel and white. A real pretty Tobiano."

"Have you advertised, maybe put a reward offer in the paper?"

"That was the same thing the sheriff suggested," Ronny said. "The problem is, I don't have any cash."

"Who said it would have to be cash?" Wally spoke up.

"Maybe you could give away sandwiches. Say maybe a couple of weeks' worth." I said.

"Do you think Lou would let him do that?" Watkins asked, looking my way.

"He could take it out of my pay!" Ronny said. "I'd give away a whole month's worth of sandwiches if it would help get my horse back."

"Are you sure, you'd like to do that?" I asked. "You'd need to be sure."

"Be sure of what?" Lou asked. He had just finished his victory lap around the room and was back at our table.

"Ronny was just telling us that he's posting a reward for finding Comanche," I said. "He wants to give away a month's worth of sandwiches from here at the Branch."

"Hey, that sounds like a good idea!" Lou agreed. "I could just take the cost out of your check, Ronny, and it'll be good advertising for the saloon."

"So you'll do it then?" Wally asked, his smile ever broadening.

"Sure," Ronny said. "I can make posters up and put them all over town." He was really getting into it now.

I picked up the meal check and handed it to Ronny. "I think I'll have a beer in celebration. How about you, Wally?"

"Don't mind if I do. Miller Genuine Draft! And Lou, will you join us?"

"It's early, but what the heck, sure I'm in," Lou said pulling out a chair and sitting down. Ronny wrote the beers in on the tab and added the total again, handing the check to me.

"This can be Ronny's first installment," I said, passing the meal ticket on to Lou. Turning to Ronny I added, "Your gelding is out at the Torrez ranch on Twenty Mile. He wandered in a couple of weeks ago." Ronny stood with his mouth hanging open and his eyes glazed over.

"Where are those beers, bartender?" Lou asked, waving the lunch check at Ronny. He slapped both Wally and me on the back. "Looks like I'll get to see a lot of you two for the next few weeks!"

Chapter 19

Load Up

A few days later I stepped out on the porch to the crisp morning air of summer when the smell of sagebrush is mixed with a hundred milder aromas: spruce and pine, larkspur and Indian paintbrush, clover and fescue. "Why would anyone ever want to live anywhere else?" I wondered aloud. I knew it would be almost impossible to stay inside and tend to the paperwork part of my job so I vowed to finish in the office as soon as possible. Three hours later I was engrossed in deciding on an order of drugs and didn't hear the truck pull up to the front of the clinic.

"Doc, you in here?" Dan called banging on the door as he threw it open to smash against the plastic chair in the waiting room. I rolled my stool away from the pharmacy cabinet, scooting across the floor to peer around the dividing wall.

"Hey, Dan! What are you up to?" I asked, getting up to greet my favorite plumber.

"Brought in a couple to worm," he said, pointing out the window to his truck and trailer sitting in the middle of the little parking area, an area I shared with four other businesses. It was just after nine, one of the busiest times for Ken's doughnut shop just two doors down and, because Dan was blocking most of the parking lot, cars were already starting to backup.

"Why don't you pull around back and unload?" I suggested, motioning in that general direction. "That way the traffic won't spook your horses."

"Already got'um unloaded and tied to the trailer. The cars'll be good for 'em. Might get that roan mare to stop kicking at anything that comes within range."

"Yeah, nothing like a parking lot full of cars and little kids when you've got a kicker!" I sprinted for the door hoping no one had already been injured. Dan followed at a more leisurely pace, his spur rowels scraping across my tiled clinic floor. Dan Jones never seemed to get in a hurry. He was short but powerfully built with a barrel chest and forearms bigger than my calves. The way

Dan slouched made it appear he didn't have a brain in his head, an opinion reinforced by the raggedy tee-shirts that he wore with logos of beer companies emblazoned on both front and back. He had a large mop of curly, unkempt hair and a half-grown beard that never seemed to change. Dan looked as if he'd not matured a day since high school, except for his eyes. There was always a knowing twinkle in his steel grey eyes.

"Would you look at that? Old lady Langnor had to park her Caddy out on the highway." Dan pointed toward the parking lot entrance. "I hate that bitch. She made my life a living hell when I replaced the water lines under their house last year." Dan was grinning ear to ear. "Hi, Ruth!" he shouted, waving at the elderly woman as she made her way shakily toward the beauty salon three doors down. Ruth Langnor was a scrawny, bony woman in her mid-seventies. A genuine blue hair, she made the trip to the salon on a weekly basis, in time for the Wednesday bridge game and luncheon of the Methodist Women's League. She looked like a zombie from a Halloween cartoon with her arms outstretched in front of her for balance. Her high heels were twisting in the gravel, causing her to lurch unsteadily. The large purse she carried banged against her thigh with every step, adding a lateral component to her already jerky gait. She peered in our direction unable to identify Dan through her bifocals.

"Hi, Ruth. It's Dan, Dan Jones!" Dan waved again, still smiling.

"Oh, hello." Ruth stumbled as she tried in vain to identify her plumber.

"Over here, dear," Dan waved both arms to attract her attention. "I hope she falls and breaks a hip," he whispered. A small crowd comprised mostly of law enforcement officers was gathering with doughnuts and coffee in hand, unable to leave since my client's rig was blocking the lot.

"Hang on to this mare," I said, handing Dan the lead after untying the roan from his old dilapidated two-horse trailer, its small front window long since smashed out. "I'll get my stuff and we can get you out of here before you get me arrested."

"We may have to run you both in for obstruction of doughnuts," Nate Trogler said, overhearing our conversation. He adjusted his holster with his free hand and balanced a doughnut on top of his coffee cup with the other as he sauntered over to watch us work.

"Like you need another doughnut!" Dan replied, sticking out his stomach and pointing to it.

"That does it! Cuff 'em, Dano," Nate said, turning to a uniformed highway patrolman. I'd gathered up all the items needed to deworm Dan's horses and was headed back to his trailer; followed closely by most of Routt County's lawmen. The nasogastric tube was draped around my neck and I carried a stainless steel bucket filled with water, a dose syringe and my nose clamp in one hand and a large container of Omnizole in the other.

"Just back her up to the side of the trailer," I said to Dan, setting the bucket and wormer on the gravel. I filled the dose syringe with Omnizole and laid it next to the bucket. Then I picked up the nose clamp and, as Dan positioned the mare, grabbed her upper lip. "Let me get this twitch on her," I said as I applied the clamp, wrapping its nylon cord around the pliers like handles. I snapped the cord to the mare's halter to keep the clamp tightly in place. The roan only pulled back slightly since her rump was almost in contact with Dan's trailer.

"That'll make her squint." I said, quickly slipping my right index finger into the horse's left nostril.

"Damn, straight! It sure would make me squint!" a highway patrolman said as he pinched his own upper lip and grimaced.

Passing the end of the long plastic hose under my finger to insure that it would stay on the bottom of the nasal passage I carefully advanced the tube. "I'll give it little twist of the wrist to keep it out of her lungs," I said as the horse swallowed allowing the tube to slide easily down her esophagus. It was visible on the left side of the mare's neck indicating that it was indeed going to the stomach and not headed down the trachea in route to the lungs. Sticking the other end of the stomach tube in my mouth I blew on it inflating the esophagus and making the tube pass easier.

"Hand me that dose syringe, if you please," I said to no one in particular. A moment later the thick pale pink wormer was flowing down the tube followed by several ounces of water to wash the Omnizole into the mare's stomach. "Where's our next victim, Dan?" I pulled the tube from the mare's nostril with a flourish in one long sweeping motion. Rinsing the hose, I drew up another dose as Jones went to tie the roan back to the trailer. The mare began pulling back before he could get her tied, so I stepped behind her and waved an arm making her move close enough for Dan to fasten the lead. She switched her tail warning me away, but stood quietly.

"The gelding'll be easier than this old bitch," Dan said, walking around the trailer to bring his rope horse to me. "Ya know," he said, casting a glance toward the Beauty Salon, "I think I'll rename the roan mare Ruth." The comment brought a round of chuckles from the audience as they brushed the last of the icing from their shirts and the corners of their mouths. The lawmen were beginning to fidget, walking back and forth in preparation for their departure.

"I can move that mare over if any of you need to back out and get on the road," I said, turning to the patrolmen.

"Oh, hell, Doc, they ain't in any hurry. We're payin' for 'em to stand around," Dan said, leading his sorrel gelding over to me.

I glanced around the circle of uniforms; no one offered to get into their car. *Dan may be right,* I thought. "How's his attitude?" I asked, moving up to rub the sorrel on the nose.

"He's plum broke, Doc. My four-year-old rides him everywhere," Dan said, smiling as he patted his rope horse on the shoulder.

"How old is he, Dan?" I asked, gently slipping my right finger into his near side nostril.

"He's only seven, but you'd think he was twenty-seven when my boy's around him." Dan stepped back and looked the gelding over. "Yes, sir, best horse I've ever owned." The gelding didn't resist when I put my finger in his nose so I quietly eased the tube up his nostril.

"There you go, fella, you let me do this and you can avoid the twitch." I continued to advance the hose and the horse readily swallowed as the end of the stomach tube touched his epiglottis. "That wasn't so bad, was it?" I finished squirting the Omnizole into him and removed the tube, rubbing him on the forehead.

"You need any help loading these critters?" I asked picking up my gear.

"No, no. They load... no problem. Maybe you could hold the roan though while I load my gelding," Dan said motioning toward the mare.

"Yeah, sure." I set the bucket, dose syringe and wormer down in the parking lot and, with the stomach tube draped around my neck went to get the mare. I had started to untie her when Dan opened the rear door on his old Hale two-horse trailer. "Whoa, now, Ruth... whoa." I jerked the knot free and the mare bolted away from the trailer. I was quick enough to get her head turned and roll my hip into the rope before it came tight, leaning on it to take the jerk as she hit the end. I had no time to think; it was just reaction. Jerking the mare toward me caused her to swing around wildly. She ran right over my bucket sending it flying. It clanged as it bounced over the gravel. The plastic jug of Omnizole rolled away only to be stepped on as the snorting mare backed across the parking area. I was able to slow her before she hit any police cars, and the officers were already waving their arms trying to stop her backward progress. "Easy, Ruth, try not to kill yourself," I said, coming hand over hand up the lead rope. "What the hell is wrong with this mare, Dan?" I asked looking at the thick wormer now coating her back leg half way up the cannon.

"She's just a little skittish, that's all, Doc," Dan said, throwing the lead over his sorrel's neck so he could jump into the trailer.

"A little skittish, my ass! She hates this trailer business." I had to keep her head pointed toward the old Hale as she tried to back away. "So she's not hard to load, huh?"

"She used to be," Dan said as he clipped the butt chain behind his gelding and stepped inside the mare's half of the trailer. "But she's not anymore!" he added, going to the front of her stall. I heard a metallic click and the unmistakable whine of steel cable against metal. Dan jumped out of the trailer and rushed toward the roan, a carabineer in his outstretched hand. Quarter-inch steel cable stretched out behind him, snaking back to the trailer.

"Are you out of your mind?" I asked. The mare pulled back as Dan snapped the cable to her halter and released her from the lead rope. I stood, mouth agape, holding a limp lead as the roan bolted across the parking area behind the trailer. Twenty feet of steel cable hissed across the gravel bouncing wildly off the rocks. All the bystanders, myself included, raced for the shelter of the clinic's porch. Dan on the other hand sauntered leisurely to the trailer's front and reached through the broken window. All the while, his mare careened through the gravel lot. She shied at my stainless steel bucket and jumped the dose syringe only to have them flipped in the air by the trailing tether. The cable made a whooshing sound as the mare hit the end of her run. The line scraped up the trailer's rear door with a squeal and she was jerked around by her head, throwing gravel into the air, her hind legs flying clear of the ground, then racing back the other direction to repeat the insanity.

"Now, boys," Dan said with a smile and a wave. "This is how you load a mare." We could hear a ratcheting sound and see Dan's arm pumping away inside the hole at the front of the trailer. As the hand wench wound in the cable Ruth became even wilder. Her head was only three or four feet from the gate when she reared. Lunging forward, she was able to get her nose over the trailer's roof. She hung there flailing with both front feet. The sorrel gelding had scrunched himself into the very front of his half of the Hale and was unconcernedly munching hay. He'd seen this before! As Dan continued to shorten the line, the mare was forced to jerk her head backward to get it off of the roof. Now her nose was inches from the dark stall. All four feet were braced and she threw her head sideways shaking it, like a dog playing tug-of-war with a towel.

"Damn, Dan, she's gonna cut her head open on the corner of the door or break a leg off under the trailer!" Nate yelled, shaking his head and starting off the porch toward the mare.

"Oh, hell no...She's too worthless to hurt herself, but if she does there's guns aplenty here to finish the job," Dan said, never missing a beat on the winch. As her nose entered the trailer all movement stopped. The only sound was the crunch of her feet sliding on the gravel and the constant clicking of the winch's ratchet. The roan's legs were locked and every muscle in her body was taut and quivering. Sweat broke out on her neck, a neck stretched to the point of separation. Her cannon bones touched the back floorboards and the mare launched herself into the trailer stall. Dan increased the speed of his pumping to take up the slack. "That's how it's done, painless horse loading by my new patented method." Dan grinned as he walked calmly to the rear of his old Hale. "You know, loading this mare used to make me crazy and I'd be the one to sweat." He patted Ruth lightly on the rump, clipped the butt chain and closed the door. "Anyone needing horsemanship lessons, my number's in the book just above John Lyons."

The plumber climbed into his pickup, waved to the crowd and pulled out onto highway 40. We were too stunned to respond and just milled around for a few seconds. I gathered up my paraphernalia, trying to save the last few ounces of wormer left in the squashed container.

"Probably did a good job killing those heel worms, Doc," Nate said, getting a laugh from the other officers as they moved to their vehicles.

"Damn, Dan got out of here before I could write up an invoice!" I said to no one in particular.

"You can probably track him down at the Wednesday night roping," Nate said as he backed from his parking place. "Thanks for the entertainment, Doc," he added, and then he was gone. Seconds later I was standing in an empty parking lot. The only evidence of the excitement was Ruth Langnor's Caddy, parked on the highway, with a few new dings from flying gravel and a splotch of Omnizole in the middle of the parking lot. Somehow, ordering drugs had lost its luster. I made a mental note to add wormer to my order list and headed over to Ken's for coffee and conversation.

Chapter 20

The Shoeing School

"Dave around?" I shouted, walking into the old equipment shed that served as the classroom for the Community College School of Horseshoeing. It was the end of the first week for the fall class of farriers. By mid-day the thermometer was in the eighties and in the tin roofed shed it was at least ten degrees hotter.

"Went to haul a horse over," came the reply yelled over the clanging of hammers striking steel as the new shoeing class pounded out their first full set of horseshoes. I picked out the speaker working two anvils over and stepped around the busy students. Black smoke hung in air pungent with the odor from a dozen coal forges.

"Clay Williams," I said sticking out my hand. "I'm a friend of Dave's. I thought maybe he'd have time for lunch."

"Charlie Knox," he replied with a firm handshake and a friendly smile. Charlie was a bit older than the rest of the class. I guessed him to be in his late twenties. Short and wiry, the muscles in his forearms stood out as he waited with his hammer poised. "I don't know about Mr. Lewis' lunch plans, but he said he'd be back before eleven," Knox said before returning with his hammer to the rapidly cooling bar stock he was using to form a shoe. Instinctively I checked my watch, although I knew it was almost twelve when I'd driven into the parking lot.

"I'll just hang out for a while and see if he shows," I said, looking around at the class. Charlie Knox nodded as he shoved the bent steel back into his coal forge. Unlike those of his comrades his fire burned brightly, almost smoke free.

"You're Dr. Williams, aren't you?" he asked above the hiss he made by dipping his tongs into a bucket of water to cool them. "Dave said you'd be around in a day or two to give us a few lectures." His shoe glowed bright orange as he removed it from the forge and began shaping it again. I nodded.

"These cool?" I asked, pointing to the three completed shoes lying next to his water bucket.

"Yeah, Doc, they're cold." Charlie stopped his pounding long enough to give me a knowing smile. "Sounds like experience talking."

"I have to admit I did pick up a hot one once... but just the one time," I said, bending over to pick up the finished shoes. "How long have you been shoeing?" I asked, noting the smooth curve, even fullering and well-placed nail holes.

"My dad's a shoer, so I've watched long as I can remember. Guess I started right out of high school. Shoeing part time got me through New Mexico State, and I've been at it full time for the last few years."

"So here you are, starting to learn all over again?" I let the question hang in the air as I examined Charlie's shoes to see if they were level.

"Dad's good, don't get me wrong, but he's 'old school.' He never saw a keg shoe that needed more than two whacks to make it fit." Charlie stopped and stared off into space. "Dad's the reason I'm here. Said I needed to learn to shoe 'em right. Said horses deserved that." He shook his head slightly and resumed forming the shoe.

"I like your dad already," I said, dropping the shoes beside his bucket. I wandered through the remaining students watching them work. Three forges over, a tall gangly kid with sweat running from his face and arms had just finished shaping his second shoe. "How's it going?" I asked.

"You tell me. I've been beating on this piece of steel so long I can't tell anymore." He dipped the shoe into his water bucket to the hiss of rising steam, then held it out to me clutched in his tongs.

"That's not sunburn, is it?" I forgot about the shoe and pointed to his forearm, covered in oozing red blisters.

"I must have had a reaction to some medicine Mr. Lewis gave me for my tendons," he said, turning his arm to examine its underside.

"Oh, I see...you developed a little tendonitis from pounding on your anvil," I said, trying not to laugh. "How's it responding to Dave's cure?"

"The damn blisters hurt so bad I can't tell about the tendon thing," he said as I took the shoe from his tongs. "What do you think... about the shoe, I mean?" The steel shoe, if you could call it that, had been pounded so much that it was almost twice as thick at what should have been the heels as it was at the toe and I doubted if it would ever be flat.

"I think it could use a little improvement, but I've seen worse. This is your first week, remember. Just hang in there; you'll get it figured out." I laid the ruined steel on his anvil. "I don't think I'd use any more of Dave's medicine on my arm if I were you. Catch me before I leave and I'll fix you up with some antibiotic cream. You don't want that arm to get infected." I moved on around the room and soon realized that "ol' tendonitis" was the second or third most talented student in the class. I'd just about worked my way back to the front of the room when I heard a truck and trailer grind to a stop out front. There was a squeak and pop that I recognized as Dave Lewis' driver's side door hanging up, its dent catching the front of the jamb.

"There's a vet-mobile out here so it must be time for lunch!" Lewis bellowed without bothering to slam the pickup's door. Sticking his head in the classroom he shouted loud enough for all his students to hear over the roar of their forges, "You'll learn that no vet ever misses a meal." Then he vanished and I heard him opening the trailer and the distinct sounds of a horse turning around inside before jumping out onto the gravel parking lot.

"Hell, I been here since eleven," I shouted back, heading out to the parking lot. "Damn horse shoers are never on time!" Dave was closing the trailer tailgate as I approached.

"How's it goin', Doc?" He ignored my jab and smiled switching hands on the lead rope he was holding so he could reach out his right paw to shake my hand. I instinctively flinched as we greeted each other; he'd crushed my hand before and I was sure he loved the fact that my nervous system had never totally recovered.

"No complaints," I said, stepping back to look at the big gelding he was holding. "What'll he weigh?" I asked as I sized up the beast, a rawboned sorrel that appeared to be half draft horse.

"Haven't weighed him, Doc; what do you think?" Dave shook out a little lead, stepping back to admire his horse. "You know what he is, don't you?"

"I didn't miss the brand," I said, raising the gelding's mane to examine the freeze brand on his neck. It was the unmistakable mark of the government's mustang program. "He must have been out on the north side of Douglas Mountain." I knew that the local ranchers had turned out a draft stud or two to run with the wild bunch on that side of the mountain, keeping the south side for their Thoroughbred and Quarter Horse stallions.

"You know he was. I picked him up last week and he's getting gentle already. I want him for a packhorse. There was another one available and he looked like a little nicer horse, but this guy was already castrated. The government boys didn't even try to explain that one." Dave motioned for me to have a look under his new horse. "He must have been caught in the roundup a year or two ago and then escaped back to the wild bunch." Lewis was rubbing him on the neck and the big horse was thoroughly enjoying it.

"What are you calling him?" I asked, slowly moving around the horse to observe him from all angles.

"Ninety-eight," Dave pointed to the number sticker still glued to his left hip. "It seemed to fit him. I figger it's his horse I.Q. He's not the swiftest beast I've ever owned."

"Well, Ninety-eight, you think you'll be able to bounce Dave on his head?" I smiled at the thought of this big, seemingly clumsy, horse bucking off my friend. "Did you bring him down for your new class to shoe?" I asked, looking at the platters he had for feet.

"Oh sure... if he kills two or three of my students the class size will be more manageable," Dave said, shaking his head as he started to lead Ninety-eight around the end of the classroom.

"I don't think you'll have to kill them off that way. Your tendonitis treatment ought to discourage a few of the weaker folks." I followed along behind to see what Dave had in store for his new pet.

"You saw Jason's arm, I take it. Some of these kids are sure soft."

"What did you paint him with, DMSO and cortisone?" I said, remembering the dauber bottle I'd left for his saddle horse.

"Naw, Doc, I just used straight DMSO and then put Saran wrap over it with a cotton leg wrap on top to keep it warm." Dave stopped and looked back expectantly. I shook my head, but failed to rise to the bait. "Jason sure stopped whinin' 'bout his tendonitis." Lewis grinned and winked at me as he turned to lead Ninety-eight into the corral beside the shoeing barn. "Works ever' time."

Opening the gate Dave walked the packhorse through and turned him around. "I brought him down so he could buddy up with my saddle horses," he said, pointing to Jake, his personal horse and a well-built gray pony just over thirteen hands that belonged to Dave's eight-year-old son. The saddle horses were peacefully munching on a few flakes of hay in the middle of the corral. The new comer's arrival brought both horses to attention, and before Lewis could unfasten the mustang's halter they had trotted up to get acquainted. "This should be interestin'," Dave said as he turned the big gelding loose. Jake and the pony had their necks bowed and were snorting a greeting that went completely unnoticed by Ninety-eight. He'd already spotted the hay, which to him was like candy to a school kid, and he sauntered down for lunch.

"He doesn't know Jake exists," I said, watching the show. The two saddle horses appeared to be totally shocked that the new-comer would ignore them, and they stood by the barn for thirty seconds or more discussing the situation. It was decided that Jake, being the larger and self appointed leader, should go and straighten the intruder out. "Here we go," I said as Jake bowed his neck and pranced down to inform Ninety-eight of the house rules. Squealing, Jake swung his hip toward the mustang in an obviously threatening way. Ninety-eight calmly munched the alfalfa, occasionally swishing at a fly, seemingly unaware of Jake's presence.

"He's a peaceful giant, ain't he," Dave said smiling while Jake continued to harass Ninety-eight. Turning in a tight circle the bay saddle horse lined up again squealed and half-heartedly kicked in the big horse's direction. Ninety-eight never flinched or raised his head, but he landed a blow to Jake's ribs that sounded like he'd swung a baseball bat. The kick was so fast and so well aimed that the bay horse's hind leg was still in the air when he was lifted off his feet. Jake maintained his footing and came stumbling back up to the barn, obviously in complete humiliation.

"Ninety-eight may be peaceful, but he doesn't take anything from anybody," I said, moving around to see if Jake's rib cage was dented. The pony followed along beside me and appeared to be making the same inspection. He touched noses with Jake, maybe to let him know he was willing to take over, and trotted down for his go at the workhorse. The pony, being older and smarter, didn't squeal to announce his arrival. He just wheeled and fired, missing by a fraction of an inch as his adversary simply leaned out of the way. Ninety-eight, head down, chewing away, caught the gray full in the belly. The impact picked the pony up laying him on his side to slide across the graveled corral. All the while Ninety-eight hadn't missed a mouthful.

"The wild bunch kick for a livin'," Dave said as he watched his pony stagger shakily to his feet. The gray stood for a few seconds, probably getting his bearings, looked at Jake standing next to the barn, shook his head and went over to quietly eat with his new best friend. "The little trader, he and Jake have been together for two years…that's loyalty for you. I didn't think horses were that much like humans." Dave scratched behind his ear and shook his head in disbelief.

Jake, for his part, didn't seem surprised at all by the turn of events. It only took him a few seconds to join the lunch feast, standing on the other side of Ninety-eight as if they were long lost friends.

"Don't you wish people could solve their differences that quickly?" I said, turning to go out through the gate. "Now that they have their lunch, how 'bout you buying mine?" I held the gate open for Dave as he gathered up Ninety-eight's halter.

"I should buy you lunch because…?" Dave let phrase hang in the air as he entered the forge room to hang the halter on a nail by the door.

"Why don't you all knock off for lunch?" he shouted to the busy students. "The Doc and I are headed for the Holiday Inn if anyone wants to join us. We'll reconvene class in about an hour and examine the set of shoes you've made this morning." Except for Charlie, no one bothered to look up, and he waved us off as he stood in conversation next to Jason's forge. I glanced at Charlie's workstation, noticing that the fire was banked and four polished shoes were hanging on the water bucket, then I followed Dave out to my truck.

I jerked my thumb over my shoulder. "You should buy me lunch to celebrate the assistant instructor you've got this time around," I said.

"Ya know, Doc, you just may be right, I think I will buy you lunch. If we take long enough Knox may have shoes made for all of them!"

Lewis laughed heartily and whacked me on the shoulder hard enough that the truck swerved as I pulled onto highway 40 and I thought, not for the first time, how lucky a man is to have just one good friend.

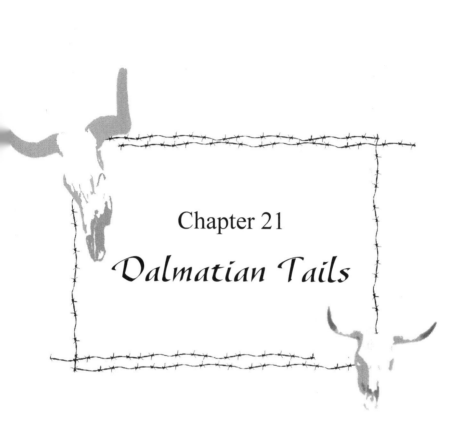

Chapter 21

Dalmatian Tails

*I*t was five o'clock, still dark on the late September morning, and I was already on the east side of Rabbit Ears Pass headed for Dillon and on to Denver. I had a transmission problem and had called the dealership for an eight o'clock appointment. My truck would be in the shop all day, so I had phoned John Makris and invited myself to spend the day at his clinic. He'd agreed to pick me up and was already planning lunch with Mary and Fletcher. As I drove I thought back to those first months after graduation and my first job as a veterinarian.

By the third week at John's clinic I'd fallen into the routine. Mary and I would clean up, get the coffee started and await the first client. I would start the history and examination while she alerted Dr. Makris. Sometimes I would be finished and the client and patient would have gone before John arrived. More often, however, I'd have made a diagnosis and would be stalling until John arrived and I could discuss the case and treatment options with him. He seldom questioned my diagnosis and often we agreed on the treatment. It was a pretty laid back practice.

"Ya know, Clay, there are a lot of ways to practice," John said one morning in those early weeks. "You'll develop your own style and that will set a tone to the practice."

"I kind of like the relaxed way you handle it," I said, taking a sip of good black coffee before sitting down across from John's desk.

"I decided early on that I would treat the clients and their animals the way I'd want to be treated if I came in without the slightest medical training." John grabbed his coffee cup and rolled his chair back, resting his shiny black Justin Ropers on the desktop. "The people who appreciate my way become clients and often friends. The others stop coming and I don't notice."

"You need a refill?" I rose, holding up my empty cup.

"Sure," John said and handed me his mug.

Mary was cleaning the counter as I started to refill our cups.

"John giving you a philosophy lecture?" she asked, adjusting her glasses.

"Yes, I guess he is," I finished, adding the mandatory three spoons of sugar to John's cup. "It's kind of interesting though."

"I'll give you five more minutes and come to the rescue." Mary smiled. "We do have a litter of pups for dew claws. You guys don't have to sit around all morning."

"Okay, I'll let John know." I started back with the fresh cups.

"Oh, he knows." She had already started down the hall with her cleaning supplies.

"What's the deal with the puppies?" I asked handing John his cup.

"Dew claws, why?"

"Mary kind of wants us to get right on them, or something," I said. John took a sip and laughed.

"Mary's upset. She thinks the quote I gave Susan Wells was too low." John scratched his forehead. "Maybe it was, but Susan is a school teacher and needs the income from her Dalmatian pups to make ends meet."

"Good pups?" I asked.

"I'll show you," John said and stood to head for the kennel. "The bitch has won about everything west of the Mississippi. Both bench and obedience."

"They look like a bunch of fat black and white sausages to me." The squirming pile of two-day-old puppies made soft little noises as they tried to position themselves to nurse. Mom, stretched out on her side, nosed first this one then that one.

"But take a look at this." John opened the large cage. "Rosie, here, girl." The Dalmatian left her pups wriggling on the blanket that served as their bed without a backward glance and came to John, assuming a bench show stance.

"Nice dog," I had to admit. She was spectacular.

"And she's just had eight pups." John released Rosie, and she immediately gave a brief check to her now squealing pups before coming back to wag and rub on Dr. Makris. "We might as well do these little guys now," John said as he started handing me an armload of sausages. He wrapped the last of the puppies in their blanket, and we carried them to the treatment room. A concerned mother was beating our legs with her tail as she circled around us trying to get a look at her babies.

"Mary!" John called, "Get a towel for the sink." She was already one step ahead of us. Mary had a thick soft towel lining the stainless steel sink. She'd also positioned the mobile surgery light to illuminate the countertop for a work area and shine into the sink for warmth as well.

"Let's put them all in the sink." John deposited his puppies and laid the blanket he'd removed from their cage on the floor in the nearest corner. We allowed Rosie to stand up with her front feet on the front of the sink and watch her brood. "I'll hold, you cut."

John picked up the first victim. He held him on his back in both hands, isolating individual legs between his fingers. I quickly removed the dewclaws and sutured the wounds with very fine 4-0 absorbable sutures. As quickly as I finished a puppy Mary would have the next puppy's feet disinfected, ready for Dr. Makris to hold. We formed an efficient assembly line, and all eight puppies were soon returned to their mother.

"I'd figured that to be our lunchtime project, so now we'll have time for lunch," John said as we returned Rosie and her brood to the large cage.

"Mary, call Fletch and see if he can meet us for burritos at Holly's." Fletcher Wood was one of John's best friends and happened also to be Mary's husband.

"You'll have to make it a quick lunch. I just spoke to Della Franklin on the phone and she's dropping off a litter. This time it's seven poodle puppies to have their tails docked and their dew claws removed," Mary replied from the front office.

"Do I know Della?" John was pouring himself another cup of the ever-present coffee.

"She has the black standard. You remember, the one that tried to bite your hand off last time you were palpating her for puppies?"

"Oh yeah," John said inspecting his fingers; then he turned to me. "I was ready for the poodle because Della had warned me, but that dog got three of my fingers in her mouth before I even saw her move. I thought I'd gotten into a quick draw contest only to find my opponent was Billy the Kid."

Dr. Makris never flinched from an attempted bite. I'd jerked away from biters on more than one occasion, so I'd been watching him closely trying to learn his technique. The only ones more impressed than I with the way John dealt with biting dogs were the dogs themselves. When a dog tried to bite John it was invariably left with a sense of awe, its mouth hanging open and a dazed look on its face.

"So, when the poodle bit you, how many stitches did you need?"

"It left a bruise that was sore for a week. I'm still not sure why she didn't break the skin, but all I got was the bruise," John said, rubbing his hand.

"Mary, you talked to Fletch yet?"

"Secretary is trying to find him now," she called from the front office. "He leaves his radio in the truck half the time, so this may take awhile."

John walked toward the office coffee in hand. "What time is Mrs. Franklin due in with the puppies?"

"I said I'd wait for her at noon." Mary covered the telephone's mouthpiece with one hand. "So I guess she'll be here soon after twelve."

"If Fletch can go late, Clay and I can do the litter first, then we won't be rushed."

"I'll see what he says. If that will work I'll hurry Della along." She removed her hand and spoke into the telephone as John and I retired to his private office.

Not five minutes later Mary came in to tell us that the plan was in place. Della Franklin would bring in her puppies as soon as she could get here and we would call Fletcher when we were leaving the clinic. At ten minutes after twelve Della Franklin dropped off Jasmine, her Standard Poodle, and a litter of seven pups all black as night. We formed an assembly line again and when we were finished seven little black tails were lined up next to each other on the counter.

Lunch was a leisurely affair with the largest burritos north of Chihuahua. After building the monster burritos the cook topped them with enough cheese to cover a family-sized pizza and smothered them in a pint of green chile sauce. Each burrito could have easily fed a family of four. Bloated but happy, we returned to the clinic just after two. I started in on some afternoon treatments while Mary cleaned up our previous mess. I noticed John quietly chuckling to himself as he came and went from his office.

"Clay, come and take a look at this!" John called from the main exam room. I dropped what I was doing and went to see what kind of case Dr. Makris had for me this afternoon.

"What do you have?" I asked, approaching from the kennel room.

"Take a look," John said. Beaming from ear to ear he pointed to a paper towel lying in the middle of the stainless steel exam table.

"What the...Where did you get those?" I asked, confused by the seven little black and white tails lying on the paper. John just stood there with a silly grin on his face.

"Do those look like they came off Rosie's puppies?" He asked.

"The Dalmatians! How did that...? Wait a minute, what is that on the tails?"

208

"Just a little White Out from Mary's desk. They look pretty good though, don't they? Good enough to fool an owner?"

"You're going to tell Susan Wells you docked her litter by mistake?" I asked.

"Heck, no. I'm going to tell her my new, fresh out of school, assistant docked them by mistake!" John laughed and I couldn't tell if the laughter was from the thought of Susan's shock or mine.

"Wait a minute, she might not think this is funny. You can't tell her that."

"All right, I guess you're right," John said with as much dis-appointment as I'd ever seen him show. "How about this? We just set them on the counter when she comes in and let her draw her own conclusions."

"Who's drawing conclusions about what?" Mary asked, enter-ing the exam room.

"John was just telling me how I'm going to give a client a heart attack," I said, moving to the side so Mary could see the tails.

"I see," Mary said, studying John's paint job. "Sorry, Clay, I forgot to tell you about this part of the practice." She quietly stud-ied the tails again. "This is how we'll pull it off," she said.

At three forty-five, on her way home from school, Susan Wells came in the front door to pick up her Dalmatians. Mary was sitting behind the front counter awaiting her arrival. Susan looked tired and bedraggled after a day of fifth graders.

"Hi, Mary, I came by for Rosie and the puppies," she said, placing her purse on the counter. "Did Dr. Makris have any trouble?"

"Actually Dr. Williams, our new graduate, took care of the puppies," Mary said as she stood and gave Susan Wells her most serious look. "And, well as a matter of fact..." At that instant I rounded the corner from the hall where I'd been lying in wait. I carried the black and white tails on a towel. They were nicely arranged in a little line and I held the towel with both hands extended in front of me.

"I think I got these all about even," I said, placing the towel on the counter next to Susan's purse. Looking Susan Wells in the eye I gave her a big smile. Her eyes flicked from the tails to me and back. I wasn't counting, but I'm sure it was at least a count of three before the sight registered. I was just starting to wonder if she realized the scam.

"Oh, my God!" she screamed, holding on to the counter for support. Her face had turned a deathly white and she was visibly trembling. The violence of her reaction was a shock, and I wasn't sure what to do.

"It was just a joke," I said, hoping she wouldn't faint.

"You cut my puppies' tails off as a joke?" Her eyes flashed and her lips pulled back in a snarl. I backed into the wall holding my arms up for protection as she lunged over the counter. Her face had gone from white to crimson in the blink of an eye. It was obvious she wasn't about to faint any more, but I was feeling a little weak in the knees.

"This sure is a nice litter," John said as he came into the waiting room. He'd placed the puppies in the basket that Susan had brought them in and he set it at the teacher's feet. "They're all so evenly sized, not a runt in the bunch." Rosie closely followed John and she quickly checked her puppies before rubbing against her mistress's legs. "Clay removed the dew claws," he said smiling. "He was so quick the puppies hardly knew what happened." Bending down, John picked up a pup and it grunted contentedly as he handed it to Susan.

The teacher stood frozen in place trying to comprehend the situation as she gazed at the long beautiful tail of her two-day-old champion. I glanced at Mary. She was shaking with contained laughter, tears rolling down both cheeks. Susan Wells began to get the picture; extending her arm she shook her finger at me. "You, Dr. Williams, you're fair game now!"

"It was just too good to pass up, Susan," John said, placing the basket on the counter so his client could see that all her puppies had their tails. The teacher checked them all and was beginning to see the humor of it all.

"I'm sure this was your idea, John." She said as she put the last of the litter in the basket. "I won't forget this, and I'm sure Mary will help me with a plan to even the score."

"I'm sure she will," John agreed. "After all, she planned this little prank." Susan's eyes got big as she turned to Mary.

"Mary!"

"Well, the idea was John's. I just came up with the plan," Mary said, starting to laugh all over again. "But it was such fun I'd be happy to help you get even."

Chapter 22

Essie Miller

I should have asked for better directions on the phone, I thought as I cruised through one of Craig's only suburban areas with the chill wind swirling leaves across the street. Small yards of brown grass and leafless trees surrounded by high fences made this housing tract look just like so many others I'd seen when I practiced in Denver. I must have gotten the address wrong. There couldn't be horses living here. I eased around a curve looking for an empty driveway so I could turn around, and there was Essie's farmhouse, just as she'd described it. Here in the midst of suburbia sat her old two-story house; white paint, now yellowed with age, was peeling from the walls. A hog wire fence sagged along on rotting posts enclosing the large horse pen. The pen, now L-shaped, had previously been divided into two rectangular paddocks by a four-strand barbed wire fence. Most of the posts had rotted off so that the fence lay over with the top wire only a foot or two above the ground. It was one of the most perfect horse snares I'd ever seen. I envisioned her poor saddle horse down with all four legs tangled and cut to the bone. The other fence, the one with the hog wire, continued around the house enclosing a front yard devoid of any grass or weeds and well covered with dog manure. A barely legible hand painted sign attached near the rickety gate announced, "WATCH OUT FER THE DOG." Essie's place was a strange sight surrounded by the newer tract homes and a sidewalk complete with modern streetlights.

I pulled up to the curb and stepped out. I'd barely laid a hand on the front gate when a chorus of barking erupted from the house. I stood transfixed, listening to the cacophony, and counted the distinct barks of at least six or seven different dogs. An elderly lady watched from the largest window. Hunched over with age, she pulled back the dingy, stained curtain with a gnarled hand as she motioned for me to come to the side of the house where a gate opened directly into the horse pen. By the time I'd gathered up the equipment and drugs I thought I might need and loosened the

214

rusting snap holding the gate, Essie Miller had come into the pen by a gate near her back door.

"Nailed it shut," she said, hobbling over to where I was trying to resnap the gate.

"Excuse me?" I turned to look at Mrs. Miller. A sweatshirt grayed from age and dust hung loosely over her dress, and I was assailed by a gamey fragrance with her every move.

"Nailed it! Damn kids let my dogs out," Essie said, pointing toward the front gate.

"You nailed your gate shut?" I pushed my hat back to scratch my head.

"Damn kids playin tricks," Essie pointed again. "Fixt 'em. Nailed it shut."

"Oh, I see," I said. "I'm Clay Williams." Giving Essie my biggest smile I extended my hand.

"You're the vet," Essie said, shuffling around so she'd be headed back the way she'd come. "Figgered it out 'cause it's Tuesday. Had the 'pointment fer Tuesday an' I don't take no vizters." She squinted in my direction through thick, square bifocals, her stringy gray hair falling over the rims as she attempted to turn her head.

"Yep, you figured it out, Essie," I laughed, moving around to make it easier for her to get a look at me. "You don't mind if I call you Essie, do you?"

"My name, ain't it? Why should I mind?" Essie squinted even harder and rubbed the side of her nose.

"Horses out here in the back?" I asked, slowly moving through the pen.

"Ponies!... Ponies in the back," Essie nodded slightly as she shuffled along behind me.

"Oh, okay. Ponies," I said as I passed the corner of the house. Her two Paint ponies spotted me before I located them, and they were off, bounding along the fence like deer; reaching the far corner of the pen they wheeled, circling and snorting.

"It's the lit'list one. There, you see?" Essie said, pointing as the ponies pawed, spinning around and kicking up dust. They pressed back into the corner bowing the hog wire out on both sides of the corner post.

"You wouldn't happen to have a halter handy, would you, Essie?" I asked, pushing my hat back a second time.

"I got something.' It's by the house. You stay here an' maybe it won't upset the dogs." Essie started for the house. "Lost ol' Scoot. I think it was his liver. Just give out. Then them boys let Daisy get hit; damn truck squashed her flat. Now I only got eight dogs left an' not a one of 'em mean as ol' Scoot. Had ta' nail the gate." Essie had reached the step and was on her way back.

"The littlest pony hurt his eye?" I asked, waiting for Mrs. Miller to totter back with an ancient yellowed nylon halter. "How long ago did he injure himself?"

"Damn kids, without Scoot I had to nail the gate. Here's the harness," Essie said, holding out a halter so stiff it stayed horizontal as she reached to hand it to me. Before I'd even touched it the odor almost made me gag.

"You've got some cats too, don't you, Essie," I said taking the halter; the stench making me squint.

"Now how'd you know that?" Essie asked, scrunching her face up in what must have been a smile. "How'd you know I got nine cats?" Her single yellowed front tooth protruded as she cackled. "You're right smart, ain't ya?"

"I just knew you had a tom cat," I said, still holding the halter, stiff with urine, at arm's length.

"Amos," Essie said shuffling off toward the ponies. "Must be nine, maybe ten, black as night, meaner'n an old bobcat, too." She cackled again and her shoulders shook with the effort.

The ponies stayed in the farthest corner of the pen, looking anything but gentle. I carefully stepped between the strands of barbed wire with the highest strand reaching to just below my knee. I felt like I was in military training camp trying to complete the obstacle course. "When did the little fellow hurt himself?" I asked again.

"Who, the pony? Musta' been a couple a days ago. "Neighbor told me about it. Damn busybody, al'az stickin' her nose in." Essie shook her head. "Yeah, a coupla' days, I think." She scratched behind an ear and looked off into space. I finished negotiating the barbed wire and turned to face the ponies. That was all the stimulus they needed, and they bounded away along the backside of the lot. They were at full speed when they reached the corner and made the turn by bouncing off the hog wire, the wire squealing in protest. Then they sprinted down the pen's long side past me jumping the canted fence like it wasn't even there. They ended their run next to the front gate spinning, blowing and tossing their heads as they trembled ready to run some more. The injured eye was obvious on the smallest of the creatures as they spun in front of me. Even from this distance I could see that pain and swelling had the pony holding the eye closed, and tears combined with a thick discharge had stained his face.

"When was the last time you caught these guys?" I asked, starting back across the downed fence.

"Shoer catches 'em real regular," Essie said as she watched the two Shetlands.

"Looks like he's about due to come," I said, noticing for the first time that the ponies feet were quite long with the walls broken out at the quarters. I was thinking that maybe I should wait for the shoer to help me capture the little guys.

"Ain't due for a while yet," Essie said pulling on her ear. "Comes ever six months regular as if he was eatin' All Bran ever' mornin'," she smiled; seeing her one front tooth made me shiver. "Catches 'em easy, no problem for him. A real cowboy, that feller," Essie said, glaring at me.

"Maybe we can get lucky," I said as I finished renegotiating the barbed wire. I watched my quarry start to tremble as I edged closer.

"Shoer runs 'em in the barn," Essie said, and when she raised her arm to point to the ramshackle shed the ponies broke clearing the fence at full speed without getting a scratch. "Brings his own help with him, no extra charge, an' they don't have no trouble."

"I'm not sure how we're going to get this done with just the two of us," I said, slipping along the fenceline to head my would-be patient toward the three-sided building.

"Ain't you got no gun?" Essie asked as she gazed at the fence she needed to crawl over.

"Yeah, I've got a gun," I said, placing one foot on a post to make it easier for Essie to cross.

"Well, git it!" Essie stopped putting both hands on her hips.

"If we use my gun the pony won't get up," I said.

"You mean ever?" She asked staring bug eyed. I nodded trying not to smile.

"Don't you have one of those shot guns?"

"If you mean a tranquilizer gun, no, I don't have one," I said, still holding down the fence for her.

"Well, yer 'sposed to, yer s'posed ta have one," Essie shook her head and clucked softly.

"Let's get you out of that fence," I said, ignoring the remark and taking Essie's elbow to get her across. "Maybe if you stand in the middle of the gap, we can get the ponies into the shed."

"I cain't run too fast, but I ken shoo 'em," Essie demonstrated by waving her arms, an act that sent the Paints flying around the old shed.

"That's good, but maybe you could be a little less vigorous with the shooing," I said, moving carefully toward the ponies. I was sure this was a fruitless endeavor, and I didn't want to quit until Essie understood the impossibility of the situation. With each step I took the ponies trembled harder and tossed their heads faster and higher. I was still a good forty feet away when they broke and raced around the shed. I stepped to my right and raised an arm as they came around the building. My slight movement caused them to slam on the brakes to stand shaking in front of the shed. The larger of the two turned, peering into the shadows of the little stall, and gingerly walked in, closely followed by his little partner.

"Yep, that's how tha shoer done it," Essie nodded, starting in my direction.

"We haven't gotten them haltered yet," I said as I tried to shake out the stiff nylon halter.

"He just slipped in thar an' put it on 'em," Essie said, raising her eyebrows.

"You stand here and we'll see how good I am at slipping," I said, gently moving toward the smaller of the two. I made sure the pony could see me out of his one good eye and carefully approached, hoping that by some miracle I could get the lead rope around his neck. The ponies quivered, snorted and stood like two statues. I slipped the halter on and buckled it thinking that any second the express train would leave the station.

"That's the way them shoer fellers do it, all right," Essie said, still nodding her head. "Ain't Billy a smart little feller?"

"Billy, this one's Billy?"

"Yep, Bronco Billy an' Big Bad Bob. Them's their names, an' Billy, he's the gent-lest one."

Essie took a step in my direction and Billy capitalized on the move. Rearing he spun away from me and was able to make one lounge before I recovered and threw my weight into the rope. His front feet were still off the ground and I almost flipped him on his back. Billy was as agile as he was quick, and he recovered by spinning back in my direction. I expected him to hit the ground and try another angle for his escape; instead he lounged straight at my head front feet flailing. The entire ballet happened in less time than it took me to suck in a breath, and now I was backing away and dodging. I was George Foreman with Ali coming out of his rope-a-dope flying like a butterfly and trying to sting like a bee. It was my turn to spin away. I threw my arm up to protect my head and the razor sharp edge of Billy's hoof grazed my shoulder, neatly ripping half my shirtsleeve away. Seeing daylight Billy gathered and lunged for the opening. I instinctively held on to the rope and braced for the impact. The pony already had his head cocked in my direction; he was jerked around to face me, his hind feet flying clear of the ground as he swiveled on one front leg. Essie hadn't moved a muscle and Billy's tail brushed her dress as he wheeled.

"Full ah piss an' vinegar today, ain't he?" Essie cackled, reaching out to pat Billy on the rump. "Bronco Billy, that's his name all right!"

"You might want to stay back a little while I start to lead this guy," I said, panting with the exertion and waiting for the pony to make another run for freedom. I gently pulled on the lead and the pony stepped forward acting like the gentlest of saddle horses. Bob stayed in the rear of the shed and continued to quiver and spin around occasionally. I slowly ran my hand up the lead and began rubbing Billy on the nose. He snorted and tossed his head, otherwise remaining calm. Pressing gently around the eye didn't seem to cause any discomfort so I attempted to spread Billy's lids open. The pony tossed his head again making further investigation impossible so I began to rummage through my jacket for a sedative.

"Like I said, gentle…he's gentle as Ex-Lax, ain't he, Doc?" Essie was nodding her head with that one front tooth showing in what I'd come to recognize as a smile. I drew up a healthy dose of Rompun, the most recent addition to our line of drugs for sedation, and quickly injected the pony; he only quivered in response to the needle's prick.

"He's gentle all right," I said shaking my head and rubbing on Billy's neck where I'd given the injection. The pony's head began to drop within seconds, and I was able to part his eyelids and get a look at his conjunctiva and cornea.

"Damn, that crap works quicker'n a enema!" Essie said, pulling on her earlobe with gnarled fingers. I rolled Bronco Billy's lower eyelid down exposing a large glob of mucus. Using a gauze sponge I carefully wiped some of it away and spotted the end of a grass stem, which I removed with a small pair of forceps.

"His cornea looks clear. I'll just put some of this stain in to see if he has any scratches," I said, slipping the orange strip of paper containing fluorescein dye behind the lower eyelid. I left it in place for a second, and Billy's tears became an amazing iridescent green.

"Now, ain't that somethin'?" Essie said as the bright green stain ran down Billy's face.

"When his tears have washed out the dye, we'll shine a light on his cornea, and if there's a scratch, the dye will stick and we can see it," I said as I flushed the eye with a little saline to expedite the procedure.

"That is somethin'," Essie repeated, scratching her head as she pulled back a stray strand of greasy hair hanging over her bifocals.

"All clear," I said, putting my ophthalmoscope back in my pocket. "Some antibiotics and a little cortisone and he should be fine." I pulled a broad-spectrum antibiotic and a few milligrams of a corticosteroid into a small syringe and attached a tiny 25-gauge needle. "I'm going to inject this right into Billy's eye so you won't have to put ointment in," I said as I rolled his lower lid down again and slipped the needle into the fleshy conjunctiva behind it.

"I could put ointment on him," Essie said as she hunched over and squinted watching me stick her pony in the eye with a needle.

"You'd have to treat the eye with ointment several times a day," I said, rubbing Billy on the nose. "I'm not sure he'd want to be caught that much."

"I'd just tie him in here," Essie said pointing to the back of the shed.

"I think the injection will work fine," I said, stepping over to push on one of the corner posts. It had rotted off long ago and the little building squeaked as it rocked under my gentle pressure. "When was this shed built?"

"My Gene, he put'er up maybe thirty years ago," Essie said, rubbing her forehead. "Yep, must'a been at least that long. Gene's been gone fer twenty, maybe twenty-five."

"I'm surprised it's still standing. What keeps it up, Essie?" I started to remove Bronco Billy's halter. Essie backed up a few steps, looking the structure over.

"Well," she said scratching behind one ear as she rocked back and forth. "I figger she's been standin' here so long she just don't know how to fall down." Billy spun away from me as the halter slipped off his nose and both ponies exploded out of the shed and raced across the pen jumping the barbed wire in unison. "You want me to call if it don't look right?" Essie asked.

"Oh, no, that's okay, Essie. Don't call me, I'll call you!"

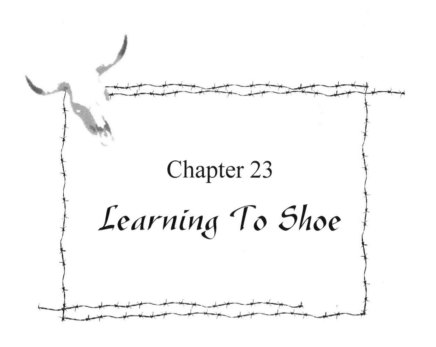

Chapter 23

Learning To Shoe

*E*very fall, immediately after the last hunting season, as the snow began to pile up, Routt Counties horse activities stopped. Most of the horse population was turned out for the winter. The better horsemen pulled their horses' shoes and trimmed their feet first, but many saddle horses were just led into a pasture and slapped on the rump. Those horses' shoes would fall off before spring, usually taking a large part of the hoof wall with them, and the horses would survive by following the feed sled along with the cattle. Dave Lewis timed his Horseshoeing School so that graduation was just before Thanksgiving. His next group of victims would not arrive until early March. That allowed him the coldest months to work with local horse owners. Dave and I agreed that the best clients were the people with the most knowledge, so each winter Dave held a class teaching local horse owners how to shoe their own horses.

"How you doin', Doc?" Dave asked as he flipped on the lights inside the shoeing barn.

"Just great," I said, stamping my feet on the concrete. "It's gotta be below zero tonight." I pulled my gloved hand from my goose down parka and bent my wrist to expose my watch. "It's not seven yet, but I'm hopin' nobody else shows and we can go on home."

"Minus twelve when I left the house," Dave said, his breath as visible as frost on a window. Wadding up newspaper he stuffed it into a coal forge. "I know for certain we'll have three more folks, and Bill Maze is hauling in four head we can use for practice." Dave turned on the blower for the forge and was looking around for a match. "It'll be warm in here in no time."

"Yeah, right. I forgot how well insulated this place is," I said, looking at my truck through gaps in the old fir boards that made up the walls. "That fire really heats up this concrete in a hurry. You won't be able to freeze an egg on it by June." I shivered thinking about the next three hours in the subzero barn.

"I didn't know you were such a pansy. You've never complained before when I've asked you to come and speak to a class," Dave said, lighting the newspaper and carefully placing several large chunks of coal into the firebox.

"Listen, partner, there's a hell of a lot of difference between rollin' in to give a fifteen minute talk before heading over to the Holiday Inn's bar and standing on this concrete for three hours."

"I didn't hear this kind of talk when you signed up for this class." Dave was grinning from ear to ear.

"Hell, you talked me into it in October. 'It'd be good PR,' you said. 'I need an expert in the class,' you said. Nothin' about 'it'll freeze your fingers off' or 'you won't be able to feel your feet for a week.'"

"Tell you what, whiner, we get done this evenin', I'll buy the first round at the Holiday," Dave said, turning the blower down on the already glowing coal.

The banging of unhappy horses in a cold stock trailer as Bill Maze pulled into the parking lot interrupted our negotiations. We stumped outside moving stiffly and slowly in the cold. Dave had the four unloaded and we'd led them into the shed before Maze got himself bundled up and out of the cab. I was busy tying up horses and looking at feet that had been neglected since the first October hunt. Shoes remained here and there with the hoof wall grown over them. The shoeless feet had the quarters broken out around the old nail holes.

"We'll have them trimmed and ready by nine-thirty; you can pick them up then," Dave said as Bill Maze came into the classroom.

"You've got some good grass hay in that feed room, don't you? I feed nothing but the best," Maze said, hitching up his Levi's as he sauntered across to warm his hands at the forge. "I've got to get back to the ranch, so I'll leave the trailer and pick up the horses tomorrow afternoon."

"I've got about two flakes of hay left," Dave said, giving Bill his biggest smile. "Pick them up anytime. I'll leave the halters in the trailer. We're goin' to Denver in the mornin' so they won't be bothering a thing."

"You just be sure to check the trimmin' on all these horses. I don't want no amateurs messin' up their feet," Bill said, sticking his thumbs in his hip pockets as he turned to go. "Eight-thirty, you said," he said as he walked on out to his truck without waiting for a reply. The stock trailer banged and rattled out of the parking lot as Bill pulled onto U.S. 40 and headed north into town.

Cars started arriving, so I returned to my examination of our shoeing candidates. The first mare, a little bay, switched her tail and shifted her weight onto the rear leg I was trying to lift. Next in line a tall thin grey gelding leaned away from me raising his hind leg before I'd even touched it. I grabbed some newspaper and crumpled it into the nearest firebox to claim my spot and rolled a shoeing box full of tools next to the gelding for good measure. Then I went looking for matches to light my forge.

"Cindy, how're you doin'? Cold enough for you this evening?" I asked, walking over to greet the jumping trainer. "Patsy, Bill, you two have all your hunting camps pulled down?" I shook hands all around as the group crowded close to Dave's forge for warmth. Dave let us stand around and chat for a couple of minutes while he sized up our victims and then came to join the group.

"I know of at least two folks that can't be here for legitimate reasons; the others are probably as scared of the cold as the Doc here. Doc Williams coerced me into buyin' the first round as soon as we're done," Dave said to laughter and applause. "It looks like he's already picked the easy horse for himself, so go to work an' I'll be around to check the trimmin' before you nail on the shoes. Then I'll grade the whole job before you pull the shoes back off so Maze can turn them out for the winter."

"Where'd you hide the matches?" I asked, picking up a bucket of coal.

"They're on the shelf," Dave pointed to the door. "Bill Maze will be back by eight o'clock. If you don't want him over your shoulder criticizing your work, I suggest you be finished by seven forty-five."

"Last one done buys the second round," Patsy said, patting the roan horse standing last in line.

"That would be me," Cindy said over the roar of the blowers as Bill and I fired up our forges. The trimming proceeded with an occasional remark or a call for Dave's advice yelled over the sound of the fires.

The grey had good feet and was cooperative so the trimming was routine and went quickly. "Take a look at my gelding," I said, glancing around to be sure I was finished first.

"I can see from here you've got some rasping to do, Doc," Dave smiled in my direction. "Look right down the foot from the heels and don't be afraid to get under your horse on both sides; I seem to remember you telling me how easy it is to spot green shoers because they can't rasp feet level."

"Okay, you're right," I said, picking up the left front to rasp it again. By the time the last foot was finished I had to wait while Dave inspected the work of two of my colleagues. I made a few more swipes with the rasp wanting the job to be perfect. Dave silently examined all four of the grey's feet.

"Doc, are you closin' your eyes when you do this? Pick that foot up and look down it."

"Looks pretty good to me," I said. Crouching, I rested the hind leg on my shoeing apron and peered down the foot.

"Put the foot down. You never miss this when you're vettin'. Now look at it like Bill Maze called you to check out a lame horse." Dave leaned against the hitching rail.

"Maze wouldn't call. First, he's too tight, and second, he wouldn't know a lame horse if it fell on him," I said, setting the foot down and stepping away to get a better view. "Ouch, looks like a green shoer did this horse." All four of his feet were out of level and each one sloped in a different direction.

"Good thing we've got a lot of foot to work with," Dave said, picking up the near forefoot. "You've got to get under your horse more. Here's what you look like." Dave straightened his knees and back rolling the foot to the outside. "There's no way you can rasp the hoof level with the leg twisted like this. You can make it flat, but it won't be level."

By the time I'd gone around my horse again my legs were shaking, my back was screaming and our illustrious instructor couldn't keep the grin off his face. I carefully examined the grey. I lined up in front of each foot, moving the horse to be sure his feet were balanced, and called for Dave. He was tied up helping Cindy with the bay mare. The little horse had turned out to be every bit as much trouble as I'd expected, and Cindy at five-foot-two and ninety-eight pounds wouldn't have been a match for the mare if she weighed twice as much. As it was Cindy had back problems on her best days, the result of years of jumping spills. Dave had come to her rescue.

"We know you're not plannin' on doin' this for a livin'," Dave said as Cindy vigorously nodded. "You just put a shoe on that left front and I'll finish trimmin' the other three when you're done." He placed the foot on the floor and turned to select a shoe from her shoeing stand. "This'll fit if you spread it just a little," Dave said as he handed Cindy the shoe and turned to me. "Just cool your heels a while, Doc, I'll be over in a minute."

"How are you two doin'?" I asked, stepping around the grey to check on Bill and Patsy.

"If I could feel my feet I'd be gettin'along a hell of a lot better," Bill said, stepping away from his anvil and stamping both feet. "I was just tellin' Patsy that I'm done with complainin' about the cost of shoeing." He bent to lift the left hind foot and check the fit of the shoe he'd just been shaping. Glancing over my shoulder I saw Dave helping Cindy hold the shoe in place as she drove her first nail and knew I'd have time to check out Patsy's progress.

"How's that roan cooperating?" I asked, moving to the next forge.

"Not too bad," Patsy mumbled, talking around the last two nails she was holding between her lips. She twisted off the shaft of a nail with her shoeing hammer before easily driving another. A few more taps, a twist and she set the second shod hoof on the floor. "How'er you comin' along, Doc?" she said, turning to face me. Patsy was lean; she had a build my dad would've called stringy, stringy and tough. She stood an inch or so taller than I am even without the down, florescent orange hunting hat perched atop her blond curls. Patsy, in her forties, did a little farming, worked as a grease monkey for one of the coalmines and ran the packing and outfitting business she'd inherited. She packed a few fishermen into the Mad Creek Lakes each summer and ferried hunters into one or another of several drop camps she maintained in the area.

"I'm with Bill," I said. "I'll sew up a few more cuts and gladly pay to have steel nailed on. I've only got three head though so it's not like I need to put shoes on a whole pack string."

"I shoe my pack horses, and I have my saddle horses done by someone who shoes for a livin'," Patsy said, bending to pick up another shoe and moving around the roan.

"Let's take a look at your work," Dave said over the forge's roar. He was already shaking his head as he moved in front of the grey.

"What?" I said, coming up behind him to try and see what he was looking at. "I'm pretty sure those feet are about as good as they're gonna' get!" Dave took his time examining each foot.

"I guess if that's the best you can do, it'll work. Nail on the steel." Dave set the last foot down and went back to check on Cindy's nailing job. I looked around casually checking my competition. Patsy was on the third foot and Dave was already letting Cindy remove the shoe, so she'd be the first one finished. My only hope was that Bill, now shoeing the second foot, would take his time.

I set to work shaping the correct size shoes. My shaping wasn't the greatest, but what the heck, I could rasp the foot to fit and besides I was going to pull the shoes right back off. Looking across to check on Bill as I nailed on the third shoe I realized I was slightly in the lead. I had him and it looked as if Bill didn't have a clue. My fourth shoe didn't seem to fit very well, and I wondered for a second if I'd switched a shoe somewhere. I was about to take the shoe back to the anvil for some adjustment when I heard the ringing of steel as Bill shaped his last shoe. *My shoe's a little narrow in the heels, but it'll be just fine,* I thought. I started nailing and was in the process of driving my last heel nail and thinking about the round of drinks I wasn't buying when the grey jerked his foot away. I wasn't ready for it and he almost picked me right off my feet. I held on and he settled down. Tapping the nail again made him flinch a bit so I finished setting the nail very carefully. I quickly dressed the foot with my rasp and called to Dave to check my work. *Winner,* I told myself.

"Better pull that last nail, treat the hole with a little iodine and reset the nail," Dave said not even bothering to come and check out my job.

"He jumped a little on that nail," I said, stepping up to rub the grey on the face. "I think I'd twisted his foot around. I wasn't getting under him again."

"Like I said, Doc, you quicked him," Dave said, walking over and pointing his rasp at the hoof.

"I'm sure I didn't quick him. He just spooked a little," I said, making myself as tall as possible. I glanced over my shoulder and saw Bill dressing his last foot. "Maybe that shoe is a little tight at the heels, but we're pulling them right back off."

"When you're shoein', you're not a surgeon, Doc, so you'd better treat that nail hole," Dave pointed his rasp at the offending foot for a second time.

"Look," I said, "it's no big deal, he's gonna' be ju…" I turned and stared slack jawed at the foot as a trickle of blood ran from under the shoe, pooling on the cold concrete.

"I'm sorry, old buddy; you should have told me," I said, patting the horse on the neck before I picked the foot up to pull the nail.

"He should have told you? He jerked you off your feet! What does he have ta do, stomp on your head?" Dave couldn't keep the grin off his face as he examined my shoe close up. "You think you can drive a safe nail as narrow as that shoe is?"

"All right, everyone," I yelled, "I'm buyin' the second round." There was laughter and applause all around as I removed the offending shoe to reshape it on my anvil.

"Just treat the nail hole, Doc, and jerk the rest of the steel; we're all too damned cold to wait for you to get it right," Dave said. "I'm sure you're better at buyin' drinks anyway."

Chapter 24

Quarantine

*I*t was late January, almost exactly a year since my arrival in Steamboat Springs, when I received a call from Dr. Redmond, the state veterinarian.

"I understand," he said, "that you drew blood on a horse for an Art Hudelston."

"Actually, I Coggins tested two horses he races on his chariot team," I said. "He's headed for Wyoming. There's a race in Evanston in a couple of weeks."

"He's only taking one of them. The other, Jetaway, a bay four–year-old, tested positive."

"Jetaway! Art's only had that horse about eight months. He was negative when he left Oklahoma," I said, stunned that the young gelding could be positive for equine infectious anemia. "Maybe it's a lab snafu. I could pull another sample."

"I already had them check the sample and rerun the test. It's the blood you sent, all right, and he's definitely positive. Maybe he'd only recently been exposed when Mr. Hudelston bought him and hadn't had time to develop a titer."

"Sounds like you're pretty sure about this," I said.

"Yes, and that's why I called. I'd like you to go out to Hudelston's and issue a quarantine on the gelding."

"You want me to quarantine Jetaway?" I said, thinking how much fun it would be to tell the rancher that his best chariot horse would either have to be killed or be quarantined for life at the ranch. "I don't think I can do that, it's not my job, and Art Hudelston's a good client of mine." I thought of Art. In his mid-seventies, still standing six-foot-six, he weighed well over 250. A full head of light brown hair and a ruddy complexion made him a handsome man in a rugged sort of way; everything about him was big, his arms, his chest, his ears and most of all, his big flat nose.

"Yes, well, then...could you go out with me, ahh...to show me the way to the ranch? I could be up on, say, Thursday."

"The ranch is easy enough to find," I said, looking at the Routt County map I'd taped to my clinic wall with clients' ranches highlighted in yellow.

"All right, okay... I'd really appreciate you going along. It would make the whole process go better. Owners with questions tend to believe their veterinarians more often than a state official."

"When you put it that way, how can I refuse?" I chuckled silently, "Yes, I'll go." I made a note on Thursday's schedule.

"Good, I'll call Mr. Hudelston today and be at your office about eleven Thursday. If...if eleven's all right with you. Having you there will be especially helpful; I'm going to try to get him to test any other horses he's got on the ranch. The disease is so rare in this state that you probably don't realize how devastating it can be in its acute form, but I assure you testing of any other horses in the area would be a good idea."

"I was in southeast Asia. I've seen a number of cases," I said, thinking back to my time in the Philippines. "I lost my share with temperatures over a hundred seven and anemia that left them with Cherry Kool-aid for blood."

"Oh, well... you know what I mean, then. I've only seen pictures myself, but it looks pretty rough. Pretty pale, aren't they?"

"White as a sheet!"

"Probably weak, too, I would imagine."

"I was taught in school that a packed cell volume of eleven percent is incompatible with life, but I've seen Swampers still standing with PCVs of seven," I said.

"Wow, well, we'll talk more on Thursday. I'll see you then."

"Okay, that sounds fine. See you at eleven," I said, hanging up the phone. I sat thinking about Art and the news he was about to receive. I knew Jetaway was feeling great and looking better. He was an asymptomatic carrier and he might remain that way for life. He could transmit the disease at any time or he might never give it to another horse. That's the hard thing for an owner to swallow, a perfectly healthy horse that must be quarantined for life or euthanized. Redmond was going to call Hudelston, so I decided to wait and talk with him on Thursday.

I busied myself around the clinic and wasn't thinking about swamp fever or Coggins tests when the phone rang two hours later.

"Clay Williams," I answered, pulling out my desk chair and collapsing into it.

"Clay, have you heard about my problem?" I immediately recognized the deep bass voice.

"Yeah, Art, I have. Redmond called me a couple of hours ago," I said, picking up a pencil and drumming the eraser on my desk.

"So, tell me, is this quarantine thing legit?" I could hear the strain in his voice.

"Yes, Art, it is. It's a federal regulation. Quarantined for life three hundred feet from any other horses or euthanized. I'm sorry," I said, windmilling the pencil between my fingers. I started to doodle short straight lines as I listened to the silent phone.

"I suppose I'll have to keep him home. I bet he had it when I bought him in Oklahoma. The other thing is I haven't had anything sick," Art said.

"You may never have an acute case or it may hit your whole herd. You can't ever tell. When I was in the Philippines we had over a hundred head of horses at the base and I saw a lot of acute cases.

"You had a hundred head of horses on an Air Force base?" Hudelston asked, disbelief evident in his voice.

"Well, Clark was an R and R center during Nam, and a previous veterinarian had sold the Air Force on a riding stable for the boys on leave," I said, as I thought of the Clark Riding Academy. I was doodling again, smiling at the memory. "The veterinarian before me finagled a six week trip to Australia to buy Thoroughbreds for the base. Anyway, I've seen a lot of cases and I don't care to ever see any more."

"Well, like I said, I'll keep him home." Art sounded tired. "What's this state fella want to come on my place for? Said he'd be here Thursday about eleven."

"I guess he needs to talk to you about the quarantine," I said.

"Hell's bells, I already told him I'd keep the gelding home." Art's voice had gone up an octave.

"I agreed to come out with him. I'm not sure why he wants me there, but I said I'd come." I was sitting straighter now.

"Maybe he feels like he needs a witness in case he don't come back alive," Art said. "I'm not real fond of the state snoopin' around my ranch."

"I don't think he'll be doin' much snooping," I said as I doodled a stick figure lying dead and another with a smoking gun. "I'll let him know how much you like the idea of the state coming for a visit."

"Thanks, Doc. I don't understand all this business. I'll see you Thursday." Art said, hanging up the phone.

I had to hurry through some routine vaccinations Thursday morning to make it back to the office by eleven. Redmond's car was already parked in front of my clinic, a white Chevy Belair with state plates and a big whip antenna. Pulling in next to the Chevy I climbed out of my truck. Figuring the smell of Ken's warm doughnuts had gotten to him, I started down the wooden porch that connected my clinic to all the units in the little center. Dr. Redmond must have heard my tread because he came out immediately with both hands full, one with coffee and the other with a cream-filled chocolate éclair.

"Dr. Williams?" he asked. I nodded and he continued. "I'm Mike Redmond, as you must have guessed." He stuck the éclair in his mouth, inexpertly wiped his hand on the napkin he'd used to insulate the coffee cup and reached out to shake my hand. "Hope I'm not sticky," he mumbled around the pastry.

"No problem," I said, taking the proffered hand. "Clay Williams, glad to finally get to meet you. Take your time; it'd be a shame to hurry Ken's éclairs, although I can't always say the same for his coffee. This late in the day it sometimes dissolves the plastic spoons."

"Not bad today. He said that he'd made a fresh pot." Redmond had removed the éclair and was speaking more clearly as I ushered him into the clinic.

"That's not always much help. Ken thinks a fresh pot means made the same day," I said, offering Redmond a chair, but the state official shook his head as he swallowed the last of his éclair.

"We can take my car if you'd like. I'm in a bit of a rush; my son is playing basketball tonight over in Greeley."

We left the parking lot and I motioned for Dr. Redmond to turn right, heading south on US 40. "Art's ranch is only about ten minutes from here and he's expecting us."

"Did you have the opportunity to speak with him?" he asked, glancing over as he drove.

"Yes, I did, and I told him that I'd let you know how much he likes 'The State' snooping around his place," I said with a laugh.

"Old time rancher, I'll bet. Some of them have a real dislike for any authority," Mike Redmond said, slowing to turn left at my direction. "The horse will have to be quarantined, however, or the state may come snooping around. You make sure he knows that." Redmond gave me a hard scowl.

I returned his stare. "Oh, he knows. I'm just glad I don't have any part in this."

"I'll need someone to verify he's abiding by the law, and you're the logical one," Redmond replied, scratching the balding spot on top of his head of silver hair.

"I might be interested in the job," I said. "How much does the state pay?" Redmond broke into a tight smile that didn't appear to be all that friendly. "It seems like something the sheriff's office

238

would do, so I should be paid at least as much as a deputy. Don't you think?"

"The state veterinary office doesn't have funds for that!" Redmond raised his voice and waved his right arm in a dismissive way.

"Sure wish I could help, but I'm real busy," I said. "Besides, Hudelston said he'd keep the horse home."

We rode on in silence and I gestured at the places Dr. Redmond needed to turn until we pulled under the ranch gate with its sign hanging high above the Chevy. A split log on two short chains sported a big slash H burned into the wood. Small pastures lined either side of the lane leading to Art and Sally's home. The ranch house stood only a few hundred feet off the gravel road. It was a new modular with a commanding view of the main hay fields that sloped down to a bend in the Yampa River a half mile away. Sally had done a great job of landscaping, planting a stand of aspen next to the large deck that faced the river. It was a beautiful spot, and the house looked so natural there that it was hard for me to imagine the huge log home, almost a hundred years old, which had fallen victim to a propane leak in the basement and burned on the exact spot less than a year ago. The driveway ended behind the house with a parking area large enough for a semi with a cattle trailer to turn around. Just beyond were the corrals and main barn.

Art came down the steps from his deck looking more like a bear in a baseball cap than a rancher. I saw Redmond swallow and pale a little. Bailing out of the Chevy, I introduced the two men, and they shook hands warily.

"You already know why I'm here. I'd like to see the gelding that reacted positively to the infectious anemia test," Redmond said, folding his arms across his chest.

"I've brought him up in the corral." Art started across to the barn and we followed. "Hasn't been sick a day since I bought him at a sale over a year ago," he said, scowling back over his shoulder.

Art haltered the gelding, and Dr. Redmond pulled a thermometer from his shirt pocket, conducting a brief exam that seemed mostly a formality. Jetaway was in perfect health. "We'd like to have blood drawn on all your horses, the state veterinarian said as he put his thermometer away.

"By 'we' you mean the state?" Art asked, straightening to tower over Mike Redmond.

"Well...yes... the state... in a manner of speaking." Redmond fidgeted with his watchband.

"'In a manner of speaking!' What the hell does that mean?" When Hudelston folded his arms across his chest he became a mountain.

"The state veterinarian's office wants all these horses tested," Redmond said, waving his arms to include most of South Routt County.

"I can't speak for the rest of the folks here abouts, but the state is welcome to test all my horses," Art said, motioning toward the river pasture where about fifteen horses were grazing.

"Oh... well, the state doesn't have funding to test your horses, Mr. Hudelston," Redmond said, shaking his head.

"Well, I sure don't have the funding to test them either." Art scraped his toe in the gravel and shook his head. "But I will keep the gelding home, just like I told Doc." Art looked over at me and winked.

"Yes, well then, there is the requirement of keeping Jetaway three hundred feet from any other equine." Redmond looked from Art to me and back.

"You know, I've been thinking a lot about that." Art raised his cap, scratching his head with his middle finger. "Look over here." He moved to the left a few yards so the barn wouldn't obscure his view. "Right down by that turn in the river." Art pointed across the hay field. "A pen down there would give Jetaway both feed and water. Cut down on the maintenance."

"Anywhere that's isolated would be fine." Redmond smiled for the first time.

"It's a hard area for me to hay anyway, so you fellas could build the fence right out there." Art pointed to some low-lying ground. "Bring it out maybe a hundred yards, then right angle it for another fifty and then back to the river on the bend there. That would be a good home for ole' Jet." Art smiled his biggest smile for Dr. Redmond.

"Mr. Hudelston, the state is not going to build any fence for you!" Mike Redmond said frowning.

"Well, I'm sure as hell not going to build any fence either."

"Mr. Hudelston, the horse must be quarantined!" Redmond's voice was getting higher and he began to pace.

"Like I said, I'll keep him home," Art said, rocking back on his heels.

"What about your neighbors? The infected horse must be three hundred feet from any other equine." Dr. Redmond repeated.

"I'll let them know in case they want to build a fence on their place," Art said, looking at me with a grin. Mike Redmond started back toward his car shaking his head. I noticed a definite redness to his ears and neck. Art and I followed along in silence walking over to the Hudelston's deck. Upon reaching the car Dr. Redmond pulled out his clipboard and removed several pieces of paper, then he came to where we were standing.

"Here are the quarantine papers." He flipped over several thin, official looking pages. On the last page a signature line had been highlighted in neon green. Pulling out a ballpoint pen he said, "I'll need you to sign here."

"I'll keep the horse home, but I'm not signing anything," Art said, taking a step back toward his house. The state veterinarian ground his teeth, the muscles in his neck bulged and his face turned a bright crimson.

"You must agree to the quarantine and sign this paper!" Redmond's voice was at least two octaves higher. He clicked the pen continuously, his hand visibly trembling.

"If you want to buy the horse then you can sign the damn paper yourself. Otherwise I'll keep him home and that's all I'll do!" Art boomed back.

"I can just drop these papers here on the ground," Redmond said, holding the agreement at arm's length. A haughty smile creased his red face.

"Yes, and I can step inside for my rifle and shoot you before you can possibly get off my ranch," Art said with a menacing glare.

"Well, I wouldn't just drop them," Redmond said, throwing his chest out.

"I wouldn't shoot you, either," Art said, the glare changing to a twinkle in his eyes.

Dr. Redmond turned and started for his car still clicking the ball point. "You'll keep him home then?"

"Said I would."

"People will be checking to see that you do," Mike Redmond said, getting into the car. I looked from Redmond to Art, and Hudelston winked again. I had to walk away to keep from laughing out loud. We roared up the lane throwing snow as we fishtailed on to River Road.

"Some of these old boys are hard cases," Redmond said, "but he'll have to sign for it when I mail it to him as a registered letter." Redmond's eyes sparkled and the corners of his mouth were turned up in a gleeful smile.

"Dr. Redmond," I said, "how many registered letters do you think Art gets from the state in a year? There's no way he's gonna' sign for a registered letter from your office. He said he'd keep the gelding home."

A few weeks later on an overcast afternoon in the middle of March I wasn't thinking of EIA or Coggins tests as I headed out to

242

the Hudelston ranch. I drove through spitting snow whirled about by an icy breeze. Art's best brood mare wasn't due for a couple of weeks, but he was afraid she was trying to abort. She'd been depressed since feeding time this morning, hardly eating at all and walking around, as Art put it, 'all wobbly like.' I pulled in the lane and recognized Art standing by the corral fence, huge in his goose down parka.

"How's she doin'?" I stepped out of my truck, grabbing a stethoscope and thermometer before walking over.

"Not so good, Doc. Thanks for coming out so quickly." Art turned to shake my hand. "She just stands there with her head down, lookin' real weak."

I peered through the fence at the mare tied across the corral some sixty feet away. She looked depressed all right. Her head was down, and she was breathing hard as if she'd run a long way. She frequently shifted her weight from one hind leg to the other swaying noticeably each time. *Interesting,* I thought. *I've seen this somewhere before.* Then it hit me!

"Art," I said, as the hair on my arms stood straight up. "You see how hard she's breathing? That's from the fever and anemia. We'll go over and raise her lip, an' she's gonna' be whiter than this new snow." I brushed the fresh powder with my boot. "When we take her temperature it'll be over a hundred and five. If that's what we find, we'll run a Coggins test. She's an acute swamp fever case if I've ever seen one." I watched as Art started to swing open the big pole gate. He was pale as a ghost and every bit as wobbly as the mare. He stood hanging onto the gate for a few seconds before starting to move.

"My best mare! Why did the son of a bitch have to give it to my best mare? I just wanted to give him a chance. He's never been sick." Art slumped, shambling slowly across the corral, look-ing every bit of his seventy-six years. He reached the mare and gently rubbed her neck. My exam didn't take long. A heart rate over eighty and snow-white mucus membranes, coupled with a temperature of 106.4, certainly fit the picture.

"I'll pull some blood for the Coggins test," I said, as I held off her jugular vein, waiting for it to fill above my finger.

"I guess you better run one, but I think you called it right. Two questions." Art said.

"Shoot," I said, sticking the jugular vein and withdrawing 5 cc of watery red fluid.

"Damn, that blood is like cranberry juice," Art said, shaking his head.

"Maybe even thinner," I said, transferring the blood into a red-topped test tube. "What was it you wanted to ask?"

"First, can you come back in the morning and test all the horses? I'll have them all up in the corral by eight." Art looked down and scraped at the snow with the toe of his boot. "And second, is there anything you can give my mare? I don't want to shoot her."

"Let's see, first things first. You might not want to put the mare down yet in case I'm wrong."

"How much pain is she in, Doc?" Art continued to rub the horse's neck.

"She's in distress and I think that scares her. She has to breathe hard and her heart is beating a mile a minute, but that's not the same as pain."

"So is there anything you can do?" Art said, clearing his throat.

"We could give her an anti-inflammatory to drop her temperature. It would make her feel better. Some antibiotics wouldn't be a bad idea in case I'm wrong, but that's about all the help we can do without trying to do a transfusion."

"I doubt you're wrong. So do you think she'll have this foal without aborting, and if she does, will the foal be all right?"

"Honestly, Art, I don't think she'll be alive by morning. Not without a transfusion."

"I think that's out of the question. If she's going to survive, she'll have to do it on her own. Why don't you make her feel better with whatever you said." Art untied the lead rope.

"I'll get some bute from the truck," I said, turning to trot across the snow-covered corral. As I gave her the injection I addressed the other problem. "What about Jetaway? There's not a whole lot of use to test all the horses if he is still in contact with them, and besides, we won't know for sure till her blood is tested. That will take a couple of days."

"I think we both know what this is, and Jetaway won't see sundown today. I'm doin' what you thought I should have done weeks ago." Art shook his head. "Being stubborn got this ranch built, but Sally always says that just because a person's stubborn it doesn't mean they can't listen to reason." Art gently slipped the halter off his mare, rubbing her on the forehead. "I bowed up one too many times on this one."

"I think we should wait a couple of weeks to test the herd, in case, like Jetaway, some other horse has just recently been exposed. It doesn't have to be mosquito transmission. Any exchange of blood can do it." We both started for the gate.

"Whatever you think, Doc. I'll check with the neighbors and be sure they won't mind if I test their horses too... I better go break the news to Sally. She really loves that mare." Art trudged on toward the house. He looked back and waved as I backed my truck around to leave.

The mare died that night, and I received a call from the state veterinarian a few days later when the lab informed him of her positive status.

"I tried to help Mr. Hudelston the first time I visited him," Dr. Redmond said, "and now, because he wouldn't listen, he has another horse to quarantine!"

"No, he doesn't," I said, shaking my head in disgust. "The mare was an acute case and she was probably exposed last summer when the mosquitoes were out. She didn't survive and his gelding's been euthanized."

"Well, at least I won't need to make another trip all the way up there; I'll send you the appropriate forms to verify those facts," he said, sounding very official.

"I'll be expecting them," I replied, hanging up the phone. Redmond didn't ask about testing the other horses and I didn't offer any information. They were, by the way, all negative when we completed the testing some weeks later.

Art won the Championship at Evanston the next year with two young geldings he bought at a sale in Oklahoma.

About The Author

Dr. Richard Perce was raised in New Mexico and attended the University of Arizona before graduating from Colorado State University School of Veterinary Medicine. He practiced in the 'high country' for almost twenty years before moving to Northern California. He now resides with his wife, Chari, in the wine country where he maintains a full time equine practice. Currently Dick is working on his second novel: 'Above Timberline'.

1208185R00136

Made in the USA
San Bernardino, CA
30 November 2012